The Killing Choice

Also by
The Burning Men

WILL SHINDLER

The Killing Choice

HODDER &
STOUGHTON

First published in Great Britain in 2021 by Hodder & Stoughton
An Hachette UK company

1

Copyright © Will Shindler 2021

A CIP catalogue record for this title is available from the British Library

Hardback ISBN 978 1 529 30175 5
Trade Paperback ISBN 978 1 529 30176 2
eBook ISBN 978 1 529 30317 9

Typeset in Plantin Light by Hewer Text UK Ltd, Edinburgh
Printed and bound in Great Britain by Clays Ltd, Elcograf S.p.A.

Hodder & Stoughton policy is to use papers that are natural, renewable
and recyclable products and made from wood grown in sustainable
forests. The logging and manufacturing processes are expected to
conform to the environmental regulations of the country of origin.

Hodder & Stoughton Ltd
Carmelite House
50 Victoria Embankment
London EC4Y 0DZ

www.hodder.co.uk

PROLOGUE

Some moments carve themselves into the memory, the decisions you make shaping the scars they leave behind. That's what Karl Suleman would later think when he remembered this part of it. Just before.

Karl shivered and hugged himself. Spring was about to give way to summer, but at seven in the evening the wind still carried a bite. The Crystal Palace dinosaur park was a place he knew well. Built in 1854, it was designed as an attraction for Victorian families to peruse, before taking in the Great Exhibition on the hill above. Dark outlines of vast granite creatures lined its pathways, the sway of the surrounding trees animating them just enough to earn the odd snatched glance from the commuters wandering home.

Karl had grown up in these parts, remembered his mum showing him the same stone beasts when he was a boy. Now he'd come full circle, he realised, as he saw the pretty young woman walking towards him with a broad smile. He'd taken her here when she was just a toddler. Now look at her, he thought. Even on a miserable night like this, she shone.

'You made it on time?' said Leah Suleman, making no effort to keep the surprise out of her voice.

'Of course I did. I even left work early tonight. Besides – a tradition's a tradition.'

'Oh, is it? Last time we did this, I seem to remember I was waiting in the freezing cold for half an hour.'

His grin met hers.

'Your old man promised you a Friday night curry, and a Friday night curry you shall have.'

That wasn't strictly true. It was Leah's mother Claire who'd come up with the idea. Karl was a workaholic, whose commitment to his job bordered on the obsessive. His wife kept a close eye to ensure that didn't come at the expense of his paternal duties. Claire and Leah were thick as thieves, so she was quite happy to sit out their monthly night of father–daughter bonding.

At first he agreed to it through gritted teeth, not because he didn't love his daughter, but because he hadn't seen the need for it. It seemed a twee idea to him, unnecessary and time-consuming. One of those New Year's resolutions that could safely be forgotten after a couple of weeks. What Claire never understood was that the more he put into his work, the more the whole family benefited. Father and daughter dutifully humoured her though – and then thoroughly enjoyed themselves. Now, to his own surprise, he found he actively looked forward to this precious time alone with Leah. And there was a grudging acceptance, too, that perhaps his wife knew him better than he gave her credit for.

'Where are we going then – up into Crystal Palace to the Punjab Express, or down into Penge to the Bay of Bengal?' said Leah.

He screwed up his face.

'Didn't like the lamb at the Express, last time. Too greasy.'

'Fussy tart. Penge it is then,' she said, shaking her head in mock despair. She took his arm, and they strolled and chatted for a few minutes as they wended their way past the huge stone lizards.

'So tell me about this new boyfriend of yours,' he said.

'Oh Dad, give it a rest, he's hardly . . .'

She stopped suddenly, her arm falling to her side. A hooded figure was standing in front of them. He was wearing a reflective mask which enveloped his whole face and was holding a large serrated knife. It was as if he'd appeared from nowhere. Later Karl would realise they'd been followed, their assailant tracking them in the tree-lined greenery which ran parallel to the path. His first instinct was to look around, see if there was anyone else nearby. A few witnesses and this little chancer might just run. But there was no one.

'It's alright, there's no need to hurt anyone,' said Leah. 'If you want money, we'll give it to you.'

Karl beat down his rising fury, the desire to pummel this piece of nothing with his own hands. Leah was right though. Better to surrender a few quid than risk something worse. It was the mathematics of sense.

'I don't want your money,' said the masked figure. The voice was muffled but sounded unexpectedly youthful. That didn't make him any less dangerous though. The younger they were, the less likely they were to listen to reason. Karl's eyes alighted on the blade again and he thought about all the times he'd read about a stabbing in the paper, heard it mentioned on the radio. It was all background noise to him. Part of the everyday of living in London. Terribly sad, but not something he'd ever thought would touch him. It's what kids off estates in gangs did. It didn't happen to people like him.

'Come on, mate, there's no need for this.'

'No *need* for it? How old is she?' The figure jabbed the knife in Leah's direction.

'What's that got to do with anything?'

'I'm twenty-three,' said Leah.

'She's my daughter. Please . . . just leave her alone.'

The masked man-child turned back to Karl.

3

'So . . . would you do *anything* to protect her?'

'Yes.'

'Say it then. Say "I'd do anything to protect her".'

'Dad . . .' said Leah, trying to intervene, but Karl held up a hand, his focus entirely on the figure in front of them.

'I'd do anything to protect her,' he repeated calmly. He was trying to find a way in, to take control of the situation, but it was difficult when you couldn't make eye contact. The impassive mask was unnerving, as it was doubtless designed to be. All he was getting back was a fish-eyed reflection of his own strained features. Leah's terrified face too, distorted like an image in a fairground mirror.

'Then walk away. You said *anything*. So walk away.' The figure pointed the knife at the pathway behind him.

'Not a chance. What are you going to do to her?'

'What do you think I'm going to do to her?' He grabbed at his crotch unsubtly. Under that mask he was smiling – you couldn't see the grin, but you could hear it. Karl stepped forwards and the knife was suddenly at his throat. 'One more step . . .' the figure whispered. Slowly he drew the blade across Karl's skin, just enough to draw blood. Karl felt the serrated edge dig and pull at his flesh, and winced. He stood still. 'If you don't walk away, I *will* kill you. That's a promise, mate. Either you die, or she stays. I won't kill her though – you know, after I'm done. It's your choice.'

The smile in the voice now sounded like a leer.

'Dad . . . go,' said Leah. Karl turned to her, his legs feeling numb.

'Not a chance.'

'Go. This way, we both walk away.'

She sounded oddly calm, but he could hear the slight pleading underneath it. The mathematics of sense again. Their eyes met, a horrific understanding beginning to form.

4

'I can't.'

'Just go!' She screamed it at him this time.

He turned to face his tormentor.

'Why are you doing this?'

'Time for talking's over. Give me your phone. We don't want you calling the feds, do we?' Karl reached into his pocket and threw his phone on to the ground. 'Now fuck off.'

Karl looked over at Leah. Her eyes were imploring him to go, making it even harder. He turned around and took a step. Then another. And then he stopped.

'I can't. I'm sorry.'

He felt the cold steel of the knife again, this time digging in to the back of his neck.

'One push . . . that's all it would take,' whispered that voice again. Karl's legs moved, almost as if he wasn't in control of them. A ginger step forwards, then another. He broke into a jog, then began to sprint – laughter echoing behind him.

He ran around the corner, trying to focus his thoughts. The stone dinosaurs were ghoulish in the dark, as if their sculpted eyes were mocking him. He was looking for people now, but the park was deserted. He tried not to think about what was going on behind him, tried not to imagine that knife at Leah's throat and what might be happening. He ran even faster. There were large Victorian houses in the street adjacent to the park, families settling down for their evening meals. The main drag of the high street was perhaps only five minutes away. He didn't have five minutes.

He saw an old woman with a pug on a lead, her face widening with fear as she saw him running towards her. He could hardly breathe, barely get the words out.

'Please, I need to borrow your phone. It's an emergency. My daughter . . . she's in trouble.'

The woman looked startled, almost unable to respond for a second.

'I . . . don't have one. My son does . . . he doesn't live too far away, if that helps?'

Karl was about to answer when he heard a scream cut through the air, high-pitched and piercing. He knew instantly it was a scream of pain, not fear. He turned on his heels, running back the way he'd come, his heart pumping, the vomit rising in his throat.

And then he saw her, lying crumpled in a heap face down, dark liquid pooling around her. He knew before he got there it was too late. But before the grief and shock even hit him there was just one thought: that when his daughter had needed him the most, he'd been running in the opposite direction.

I

Alex Finn looked around the wine bar gloomily and wondered if it wasn't too late to turn back. He was hoping this would be quick and painless. If he could keep it to under an hour, it'd be a result. Caroline Hunter, universally known as Cally, was an old friend of his late wife. It was around a year now since Karin had died from a brain tumour. There were some reminders of their life together that helped with his grief and others that didn't. Cally was definitely the latter.

She reminded him a little of the Lucy character from the old Charlie Brown comic strips: bossy, opinionated and something of a conversational bully. He'd always felt a certain empathy for her rather drippy husband Eric who used to escort her, barely saying boo to a goose. They'd sent him a card with condolences after Karin's death, and he'd assumed they'd quietly fade away after that. He'd thus been rather mystified when Cally texted out of the blue, asking to meet.

The bar in Clapham was the sort of place Finn went out of his way to avoid, and it struck him how odd it felt to be meeting Cally without Karin beside him. Usually, as Cally was oh-so-wittily dissecting his personality, his wife would catch his eye; a knowing look between them which dissolved his irritation, forced him to stifle a smile instead.

He couldn't pretend he was even close to being over Karin's death. The experts say there are five stages to bereavement: denial, anger, bargaining, depression and acceptance. By his estimation he'd moved through the first three and was now stuck rather depressingly in depression – something he tried not to think too hard about. In short, there was awareness – a realisation she was gone – but no acceptance yet. Not by a long chalk.

His job, as a detective inspector with a major investigations team at the Metropolitan Police, gave him ample distraction. Whether that was positive or not was debatable. Diversion was good; not giving yourself enough space to move on wasn't. He knew that, but preferred not to dwell on it. Instead, the multiple investigations he'd taken on helped him make sense of the post-Karin world.

The one certainty in his life was that, unlike certain professions, his work wouldn't ever dry up. The official statistics claimed violent crime was on the wane. The amount of overtime he and his team were doing suggested otherwise, and Finn wasn't complaining. Work gave him routine, routine gave him structure, structure provided distraction. And distraction numbed the pain.

He looked around the wine bar with little enthusiasm. Soft jazz played in the background, mingling with the low hubbub of courting couples. It was a world he felt no connection to. He longed to be at home, with a cup of coffee and his paperwork spread out in front of him.

'I hope you haven't been waiting long?'

He recognised the cultured voice immediately, and turned to see a tall woman in her early forties with dark blonde hair smiling at him.

Cally Hunter certainly cut a distinctive figure, her fashion style very much rooted in French New Wave. She wore a simple buttoned-down blouse with a black jacket, black denim trousers and black shoes. The Gallic look wasn't accidental – she ran a small French restaurant in Islington which somehow managed to survive and thrive despite the harsh economic climate. She was looking at him with a curiosity he'd come to recognise in recent months. He'd seen that expression on a lot of faces and was well versed in it. People, it seemed, never lost their interest in where you were at with your bereavement.

'No, not at all. I only got here about ten minutes ago,' he replied. She took a seat opposite him and he pushed one of the two glasses of Burgundy on the table over towards her.

'I hope it's okay ...' He'd been assured by the waiter it would impress even the most knowledgeable pallet, and was pleased to see an appreciative look as she took a sip.

'More than okay. Very nice indeed. I'm assuming you must have taken the waiter's recommendation?' There was just enough of a sarcastic undertone to get his hackles up. The fact she was absolutely right was completely irrelevant.

'Of course.'

She smiled at him again, warmer this time.

'So, how are you doing, Alex?'

'Getting along. I miss Karin, of course. Every day – goes without saying.'

The gruffness of his response gave him away, as did his instinctive glance down. She was scrutinising him carefully, he noticed, but there followed another kind smile.

'Me too. You get plenty of fair-weather friends in life. Karin wasn't one.' He nodded and there was an awkward silence. He wasn't quite sure if she'd called him out of a sincere desire to see him, or whether there was something else to it. He couldn't think what it might be, but there was a mild flickering of curiosity.

'How are you, anyway?' he asked.

'Busy. But in my line of work you learn to be grateful for that.' She took another sip of her wine and ran her tongue over her top lip for a moment. 'Look, I won't waste your time; you're probably wondering why I suggested this.'

'We haven't seen each other since Karin's wake. I assumed—'

'Oh come on, Alex . . .' she said, immediately interrupting. 'We've never really hit it off, have we? I wind you up.'

Finn didn't know what to say. No argument there. 'I'll tell you a secret though,' she added. 'I've always rather enjoyed getting under your skin.'

'I'll tell *you* a secret – I know.'

They both chuckled and it helped break the ice.

'I do respect you though. Karin was *so* proud of you. I just found you . . .'

'. . . a humourless stick-in-the-mud?' he said, allowing just the slightest hint of a wry smile.

'Well, since you put it that way, yes. Anyway, I received a letter yesterday. This is going to sound crazy, but it was from Karin.' Finn tensed, his steel-grey eyes suddenly lasering into her. 'It turns out it was in her will. There was an instruction for her solicitor to send it exactly eleven months after her cremation.'

His gaze seemed to intensify until he broke it off and looked away sharply. There was a long silence as he took in what she was saying. The room suddenly seemed short of air.

'Alex?'

He looked back at her slowly, smiling as pleasantly as he could manage.

'I'm okay. She never did like round numbers. Six months or a year would have been too obvious. I should have guessed she'd pull something like this,' he said. The words were affectionate but inside he felt like a fist was holding his heart and slowly squeezing it.

'Don't you want to know what it said?' For an instant it was almost as if he didn't.

'Oh, go on then,' he said, trying and failing to make his words sound light.

There was a tilt of her head, an appreciation of how big a moment this was for him.

'She was worried about you. That you'd retreat into yourself after her death. She said she'd talked with you about that, but was convinced you'd ignore her.'

Finn tried to mask his reaction. He didn't quite know *what* he was feeling yet, whether this was a welcome or unwelcome development. But he felt overwhelmed. At work he thought he did a decent job of keeping his emotions disguised from his colleagues. But right now he was aware Cally was reading him like a children's book written in particularly large capitals.

'I'm guessing she sent you to check up on me?' he said finally.

'Sort of . . .'

She let it hang, inviting the follow-up.

'Can I see this letter?' he said with a sudden burst of irritation. If Karin wanted to communicate with him, then he wanted to hear the words directly from her, not her surrogate.

Cally laughed unexpectedly. Loud and throaty.

'Actually, no. She said you'd ask and instructed me to refuse – said you'd know exactly what it was about, and to remember Berlin.'

Berlin was the place Karin had chosen in the months before her death to have a conversation with him. It was where she'd shared her concerns about what would happen once she was gone. There was no danger of him forgetting – that conversation was burnt on his brain.

'So, is she right?' asked Cally.

'I suppose. I'm very busy with work though. It's hard to know whether I'm "retreating into myself", as Karin puts it, or whether I've just got a lot on my plate. Did she give instructions on what you're supposed to do about this?'

'No. She did not. Which is rather unhelpful,' said Cally with some degree of deadpan. 'Look, I know we've never been close. Maybe that's why she chose me. She knew I wouldn't give you an easy ride.'

Finn exhaled, and ran a hand over his scalp. This felt *huge*. He knew it wasn't, not in the grand scheme of things. But it was still a shock, and as a rule he wasn't a man who liked surprises. Even ones like this.

Cally was studying him again. She meant well, but he hated the scrutiny. Only one person got to look at him like that. Or at least, used to.

'So what do you want to do?' he said, throwing the ball back to her.

'I think we have to listen to Karin, don't you?'

Finn shrugged impotently. 'And what does that mean?'

'That I think we're going to have to do this again. Meet up – you and I. Because that's what she wants . . . wanted. For you to have someone to talk to – someone she trusted. Whether you like it or not. I think that's what she was after.'

Despite the words there was a kindness in her eyes.

'That . . . is *very* Karin,' he said.

Finn's phone buzzed on the table. He held up a hand in apology and took the call.

'Sorry to bother you, boss.' He recognised the slight Scandinavian lilt of DC Mathilde Paulsen. 'A woman's been murdered in Crystal Palace Park. I'm just on my way over. Do you need a lift or do you want to meet me there?'

Finn looked over at Cally, whose eyes hadn't left him.

'I'll take a lift if you're offering.'

He smiled politely at Cally.

'*Coward,*' said Karin.

*   *   *

Mattie Paulsen watched from her car as Finn said his good-byes to the rather striking blonde he'd just escorted out of the wine bar. His body language was stiff and awkward – no surprise there. She supposed it could have been a date, but instinct told her otherwise. Whatever it was, it was an interesting development, though it went without saying that interviewing a serial killer would be easier than extracting information from Finn.

The state of the DI's personal life was the subject of much conjecture at Cedar House. The strong suspicion was that he didn't *have* one. Most days he seemed to be in before anyone else, and no one knew when he left, because no one was there to see.

Paulsen, no stranger herself to brusque introversion, had noticed a change in recent weeks. Finn's usual cool detachment had crossed a line into overt snappiness, and most uncharacteristically – for him, anyway – some small slips. Misremembering the odd name, repeating the same instructions, getting the times of routine meetings mixed up. Others were noticing too, but things hadn't quite reached the stage where it was being discussed openly. Perhaps because they collectively knew what was at the heart of it.

Paulsen saw him glance over nervously at her as he awkwardly embraced the blonde. The tall woman left, heading off towards the tube station, and Finn began to stride over. In his mid-forties, he was an imposing figure from a distance, but up close the high cheekbones and horn-rimmed glasses suggested a more scholarly personality. He'd quickly re-adopted his best poker face but Paulsen knew him well enough to see he was unsettled. What was harder to read was whether that was because of the blonde woman, or because he'd been observed.

They'd been working together for almost a year. She'd joined Cedar House the day after Karin Finn's cremation.

The two of them had got over a difficult start to build a strong working relationship. They weren't friends as such, and certainly didn't socialise away from the job. She was in her mid-twenties and their worlds were completely different – if you asked him about Drake, he'd probably assume you were talking about Sir Francis. Nevertheless, there was an undeniable connection between them. She often struggled to define it. It just was what it was. Aside from her partner Nancy, she considered him one of the few people she genuinely trusted. Though that didn't stop him from being as moody and irritable with her as he was with everyone else.

He got in the car, strapped himself in and glowered at her, well aware of what she was thinking.

'She looked nice,' said Paulsen lightly.

'An old friend of Karin's. We were just having a catch-up.'

The second sentence carried something slightly defensive and she knew better than to push it. She started the engine and moved off.

'So bring me up to speed – what's happened in Crystal Palace?'

'Sounds like a mugging gone wrong. A young woman out with her father – Leah and Karl Suleman. They got jumped by some bloke in a mask. Multiple stab wounds apparently – she was dead before the paramedics got there.'

'And the father?'

'Wasn't hurt – or at least there aren't any physical injuries.'

'So what happened? Did the daughter try and take this guy on?'

Paulsen shrugged. 'The only witness was the father and he's not making much sense according to DS Ojo – he's still in shock.'

Finn digested the information and Paulsen saw him glance across curiously at her. In a jacket and jeans, she'd changed since he'd last seen her in the incident room earlier that day. Tall, mixed race, with a distinctive jet-black bob of hair, her work attire was usually impeccably formal.

'So has this interrupted your evening too?'

She nodded.

'My brother was coming round for dinner. Nancy's furious – she spent half the afternoon cooking.'

'I'm sorry.'

'Don't be. It's a bit of a relief, if I'm honest. Don't ask.'

He didn't. He frowned instead and stared with some intensity out of the window. Whether that was because of the woman he'd just been with or because he was refocusing on the task in hand, Paulsen couldn't tell, but they drove the rest of the way in silence.

2

It was the perfect place to kill someone. Finn and Paulsen parked on a nearby street and walked up through the park in near darkness, Paulsen using her phone as a torch. There was no street lighting, no CCTV, no flats or houses directly over-looking. You could just about make out the silhouettes of the huge stone dinosaurs in the murk, circled off by a vast oval boating lake. If they'd arrived another ten minutes later, the Sulemans would have found the place closed. Instead of short cutting through the park, they'd have walked up one of the adjacent streets and be enjoying a chicken balti somewhere in the warm now.

It wasn't hard to spot the crime scene. Leah Suleman's body was hidden behind a forensic tent, with temporary floodlighting in place to allow the crime scene investigators to do their work. From a distance, against the backdrop of the stone monsters, it looked like some sort of film set. Finn and Paulsen followed the dirt track around the perimeter of the lake, and headed towards the lighting array. The area was cordoned off and protected, slightly unnecessarily, by a solitary police constable as blue-gowned SOCOs went about their business.

The wind blew through the trees and Finn shivered. He could hear what sounded like geese squawking down by the waterside. Doubtless it possessed its charms by day, but south London's miniature take on Jurassic Park felt like a cold and lonely place to die. As he got closer he could see DS Jackie Ojo sitting on a bench with an expensively dressed middle-aged man, who he guessed was Karl Suleman. Finn wondered how long he'd been here, waiting for the emergency services to arrive. Alone in the dark with his daughter's dead body, and only the dinosaurs for company.

'The killer could have got out anywhere, this place is huge,' muttered Paulsen, looking around, hugging herself as the wind gusted again. She was right. Even in broad daylight the park offered plenty of exits. At night, the killer wouldn't have even needed to run. He could be watching them right now just yards away and they wouldn't have a clue. Chances were though he'd long since disappeared. Finn focused his mind. Every crime scene possessed its own unique challenges and this one was no different.

'There's four sides to this park and it's a big area, so we need to be thorough. Whoever did this may well have been splashed in blood – so let's get the CCTV from the surrounding streets, and get uniform doing as wide a spread as possible of door-to-doors. Someone might have seen something. If we can identify which exit he took, that'll give us a starting point. Hopefully he's left some sort of footprint in the mud as well, and we can get an idea which way he went. The railway station's just up the hill too – once we've got a proper description off the father, we can cross-check it with their cameras.'

Paulsen nodded and scurried away. Finn turned his attention to Karl Suleman, still sitting on the bench talking with Ojo. Jackie looked tired, another one whose evening must have been turned on its head – her mother, he guessed, press-ganged at short notice into babysitting her seven-year-old boy.

Ojo saw Finn watching, murmured something to Suleman, then rose and walked over to join him. He guided her to the floodlit area, which aside from giving off some welcome warmth, was also out of Karl's earshot.

'How is he?' said Finn.

'Not making a lot sense, to be honest, guv. He's refusing to leave until the body's been removed.'

'That might be a while. Do we know a bit more about what happened yet?'

'He says a kid in a mask ambushed them, threatened them with a knife. Then it gets a bit weird. He claims the boy wanted his phone, but then says it wasn't a robbery. He also says he threatened to sexually assault the girl.'

'Any sign of that?'

'Doesn't look like it – we'll have to wait until the PM for confirmation obviously – but her clothes don't appear to have been removed or tampered with.'

'Didn't he see?' asked Finn, not quite understanding.

'That's what I mean about weird – he's gabbling a bit. Says he was trying to find help when the murder actually happened.'

'He *left* them? *Left* his daughter?' Finn tried to keep his voice down, but couldn't help shooting a look at the man sat on the bench.

'Sounds like it. It's not entirely clear. We need to get him into an interview room and take a statement ASAP. He's the only witness and as you can see, there are no cameras around here.'

She was right, thought Finn. Traumatic events often played strange tricks on the memory. By the following morning, Suleman's brain might well be blotting out some of the critical details. It also appeared some sort of dialogue took place with the killer before the murder. What was said to make Karl leave? He'd encountered situations where parents ended up getting hurt trying to *protect* their children, but this was unusual. Fear and panic could often produce unpredictable behaviours though. Maybe he'd assumed there'd be a few more people around to help. Or maybe he'd run in terror, thinking his daughter would follow – or maybe the killer was someone he knew. Experience taught Finn not to judge, whatever it might look like.

'What do we know about them?'

'He runs an advertising agency near King's Cross. His daughter – Leah – was twenty-three and worked as a fundraiser for a local charity. He was taking her out for dinner.'

'Any other relatives?'

'Yes – the mother ...' Ojo referred to her pocketbook, 'Claire Suleman, was having a night out with some friends apparently. She's been informed and is on her way over.'

'Any sign of the murder weapon?'

It was an optimistic question given the darkness, but it wasn't uncommon in situations that escalated unexpectedly for a weapon to be discarded in panic.

'No, but we might have more luck in the morning obviously.'

Finn peered across the large oval boating lake. It seemed vast at night, moonlight rippling across it with a white-silver glow.

'He might have chucked it in there – I want the underwater search unit here early.'

Ojo nodded.

'Something else you should know, guv: he stabbed her multiple times, then cut her throat. Karl heard her scream, so we know it was in that sequence.'

Finn frowned – they both knew that was unusual. Robberies that went wrong tended to produce a single, lethal stab wound; the perpetrator keener on escaping than making a meal of things. This kind of frenzied attack suggested either a psycho or someone on something.

'Let's see if there've been any addicts hanging around the park recently. Have some uniforms ask around tomorrow morning – the local dog-walkers and joggers might remember something.'

'That reminds me – there *was* one witness. An old lady walking her dog. Karl says he tried to borrow her phone, but she wasn't carrying one. We've got a description, and we're trying to locate her. There's a chance she might have seen the killer on his way out.'

Paulsen emerged from the gloom and re-joined them.

'The park ranger says the gates were locked on time, nobody saw anything unusual. Have we got a proper description of the suspect yet, sarge?'

Again Ojo referred to her pocketbook.

'Only a sketchy one. Medium height, average build, he was wearing a dark jacket, blue jeans, wore some sort of reflective mask. The only distinctive thing was the voice apparently – said he sounded young. From the description of it, I'm fairly sure the murder weapon was a zombie knife.'

Finn nodded in resignation. It would have been an agonising death – the blades were long and serrated, designed to damage organs internally as they were pulled out.

He paused to take stock. There was precious little to work with here. A seemingly motiveless murder in an isolated location by a well-disguised killer. They were literally stumbling in the dark.

Karl turned to look at them, as if sensing their uncertainty, and Finn decided it was time to engage. As they approached he began to see the man's face in detail for the first time, the trauma written across it.

'Mr Suleman, I'm so sorry for your loss. I'm Detective Inspector Finn, this is DC Paulsen. I know this is very difficult, but would you feel able to come back to the station and give us a statement tonight?'

He seemed to think about it for a moment, but Finn knew that look. When people were in shock, words always took a few extra seconds to penetrate.

'Sure.' He nodded over at Leah. 'How long is she going to be here?' He spoke briskly, visibly trying to hold himself together.

'Karl!'

The voice cut through before Finn could answer and they all turned. A smartly dressed middle-aged woman with short brown hair was walking towards them. Finn recognised DC Sami Dattani's hunched figure next to her. The woman saw the forensic tent illuminated on the footpath, saw the wine-coloured ground surrounding it and put her hand to her mouth. She tried to go over, but Dattani gently restrained her.

'I'm sorry, I need you to stay outside the cordon,' said Dattani.

'That's my daughter ...' She tried to wriggle free, but Dattani held her.

'Please, Mrs Suleman. It's critical the crime scene isn't contaminated.'

'Claire ...' said her husband. As she saw him she shook free from Dattani's grip, sank to her knees and howled. The sound echoed around the park. Karl ran over, standing helplessly above her, not knowing what to say or do. His wife was sobbing now, huge uncontrollable gasps of pain. His head dropped into silent juddering tears of his own, the dam finally releasing. He slowly knelt in front of his wife and tried to put his arms around her.

Paulsen caught Finn's eye, and he shrugged. He'd seen all too many people at the very worst moments of their lives. He knew these seconds were precious, would hold a lifetime's memory for both of them. It wasn't yours to stamp yourself over; you had to let things play out.

'What happened?' said Claire through the tears. For a moment Karl could barely speak.

'I don't know. It was all so quick. I should have been there.'

'What do you mean?'

'This is my fault.'

Karl tried to find the words, but couldn't. He put his hand over his mouth suddenly, and quickly brought himself to his feet again. He stumbled towards a nearby bush and began to retch. His wife turned to look at the sight beneath the lighting again, and howled for a second time.

'There's something odd about this,' whispered Paulsen. She and Finn were standing alone now, watching the Sulemans, while Ojo briefed Dattani by the cordon.

'Go on . . .' Finn replied.

'If I'd been walking through this park with Nancy, and some little psycho jumped out with a knife, there's nothing – and I mean *nothing* – which makes me leave her alone with him.'

'Don't judge him. Not until we know exactly what happened.'

'I'm not judging him. It's a fact. Imagine if it was your daughter.'

Finn pursed his lips. He didn't have children; he and Karin had never got around to it. She'd wanted him to have them though, made him promise her before she died that he would one day. He'd certainly been told enough that you didn't really know what it meant to be truly selfless until you were a parent. To his very ordered mind, it was simply a dispassionate fact; he didn't have children, so couldn't put himself in Karl Suleman's shoes. Instead, he tried to imagine what he would have done if it'd been Karin there.

'There's no way I'd have left her,' he said.

'My dad wouldn't have left me either. Wouldn't leave me now, and he's seventy-four. There's nobody I know who'd do that. So why did he?'

They watched the Sulemans for a moment. Claire, kneeling in the mud, unravelling; her husband, a silhouette coughing and spluttering in the nearby vegetation. They needed to get this moving – to get her away from here, to get him back to Cedar House. Karl finally stood, wiping his chin. And that's when Finn saw it. The look in his eye. The look that would one day kill the man. The guilt.

3

'He was just a kid. If I saw him in the street during the day, I probably wouldn't give him a second look.'

They were now back in the relative warmth of one of the interview rooms at Cedar House. Sami Dattani was with Claire Suleman, having persuaded her to let him drive her home while her husband gave his statement. Karl was still palpably in shock, turning down offers of hot food or drink. Every now and then he'd start shaking and the words would dry up and they'd wait as he'd gathered himself again.

'Just start at the beginning,' said Finn, 'so we've got it all on the record. What time did you meet your daughter this evening?'

'I caught the 18.36 from Victoria, so I guess just after seven.'

'You work in central London – what about Leah?'

He shook his head.

'No, she works in Crystal Palace, so it was just a short walk for her.'

'Did anyone else know you were meeting?' asked Paulsen.

'My wife obviously, a couple of people at work I mentioned it to. I can't speak for Leah – she might have posted something on Facebook. She's all over her social media . . .' His face started to crumple again, but he just about managed to rein it in.

'So you met in the dinosaur park, then what happened?'

'We decided to walk down to a restaurant in Penge.' He shook his head. 'I can't even remember what we were talking about in those two minutes. Then this guy just appeared out of nowhere. He must have been waiting in the bushes.'

'What did he look like? Was he tall or short, for example?'

'Average height, I suppose. Maybe five foot seven or eight? As I said before, he was wearing a mask so I couldn't see his face.'

'Tell us more about the mask – what exactly did it look like?' said Paulsen.

His eyes narrowed at the memory.

'It was weird. Kind of chrome-like. Some sort of reflective material. And he had a hood up too.' He shook his head, palpably shivering at the memory. 'It was like talking to a fucking alien.'

'What about his hands? Could you see if he was black or white?'

Karl frowned as he tried to remember the brief flash of skin he'd seen on the wrist holding the knife.

'I don't know – I couldn't be sure.'

'What about his clothing?'

'He was wearing a dark blue metallic jacket . . . and jeans, I think.'

He said the words slowly, as if disbelieving his own memory.

'Expensive trainers, tatty jeans? Anything distinctive at all you can remember?'

He concentrated, then shook his head.

'Can you estimate what age he might have been?'

'A teenager, I'd say.'

'Early, late teens?'

'Sorry, could be either. It was impossible to tell under that mask.'

He reached out in front of him and took a sip of water from a paper cup, gulping it down loudly. His face looked hollow, white as the walls around them.

'What about the knife he was carrying, can you describe it?'

'It was huge, serrated. Oh God . . .'

He put his hand up to his mouth as he remembered the feel of it tugging on his skin. It was impossible not to imagine that blade cutting deep into Leah's flesh. The shark-fin steel tearing through her organs as it came back out. He dropped his head and began to sob silently. Finn gave him a moment.

'We can come back to the knife later. I don't want to make this any more difficult for you than it already is.'

Karl looked back up and swallowed.

'It's alright . . . I want to do this.'

Finn nodded.

'Tell me about the conversation – what did he say to you?'

'That's just it – he didn't seem to want anything. He told me either he'd stab me, or . . .'

He stopped again, caught in another memory. 'Or he'd rape Leah.'

The words hung there as their meaning sank in.

'He made you *choose*?' said Finn slowly.

'Yes. Leah wanted me to go. She said at least that way we'd both live. It seemed to make sense in the moment.'

'You trusted this guy's word?' said Paulsen, her tone even and neutral.

'I didn't have time to think. It all happened in seconds. One minute we're walking along, the next . . .'

He tailed off and shook his head again. Paulsen's eyes were blazing. Finn couldn't tell whether it was fury at a man who'd deserted his daughter, or rage at the individual who'd put them in this position. There was an awkward pause which inadvertently felt judgemental. In truth Finn was still processing the awfulness of the choice this man had been presented with. Suddenly the expression on his face was not so much

26

haunted as damned, the imploring tone in his voice taking on a whole new dimension.

'I went to get help. That's the only reason I left her. It was a gamble – I thought if I could find someone I could stop it. I should have gone back up to the station – there were people there. I don't know why I didn't, I wasn't thinking straight. I should never have gone. What sort of father leaves their child?'

Karl flinched, almost in physical pain. The reason he hadn't been there when his daughter died was now so much clearer to Finn. A snap decision, an equation he'd got horribly and terribly wrong. His hand rose up to his mouth again and clamped itself there. It was hard to tell if he was about to retch again, or whether it was to simply stop the incriminating flow of words. Once more they patiently waited, until the hand slowly released.

'What happened next?' said Paulsen.

'He told me he wanted my phone to stop me calling the police. At that point, I realised it wasn't about robbing us – he wanted Leah. There's a pub down at the bottom of the park – it's usually packed on a Friday night. I thought if I could get there, you know?' Again that pleading look in his eye, thought Finn, but it wasn't the two detectives he was trying to convince. 'What could I do? I'm forty-six years old. This kid was holding a knife . . .' He automatically put his hand to his throat, and Finn noticed for the first time the small dot of dried blood there. Suleman saw him staring at it. 'He warned me – put the knife to my throat. Like I say, I just wanted to get help. Do you understand? Do you see why I went, *why* I wasn't there?'

He was going to feel this for every single second of every single day of the rest of his life, that much was clear. They weren't quite fast enough in answering him.

'Of course,' said Paulsen. He looked down in shame.

'So you ran, and that's when you saw the woman with the dog?' said Finn quickly.

27

'Yeah. I asked her if she had a phone, but she wasn't carrying one. I was talking to her when I heard Leah scream. I turned and went back. The rest you know.'

'We're trying to locate that woman, based on the description you gave us earlier. She might have seen the killer too. She's probably a regular in the park, so we're hopeful,' said Paulsen. Suleman didn't really seem to be taking it in.

'If I'd have stayed, he'd have stabbed me and done what he was going to do to Leah anyway.'

Possibly, thought Finn, but didn't say it.

'And you're sure at no time did he ask for money or anything else?' he said instead.

'No – he just told me give him my phone and leave.'

'At this stage – and we haven't confirmed this forensically yet – there doesn't seem to be any sign of sexual assault.'

There was a long pause as he digested this, a tiny flicker of relief somewhere in the torment.

'Why didn't he take her bag then? It had her credit cards in, some cash. And my phone – her phone – why didn't he take those?'

'They're savvy these days – they know phones can be traced, so some of these kids prefer not to touch them,' said Finn. 'Look, I hate to ask you this, but we need to consider every possibility. Is there anyone who might have wanted to hurt either you or Leah?'

'No. Of course not. Everyone adored her. I know I would say that, but it's true. As for me – I'm a businessman. I've probably made enemies, but not to this extent. And they'd hurt me financially, not by stabbing my daughter. And none of them are teenagers, for God's sake.'

'Did she have a boyfriend?'

'No, not really. She split with someone a few months back – but that was his choice, he'd got a job in Glasgow. She'd been dating someone new recently. Some data analyst, I think. Very early stages though.'

'Do you have his details?'

'No, of course not.'

'No problem, we'll be looking through her phone anyway. But if there's anything else that comes to mind later . . .'

Suleman nodded.

'I'd never have deserted her. I was trying to find help. You have to believe that.'

Again, his tone held the same mixture of shame and pleading, but this time he didn't wait for their reaction, and this time the tears weren't silent as he broke down again.

'It sounds like out and out sadism without a motive,' said DCI John Skegman, as he tried to make sense of the story he was being told. He'd been on his way out of the building when word came through of the incident in Crystal Palace. A small wiry man, he often projected a slightly shifty demeanour to those who didn't know him. Finn knew better though. The darting eyes, and what could be perceived as a slightly condescending attitude, belied a dispassionate mind and a thick skin. By and large it was a supportive relationship, with only the occasional moments of mutual stubbornness causing friction between them.

The detritus of a half-eaten pizza crust was sitting in a square green box on his usually immaculate desk. Yet another Friday night that'd been torpedoed, thought Finn.

'Sometimes people just find themselves in the wrong place at the wrong time. The kid was probably off his tits or there was something about these two he took against,' he said.

'I'm not so sure this was an addict,' said Paulsen. 'But sadistic is the right word for that choice – there was something unnecessarily cruel about it; making this guy leave, then killing his daughter anyway. It was cold-blooded, not hot-blooded.'

Finn nodded, agreeing with her logic, the words jogging a memory at the back of his mind. It'd been nagging at him since they'd left the interview room. And now he remembered why – another man with haunted eyes, also tortured by a choice made in haste. The last time Finn had seen Martin Walker he'd been in a hospital bed, wrapped in bandages. Walker was a retired firefighter who'd crossed paths with a particularly dangerous underworld figure. He had eventually committed suicide, leaving a note behind saying he'd been given no alternative. He claimed if he hadn't, his wife would have been killed instead. But seemingly unlike this new case, Walker had been targeted for a reason – he'd stolen money from the wrong man. It was unlikely there was any connection between that tragedy and this one, though it had gained a lot of press coverage at the time. It was chilling to think it might have inspired someone.

'What do we know about the victim?' said Skegman.

There was nothing extraordinary about Leah Suleman. She'd been a charity fundraiser who lived locally. A quick check of her social media had showed nothing other than the usual ups and downs of a twenty-something Londoner. She seemed to have plenty of friends, liked to travel, and clearly enjoyed an amusing animal video judging by her tweets. Finn shook his head.

'Nothing out of the ordinary.'

'And the father?'

'Looks quite well heeled – expensive clothes, runs an ad agency in town. That's as much as we know so far.'

'Alright, let uniform and forensics do their work. Hopefully it'll give you a bit more to work with in the morning. Who's looking after this overnight?'

'DS Collier, and Sami Dattani's with the mother at the family home in Dulwich. I've asked Nishat Adams to drive Karl home.'

Skegman nodded, and absent-mindedly closed the lid of the cardboard box containing the remains of his dinner. Paulsen looked at them both.

'Are we done for now?' she said.

Finn nodded.

'Get going, Mattie, and thanks for tonight. I'm sorry it messed up your evening.'

She gave a tired shake of the head and left. Finn waited for the door to shut behind her, then turned back to Skegman.

'Just a thought, but what about making her one of the Sulemans' FLOs?'

Skegman's eyes narrowed and Finn could guess what he was thinking. Family liaison officers were usually deployed in pairs as a matter of policy. Dattani and Adams were both experienced in the role and natural fits. Paulsen was neither.

'Really?'

'She's done the training.'

It was an idea that had been sitting in the back of Finn's mind for a while now. He'd seen enough over the past twelve months to know she was both empathetic and sensitive, despite her outward moodiness. She'd hate it, of course, but that didn't bother him.

'What's your thinking?' said Skegman.

Finn had been here many times before and knew exactly how to play this. Done properly, with a little prodding, the DCI would later think the idea had been his from the start.

'I think it might help improve her all-round skillset. We both know she's got promise – but you don't realise potential without getting proper hands-on experience. Sami can help her and I think it's a good opportunity to try her out.'

Skegman's frown deepened.

'As I recall, Sami's workload is already pretty full. And hasn't he got some court commitments coming up?'

'All our FLOs are busy. It's just another reason to bring Paulsen on.'

'I'm all for bringing her on – it's using the Sulemans as guinea pigs that concerns me.'

'Don't worry, I'll be all over it. I wouldn't have suggested it if I thought there was a risk.'

Skegman looked up suspiciously.

'Is there another reason for this? Half the building thinks you show her too much favouritism as it is.'

'Then half the building can fuck off. I rate her and I care about seeing people develop – that's all.'

Finn kept his face neutral. The emphasis was now as much on whether Skegman trusted Finn's judgement as on whether Paulsen was suitable. The DCI straightened up some loose paperwork, threw it into an in-tray and leant back in his chair. He didn't look ready for a long debate.

'Alright, we'll see how it goes. Do the risk assessment for her and Sami. But I want to hear *very* regular updates. Any sign she's struggling . . .'

Finn nodded firmly, and turned for the door. The drink with Cally Hunter earlier that evening felt an eternity ago. His stomach was rumbling and his mouth was dry as a bone. Something about Karl Suleman's shame wouldn't wash off him either. He just wanted to get home, eat and sleep.

'Don't rush off just yet, Alex,' said Skegman.

Finn sighed and turned back round.

'You're quite . . .' he searched for the right words, '. . . diffi-cult to pin down these days. How are things?'

Finn sighed again, this time inwardly.

'Absolutely fine. Nothing a good night's sleep won't put right. It's been a long day.'

It was a good try, but he wasn't going to get off that easily.

'Aren't they all at the moment? If you come in at the crack of dawn that's what tends to happen. I wasn't just talking about today.'

Finn really wasn't in the mood for this. It also vaguely irritated him that someone had clearly been in Skegman's ear.

'Just organising my time efficiently, that's all.'

'Fine, if that's the reason.'

'It is.'

Finn knew what Skegman was driving at. The unspoken insinuation that his behaviour was linked to his bereavement. He stared him in the eye, as if daring him to address the subject head-on. He was betting he wouldn't.

'You could always delegate some of it. Working yourself into the ground isn't ultimately helping anyone, is it?'

'I'm just trying to be conscientious. Leading by example, if you like.'

The other man nodded, but still met his gaze directly.

'When was the last time you took a day off?'

Finn was struggling to contain his rising irritation. As far as he was concerned, his personal life was just that – personal – and nothing to do with anyone here. The longer this conversation went on, the more certain he was that no good would come from it.

'I'm probably due one soon. I'll bear it in mind. And on that note, I really ought to be going – it's going to be pretty full-on tomorrow.' He smiled pleasantly. 'Good night, John.'

He didn't wait for Skegman to answer before exiting. Another old trick he still enjoyed deploying when he felt he could get away with it.

'*You're not fooling anyone,*' said Karin, as he headed down the corridor. Nothing a good night's sleep wouldn't put right, he repeated to himself, and he walked out into the cold.

4

Mattie Paulsen arrived early outside the large block of Victorian houses tucked a street or two behind Dulwich Village. There hadn't been much time to get her head round things. A terser-than-normal Finn had rung early and asked for a straight yes or no about the FLO role. She'd accepted, largely because she couldn't think of a reason not to. Something about Karl Suleman also piqued her interest. She wanted to know more about the man who'd turned his back and ran. But as she'd made her way into south London, her suspicions had started to grow. Finn's gruffness, she'd decided, was cloud cover for something else.

The one aspect of her life at Cedar House that irritated her was the constant sense of scrutiny from both Finn and Skegman. She felt patronised, convinced other officers of her rank and experience weren't put under the same spotlight. One of these days a conversation would be had, but for now there was a job to do. She'd spoken briefly to Dattani before setting off and the scale of the task was beginning to dawn on her.

He'd stayed with Claire Suleman the previous night until her husband returned home. The grief he'd described had been visceral. She'd cried, talked incoherently or simply rocked gently on her sofa, numb with shock. He hadn't felt he'd done much good, but knew it was more his presence that mattered than his words. It was a thankless job in some ways, the only true measure of success the degree by which you didn't fuck it up. There was a slight knot in her stomach as she approached the front door.

She was no expert but reckoned any one of the homes she could see would set you back at least a seven-figure sum. The multistorey building in front of her, all period brickwork and gleaming white windowsills, looked beautifully maintained. She rang the doorbell and was greeted by a wan-looking woman wearing a sweatshirt and jeans. Her brown hair hung lifelessly around her neck, while her eyes looked red from crying. Paulsen smiled reassuringly and introduced herself, and Claire Suleman ushered her in. Expensive-looking paintings hung on the walls of the hallway, a far cry from the few odds and sods from Camden Market that decorated Paulsen's small flat in Tufnell Park. In any other situation she would have cooed with admiration, but she doubted material possessions mattered much any more to the Sulemans. Or ever would again.

Claire offered her some coffee, the words coming out mechanically. She politely declined and they went through to an opulent living room. Her eyes were immediately drawn to the large family portrait which hung in an alcove next to the fireplace: a professional-looking black-and-white shot of Karl, Claire and Leah taken maybe only two or three years earlier. The smiles looked genuine, from contented, happier times. Claire sat down on a large grey sofa and Paulsen took a nearby armchair.

'You've just missed Karl, I'm afraid. He's gone for a walk – I think he just needed to get out of the house for a bit.'

'That's understandable. How are you?'

She opened her mouth to answer but no sound emerged, and she closed it, looking down and shaking her head before trying again.

35

'It's unreal. I can't . . . haven't really processed it properly yet. I still don't actually believe it's happened. You keep thinking she's going to call or come through the door at any minute. I take it you haven't caught the person who did this yet?'

Paulsen shook her head.

'It's still early days, but we've got a major investigation underway.'

Claire nodded almost imperceptibly.

'Can you thank the officer who was here last night, by the way? Sami? He was very kind. It can't have been easy.'

'You'll get the chance to thank him yourself. He and I are your family liaison officers.' There was another brief nod of acknowledgement, but Paulsen could guess what she was thinking: that she didn't want more police officers sitting in her living room. Because she desperately wanted it to be yesterday afternoon again, when her daughter was still alive. But that, in part, was why Paulsen was there: to help the Sulemans deal with some of the hard realities of what was happening.

She explained that she and Sami would be keeping Claire and Karl up to date with how the investigation was progressing and could answer any questions they might have. They could also provide information about support agencies, the complexities of the criminal justice system, and coronial procedures. If the Sulemans had any complaints, queries or worries of any kind, they'd be there to field them. Human faces in the tide of confusion which often followed sudden and unexpected horror.

Claire turned to her – a question seemed to be bubbling to the surface, one she was struggling to articulate. Paulsen shuffled in her seat uncomfortably as she waited.

'When can we have her back?'

'The post-mortem's scheduled for tomorrow morning. We'll look to try and hurry things up after that, so you can get on with organising the funeral.'

Claire suddenly looked very small. The language of death – post-mortems, funerals – all emphasising the new reality again.

'I'm sorry to ask you, but is there anything we ought to know about your daughter?'

'How do you mean?'

'We're working from the assumption that this was a random attack. But we have to cover all bases – is there any reason someone might have wanted to hurt her?'

The thought clearly hadn't crossed Claire's mind. She shook her head in horror.

'She fell out with a friend a few months back, I don't think they've been talking since, but that was over some festival tickets. It's hardly a reason to kill her. Otherwise – no, she was a very happy and popular person. Unless there was something she wasn't telling us.'

'I gather she'd just split from her boyfriend?'

'Ross? That wasn't serious. He was a nice lad, but he got himself a job in Scotland and it just sort of petered out.'

'Your husband also mentioned she'd met someone new?'

'I wouldn't go that far – she'd been trying those dating apps. I think she'd gone on a couple of dates, said the last guy seemed nice but that was it.'

'We've got her phone, so we'll look into him. What about your husband – does he have any enemies?'

'Karl? I don't understand.'

'It's possible – however unlikely it may seem – that the killer may have deliberately targeted them last night.'

Claire took in the implication for a moment.

'He's not an easy man. I wouldn't like to work with him. He's very single-minded and very dedicated. He's certainly made enemies over the years, but no one who'd want to do anything like this. Surely they were both just in the wrong place at the wrong time?'

'That's the most likely explanation.'

'What do you think happened?'

'As I say, our starting point is—'

'No, that's not what I'm asking,' said Claire, cutting in. 'I don't want the official answer. I want to know what *you* think happened.'

Paulsen shrugged.

'I've no reason to disbelieve your husband's version of events. I think it happened exactly as he described it.'

Claire was impassive, but Paulsen could sense where this was going, remembering her own first impressions.

'I just don't understand why Karl left her. I can't get my head around it.'

She seemed to want Paulsen to answer the question, and Mattie wasn't sure what to say. Did Claire *know* about the choice her husband faced the previous evening? Had they had that conversation last night? Or had he been too ashamed to tell her? What was asked of him. And what he did. Was it even in Paulsen's province to tell her without having that conversation with Karl first? If Finn and Skegman were testing her, then this was challenge number one.

'It sounds like . . . they didn't have much time to think about it. In that moment, it seemed to your husband . . . like the right thing to do.'

'Except it wasn't, was it? He ran away and my daughter's dead.'

'Don't be too hard on him. From what he told us, he was trying to find help.'

'But he didn't find help. He left her to die alone in the dirt . . .' she faltered again, her eyes beginning to well up once more, 'and no one should die alone, should they?'

They were interrupted by the sound of the front door open-ing and slamming shut. Karl walked into the living room, sharing the same gaunt expression as his wife. But for a fleet-ing moment Paulsen saw something else on his face, a dark-ness which swiftly vanished as he sat down next to Claire.

'Is there any news – have you got the bastard yet?'

Paulsen shook her head and gave an abridged version of the same speech she'd given Claire earlier. He listened carefully then sagged into the sofa. He looked utterly exhausted and it was only ten o'clock in the morning.

'Is there anything else that's come to mind overnight?' said Paulsen.

'No. I just wish I'd done things differently. I keep playing it over and over in my head.'

He looked over at Claire, as if expecting some reassurance. But if he thought she was going to say 'You can't blame your-self' or 'It wasn't your fault', then the words didn't come. Claire was focusing her gaze on the corner of the room instead.

'That's a very natural reaction,' said Paulsen. 'Look, I know it's very soon, but after what you've been through – *both* been through – there's people I can put you in touch with. Counsellors, who've great experience of helping with these situations.'

Karl made a dismissive gesture with his hand.

'*These situations?* Because this sort of thing happens all the time . . .'

Claire looked over sharply at him.

'Don't just dismiss it like that.'

'Come on, Claire, I solve my own problems. Always have. I'm sure it helps some people, but counselling's not for me.'

Husband and wife stared at each other, and Paulsen remem-bered her earlier butterflies. This was why she'd had them. She took a sip of her tea and didn't dare look up. There was heavy breathing, but it was hard to tell which one of them it belonged to. She felt a burning desire to get out of this claustrophobic house. The silence was broken as Karl began to vent again.

'A counsellor can't change what happened, can they? Do you know Leah wanted to go to a restaurant in Greenwich? It was me who suggested meeting in Crystal Palace. I texted her on a whim yesterday afternoon. It was easier for me to get to from Victoria. I was being selfish. If I'd have known . . .'

He put his head in his hands, and once more Paulsen noticed there were no words or sympathy from his wife. It was too early to judge what the future held for the Sulemans, but Paulsen could see Karl was struggling. He needed Claire, and she could barely look at him.

'So what are we supposed to do – just sit here now? Wait for something to happen?' he said.

'I'm here for as long as you want me to be. If you'd prefer to be alone, that's absolutely fine too,' said Paulsen.

Karl slammed his hand down on to his thigh and Paulsen jumped, despite herself.

'What really gets me is these little shitheads are allowed to run around unchecked. We don't need you here *now*, do we? We don't need police saying "There, there, there" after the event. We need officers out on the street stopping these bastards before they hurt people.' There was a slight hysteria in his voice and Paulsen smiled sympathetically.

'I promise you – we're throwing a lot of manpower at this investigation. They're all good people.'

'How many officers?'

'I can't tell you the exact number, but like I say . . .'

'You don't know, do you? I knew it – cuts. Not as many as there should be, I bet.' He smiled sarcastically. 'It wasn't just that no-mark last night, was it? The politicians killed her too.

Go on, tell me I'm wrong. When you catch this kid, he'll have been in some institution. Some idiot will have let him loose—'

'Don't take it out on her, Karl,' interrupted Claire, who had been watching his rant with a detached iciness. 'She's only doing her job. It wasn't *just* the politicians who let Leah down, was it?' said Claire. He visibly recoiled, the words hitting him like a punch to the solar plexus.

'And what's that supposed to mean?'

Husband and wife looked at each other. She rose and walked out of the room, shutting the door firmly behind her, just short of slamming it. The anger was swiftly ebbing out of him. He looked lost and defeated, and Paulsen felt the same – unable to find the words that would even come close to helping.

5

Finn liked his new flat, and that was half the problem. Not long after Karin's death he'd sold their two-bedder in Balham, and bought himself a more compact place close to Wandsworth Common. It was part of a conscious effort to move on – that much Karin would have approved of. But the way he'd turned his new home into an out-and-out bachelor pad would have infuriated her. There were still pictures of her, of course, but he'd deliberately kept those low-key. He didn't want a shrine. There was no need for copious visual reminders, not when he carried her as close as he did.

The fact was, he enjoyed his own company. The best way to unwind, he found, wasn't in a pub, cinema or restaurant with others, it was within his own four walls – alone. He savoured his privacy, preferring to process the day's events with some good food and a glass of single malt. And there were no take-away boxes littering the living room, no stacks of dirty plates in the kitchen, no unironed shirts draped on radiators. He ran a tight ship, but Cally Hunter's words of the previous night still resonated with him as he went through his usual breakfast routine: 'She was worried you'd retreat into yourself after her death.'

They weren't Cally's words, of course. They were Karin's, and much as he hated to admit it, he was starting to think the unthinkable: what if he ignored Karin's wishes? What if he stayed like this? He was, after all, happier living this way. And hadn't she wanted him to be happy after she'd gone? Wasn't that the point?

He was also irked by the conversation he'd had in Skegman's office. Everyone wanted to poke their nose in. It was none of their business; he didn't stick his oar into his colleagues' personal lives. They may have a view about how he chose to live, but that didn't mean he had to tolerate it.

'Listen to yourself,' said Karin. For an instant it was like he could see her, leaning against the kitchen counter, arching an eyebrow. He shook his head, ignored her, took a fresh cup of coffee from his expensive machine and sat down at the kitchen table. His phone buzzed with a text and Cally's name flashed up on the display. He sighed. It was as if he'd summoned her.

Have you given any further thought to our conversation?

'Not really' was the honest answer. He'd hoped she'd just go away. It would be quite easy to lose her, after all – to simply ignore her. He suspected Cally wouldn't fight him too hard either. Her honour would remain intact; she'd done just as Karin requested, made the effort. If Finn wouldn't play ball, she'd no reason to keep knocking on a closed door. She'd disappear again, leave him to his splendid isolation. His fingers hovered over his phone but he couldn't find an answer for her. He put the handset down and began tucking into his porridge, his thoughts already turning to the events in Crystal Palace Park.

'Fucking dogs. I'd ban them. And their owners,' muttered Jackie Ojo around an hour later in the incident room. She'd come fresh from the crime scene. The usually serene detective sergeant was glaring and swearing because she'd managed to put her right foot straight down the centre of a freshly laid

43

turd. Despite having cleaned the offending sole several times over, a faint waft still accompanied her. With the park closed as the forensic work continued there, Finn assumed it was more likely to be fox shit but decided against correcting her. He took a breath, both literally and metaphorically, and asked how things were progressing instead.

'There's nothing from the scene. We haven't found a weapon in the surrounding shrub land and the underwater search unit didn't find anything in the boating lake. But it's a big park, so we're a long way from done. There are footprints in the ground close to where the murder took place, but half the world must have passed through there yesterday – it's literally clear as mud. The door-to-doors around the perimeter of the park haven't produced anything either. We did get *something* though – there's CCTV on the main road, north-east of the park . . .' she glanced down at some paperwork she was holding, 'that's Crystal Palace Park Road – the cameras picked up someone around ten minutes after Leah met Karl in the park.'

She passed the black-and-white print-out to Finn. It was dark and extremely blurry, but showed a figure walking next to the fence separating the park from the road. What was clear was the figure's clothing: a dark jacket and jeans. The person wasn't wearing a mask, but with the hood up and the face pointing away from the camera, the image was too pixelated to make out anything useful. There was a murky patch across their midriff, which could have been Leah Suleman's blood or just a shadow – it was impossible to tell. This might just be an innocent member of the public, wearing very similar clothing to the individual they were looking for, but Finn doubted it. He was fairly sure the person in this picture was the same one who'd stabbed Leah Suleman multiple times, just minutes before.

'I think this might just be him. The timestamp, the rough description, the location all work. Is this the clearest image we can get?' Finn asked.

'Afraid so. He goes up the road a bit further then turns into a street where there's no coverage. We haven't managed to pick him up after that. Looks like he was heading down towards Forest Hill though.'

'Shame. Still, it's a good match for the description Karl gave us.'

He studied the image closely again. 'There's no sign of a knife, though he could be carrying it under the jacket. What did SOCO tell you?'

'They're reasonably positive. Given how frenzied the attack was, there's a chance we might get a DNA or print match. Now we know which part of the park he used to exit, we can track his route from where he ambushed the Sulemans. He might have chucked the knife into some bushes on his way out. I've got uniform doing a sweep.'

'When's the post-mortem?'

'Eleven-thirty tomorrow morning. I'm not sure how much Leah was able to fight back, but if she did manage to scratch his skin . . .'

Finn was about to respond when Paulsen swept into the incident room. She came straight over, her face instantly creasing into a frown.

'What's that smell?'

Ojo eyeballed her.

'What?' asked Paulsen, bemused.

'How did it go with the Sulemans?' said Finn quickly.

'Not great – they're in bits. Don't think it's properly sunk in yet. There's nothing new, I'm afraid, Karl hasn't remembered anything else overnight to add to his statement. What's that?'

She pointed at the print-out Finn was holding and he passed it over.

'Could be our guy. Cameras picked him up on the main road next to the park shortly after the murder.'

Paulsen squinted at it, the same way Finn had.

'Want me to take it back to Karl to look at?'

Finn nodded.

'Just a thought, but if this guy was heading down from Crystal Palace towards Forest Hill, it's not far from the Hope Estate, is it?' said Ojo.

The Hope Estate was a name familiar to everyone at Cedar House. A hub for one of south London's largest county lines gangs, a few months before it'd been the subject of a major operation. A significant number of drug suppliers and dealers had been taken off the streets, but even the police knew it was more a short-term measure than a long-term solution. Like mould on a damp wall, the problem was always going to return.

'Could be purely coincidental,' said Finn.

'It's been three months since we raided the place. Plenty of time for someone else to take control down there,' said Ojo.

She was right and Finn knew it. The business of county lines – in which organised criminals used vulnerable young people to courier heroin and crack cocaine from London out to the regions – was an incredibly profitable one. It earnt its name from the dedicated mobile phone lines that were used to take orders from local drug users. Some individual lines were worth as much as five thousand pounds in a single day. Children as young as eleven were being coerced into travelling across the country, carrying just a cheap mobile phone, a bag of class A drugs and a knife. As people poured into London every morning, a new breed of commuter was heading out in the opposite direction.

46

'But why would a county lines gang want to hurt a father and daughter having a Friday night out? Doesn't make sense,' said Paulsen. Ojo shook her head slowly too.

Finn knew how they felt. On the surface it was a murder that looked eminently explicable. The wrong people in the wrong place at the wrong time. But the more he thought about it, the more the pieces didn't quite fit together. The further back you stood, the more unclear the picture became. He cleared his thoughts and focused.

'Let's not jump to conclusions about gang involvement – they tend to keep things between themselves. It's rare civilians get caught up in it,' he said.

'Is it though?' said Ojo. 'What if this kid was dealing? Or buying. Something about the Sulemans pisses him off and it escalates from there?'

'Except according to Karl they were ambushed. Why do you ambush someone unless you want to steal from them? And this guy didn't take a thing. And then there's the mask – why wear that? Why bring it if you're buying or dealing? It smacks of premeditated.'

'Mistaken identity?' said Ojo.

'What – you think there was another father and daughter he was waiting for?' said Finn.

'No – but maybe this guy was waiting for someone else, and decided for whatever reason to target the Sulemans instead?'

Finn thought about it, but it still didn't quite add up. He was also aware there could have been any number of reasons to explain what happened. He knew only too well the triggers for violent crime could be ludicrously small and idiotically petty. Impossible to second-guess.

'A kid with a zombie knife though – it's not like it's something you can just buy in Sainsbury's. He must have got it from somewhere, been *given* it,' said Paulsen. 'How many knives did we pick up during the raids on the Hope Estate?'

Finn nodded. She was right, and there'd been plenty of zombie knives in that trawl.

'I know a guy down there – Isiah Simms. He's a mechanic, I think, but his brother was stabbed to death a few years back. He's become a bit of an unofficial knife-crime campaigner and he's helped us before,' he said. 'He's a good guy and he's got his ear to the ground. If there is any kind of gang link to Leah's death, he might have heard something about it. I'll go down and talk to him. If nothing else, someone that way might have seen our guy – he must have been covered in blood.'

'There is one other thing,' said Paulsen. 'I just rang both Karl Suleman's ad agency and the charity Leah was working for. I was wondering if someone might have seen or heard anything unusual in the last few days. Somebody hanging around, that kind of thing ...' She tailed off, as if unsure whether to continue the point.

'And was there?' said Finn.

'No, but the guy I spoke to at the ad agency was interesting. Karl's just laid a whole bunch of people off. A lot of them are pretty upset. One in particular made allegations of bullying – it got nasty; the two of them almost came to blows apparently. Not the first time Karl's lost it either, so this guy says.'

'Interesting. How does that tally with what you've seen?'

'He's certainly got a temper – I saw a flash of it this morning. But I put it down to stress.'

'Someone could have paid to have this done to punish him, someone who didn't care whether it was Karl or Leah who got hurt,' said Ojo.

Finn nodded.

'I agree. It's worth looking into. Do you have a name for this guy who made the complaint?' said Finn.

Paulsen checked her pocketbook.

'Yeah, Phil Wadham. He was a marketing exec, lives in north London. I've got a number and an address.'

'Good, give me his details. And go back to Karl and show him that photograph. Have a dig while you're there, see how he reacts to Wadham's name.' He turned to Ojo. 'Jacks, I'd like to know more about Leah. We know she was using dating apps – there's just a chance this is some crazy she met on one of those. We've got her phone, see what digital forensics have found. We know she'd just met someone new – see what you can pull up on him, and also this ex-boyfriend who moved to Scotland.' Finn grabbed his coat from the back of his chair. 'I'll go and talk to Wadham, then head down to the estate and find Isiah.'

'Are you sure you don't want me to meet with Isiah? It might save a bit of time if Wadham's in north London?' offered Ojo.

'No, I'll be fine. You stick with what I've given you. Let's regroup later.'

He marched to the door and left without another word.

Ojo watched him go, less than impressed, and began to shake her head.

'This is getting silly,' she said to Paulsen.

'What do you mean?'

'Oh, come on, Mattie. He's trying to do everything. It's pure control-freakery. Haven't you noticed?'

She had, but instinctively didn't want to be disloyal.

'It's just Finn being Finn, isn't it?'

'No, he's getting worse and it's pissing me off. I could be on the Hope Estate in ten minutes. He won't be back now until early afternoon – it's an idiotic waste of time.'

Paulsen spread her hands, unsure of how to react. It was rare to hear Ojo openly criticising Finn.

'He did say he knew Isiah Simms . . .'

'Yeah, he did,' said Ojo, standing up. 'There's always a good reason . . . just like I'm sure there's a good reason why he comes in at the crack of dawn and doesn't leave here until God knows when.' She shook her head again. 'And we both know her name.'

6

Karl looked out of his living room window and saw a well-dressed woman unloading some supermarket bags from a people carrier. She saw him watching, smiled and waved. A neighbour – she clearly didn't know about Leah yet. After discussing it with Claire, he'd given the police permission to release their daughter's name to the media. The first text arrived on his phone after the 7 a.m. news on the radio. The police had returned the handset to him after they'd finished checking it for prints. He hadn't even got round to wiping the dirt and blood off it yet. A slew of calls and texts followed and he'd ignored them all. Well-meaning people hot off the blocks, wanting to know if he and Claire were 'alright'. But he wasn't ready for the sympathy of others yet. He forced a smile and waved back at the woman outside.

Claire was upstairs taking a shower. Neither of them knew quite what to do with themselves; whether to stay in and batten down the hatches, or go out and try and clear their heads. They were tired and couldn't sleep, hungry and unable to eat. And all he could think about were the events of the previous night. The echo of his daughter's dying scream. The choice he'd made. When he'd arrived home from Cedar House, he'd tried to explain it to Claire, going through it in detail. The decision to leave Leah – that calculation of logic in the moment – became something altogether different in the quiet of their living room. An act of inexplicable cowardice.

'You weren't there,' he found himself saying, the words sounding pathetic even to him. The look in his wife's eyes was something he'd never seen in twenty-four years of marriage.

He kept fighting the irrational desire to call Leah's mobile, and shook his head at his own absurdity. It really did feel like she might answer and end this nightmare with a single cheery greeting.

'You should see this,' said Claire, her voice cutting through the silence. He turned and wondered how long she'd been watching him. She passed him her iPhone, the *MailOnline* logo clearly visible on its display, a headline screaming out.

FATHER RUNS AS DAUGHTER IS SLAYED IN PARK HORROR

It took a second for the words to penetrate.

'How the hell could they know?'

The words came out in a husky whisper. He read the article, scrolling through it with increasing dismay. It was all there – all the details that mattered anyway, couched in suitably woolly language: 'The father-of-one reportedly fled the scene after the killer allegedly threatened to sexually assault his daughter.' He looked at some of the comments beneath the story.

Men like that shouldn't be allowed to have kids.
Spineless cowardice – pure and simple.
I hope he's feeling proud.

The story had only been up for an hour but the column of comments seemed to go on forever.

'I was trying to find help . . .' he said, answering the question his wife's eyes were asking.

'I thought you said you'd decided to save yourself? Not go and find help. You were happy for our daughter to be raped, as long as you weren't hurt? That was the deal, wasn't it?' said Claire.

'I didn't know he was going to kill her. Leah wanted me to go – *told* me to go.'

She looked at him pityingly, as if listening to a schoolboy explaining how he'd been scammed of his pocket money.

'Wow . . . just wow.'

'Claire, please. This is hard enough to deal with. We have to stick together. If we're going to get through this, you and I have to be rock solid. Come on, we can't fight. Not now.'

The hard expression on her face gave way slowly, the grief reasserting itself. He moved gently to embrace her, but she'd already begun to flinch.

'I'm going out – I need . . . to not be in here for a bit,' she said.

'Balls,' said Jackie Ojo as she stared at the *MailOnline* headline on her PC.

'I thought you'd want to know,' said Paulsen.

'How did they get it?'

'There's a local resident quoted in the piece – says a policeman was asking her about it, told her what happened.'

Ojo face-palmed. It wasn't hard to work out what had happened. A well-intentioned uniform officer conducting door-to-doors saying just a bit too much to the local busybody, who fed it straight to the press. All it took was a quick email, the old days of an anonymous tip-off from a phone box long gone.

'You better talk to the Sulemans. I'll get on to the media office – we need to issue a press release with that CCTV image anyway. In addition to a request for information, I'll get

53

them to add a line asking the media to respect the family's privacy.'

'You think that'll work?' said Paulsen.

'No, but we can only ask. You better warn them the press interest might escalate after this. It's no longer just a crime – it's an *issue* now.' She all but spat the word out.

'How do you mean?'

'What have we been doing since yesterday evening, Mattie? You? Me? All of us?' Ojo answered her own question: 'Putting ourselves in that poor sod's position. Trust me, I've been around the block enough to know which stories the media pick up and run with, and the ones they don't.'

'Really?'

'Yes, and there are lots of dimensions to this one. I hate to say it, but one middle-class white kid gets stabbed and the press goes all state-of-the-nation. If it's a black kid on an estate, it's just another routine line for them. I've seen it happen before. You watch, this'll be like catnip.'

'Do you want me to let the DI know?'

'No, you can leave that pleasure to me. You're going to have your hands full with the Sulemans. Another reason why it would have been better if he wasn't trying to do everything himself.' She shook her head and reached for her phone.

Karl paced the living room, unable to stop his mind rolling back to the previous night. He was trying to recall exactly what he'd felt when the devil in the mask made him choose. That was the pivotal moment, the instant in which his daughter's fate was sealed. He remembered his fury, the fear and the indecision. But underneath it all, hadn't there been relief at being offered an out? A primal desire to run and save himself?

As time passed he wondered how he'd remember those few minutes. He'd betrayed the one person he always swore he'd protect with his life. He could still remember how he'd felt when she was born, watching her play as a toddler and the grief she used to give them when they put her to bed. The idea he'd one day fail that little child . . . He let out a noise – half whimper, half wail – and gripped his skull with his hands again until his head hurt.

He was interrupted by the sound of his phone ringing.

'Hey Karl . . .'

He froze. He recognised the voice immediately because he'd been hearing it constantly for almost eighteen hours: the devil in the mask.

'How did you get this number?'

The words came out in a hoarse whisper.

'Can you still hear her screaming?'

That tone, the taunt of it, the London accent. Here, impossibly, right now – the person who killed Leah.

'What do you want? Who are you?'

'Don't you remember me? I remember you.'

'I don't understand. What do you mean?'

'Be seeing you, Karl . . .'

The line went dead.

7

'The man's a piece of shit. What more do you need to know?'

A short, squat figure wearing an Arsenal training top, Phil Wadham looked slightly older than his forty-three years. They were sitting in the kitchen diner of a messy basement flat in Holloway, which Wadham shared with his partner. Or at least Finn assumed he did. Judging by the way her clothes, shoes, bags and other accessories were scattered around, it was hard to tell if he lived there too. The place smelt of stale chip-fat oil and unwashed bodies. Finn wasn't in a particular hurry to extend the conversation if he could help it. Wadham took a casual sip of a soupy grey cup of tea, and Finn watched with mild disgust as he splashed some down his top.

'What's Karl done for the police to get involved? Nothing too serious, I trust?'

He ladled the sarcasm on with a trowel.

'His daughter was murdered last night, I'm afraid.'

Finn watched as Wadham took it in, and began to row back.

'Well, obviously I'm sorry to hear that. I mean, I didn't like him, and we clearly had some differences but I wouldn't have wished that on him.'

'Can I ask where you were last night?'

The man's discomfort morphed into outright alarm.

'I was here. Job hunting – I was online all night.' He was gabbling now. 'Is this why you've come – you think I had something to do with it?'

'We were told there was some bad blood between you and Mr Suleman. That you made some threats? Is there anyone who can verify you were here last night?'

'No, Julie – my girlfriend – she was out with some friends. So, I can't prove it. But you can look at my browser history if you like. Talk to my broadband provider – surely it must show when I was online? As for the threats, I didn't mean them. Not literally. I'd just been fired, for no good reason. I was pretty emotional. But I wouldn't have actually hurt him, and certainly not his daughter. God . . .'

'We'll check with your service provider, but it'll only prove *someone* was online. Not necessarily you.'

Wadham's eyes widened. Finn was toying with him rather unnecessarily. It was a bad habit when his first impressions weren't great. The description given by Karl Suleman of the attacker certainly didn't match the slightly overweight figure sitting in front of him, whose voice was more whiny and Estuary than youthful. It was still possible Wadham was behind it, though usually in those circumstances the perpetrator made sure they possessed a cast-iron alibi to boast about.

'I'll be getting a warrant to check your phone records and your email.'

'Fine. Do what you need to, you won't find anything. I've got nothing to hide. I've a very low opinion of the man, but that's not a crime, is it?'

Finn nodded, deciding to row back a little himself.

'Thank you; cooperation's helpful and there are a number of lines of enquiry we're pursuing. That's the other reason I'm here. We think there's a possibility Karl might have been targeted. Can you tell me a bit more about him – why someone might have done this?'

'What – kill his daughter?'

'Perhaps, but maybe *he* was the intended target and she just got caught up in it.'

Wadham took another slurp of tea, looked up sharply.

'Have you met Karl?'

'Yes, but it's hard to get a sense of him in these circumstances. He's pretty traumatised.'

Wadham exhaled, some sympathy on his face. There was genuine perspective now. He didn't look like a man with enough hatred to have paid someone to rip Leah Suleman apart with a zombie knife.

'He's very good at what he does. He's built a really successful business, works all hours of the day and is very dedicated. But there's another side to him: the coked-up little Hitler who makes his employees' lives a misery. It wasn't that he was unpredictable on a day-to-day basis – it was more like hour to hour. Temper tantrums at people if they didn't come in early and leave late. God help you if you actually took a full lunch break. That's the sort of bloke he is.'

'If it was that bad, why didn't you look for another job?'

Wadham looked at Finn as if he was mad.

'Because it was my *career*. I gave him my best, and he treated me like a dog. Now look at me – on the scrapheap at forty-three.'

'And why did he sack you?'

'Said I wasn't pulling my weight – what he was getting back wasn't matched by what he was investing in me. Absolute joke of course, on both fronts.' He shook his head. 'Look, it wasn't all bad there. When he was on an up he could actually be quite inspiring. He had a scare a few months back and was actually decent to everyone for a bit. Didn't last though, did it? Soon went back to his old ways. That's Karl for you.'

'What kind of a scare?'

'Do you remember when it was snowing back in January? His train into work derailed somewhere near Brixton. Only a

58

minor thing, nobody was hurt. All the passengers ended up walking by the tracks.'

Finn nodded, recalling seeing something about it on the news.

'Why did that bother him?'

'He said – when it happened – that it felt like his number was up. Obviously turned out to be nothing too serious, but it definitely shook him up. He seemed to have a different take on life for a bit. Like I say, didn't last.'

'You say he uses cocaine – is that a suspicion, or do you have hard evidence of it?'

Wadham gave him a knowing 'we're all men of the world' look.

'Come on, mate, I wasn't born yesterday. A man who works all hours of the day but doesn't get tired, has an explosive temper and a permanent sniffle – I don't need to do your job to work it out, do I?'

'But you've never actually seen him using?'

Wadham shrugged. 'No, to be fair, I haven't.' He left a pregnant pause. 'Maybe it was just a bit of sugar off a doughnut on his upper lip. On the odd occasion . . .'

Finn ignored the crack.

'And, specifically, can you think of someone who might have had enough of a grievance to want to hurt him?'

'Look, there's a lot of people like me. People he's screwed over. But I can't think of anyone psycho enough to respond by trying to kill him or his daughter – that's mental. Then again, I might not know the whole story. Who knows what he's done over the years? His attitude to life is he'll do what he has to do to protect himself, and damn the consequences.'

Karl was sat alone in his living room, thinking. Everything was quiet, the only sound the gentle ticking of the wall clock behind him. But the noise in his head was only getting louder. He was feeling exactly the way as he had in the park. The same heightened terror, caused by the same person. He knew he should tell the police about the call he'd received. But it was the killer's insinuation that he knew something about Karl that was troubling him. That what happened last night *wasn't* just a random attack. Karl knew there were skeletons in his closet. The media were already circling and the last thing he wanted was for them to start digging into him. That just couldn't happen.

Karl's eyes alighted on one of the many pictures of Leah that adorned the walls and he felt instantly ashamed. Less than twenty-four hours after her death and he was already only thinking of himself. The tears started to well again. The life he'd worked so hard to build for his family was being torn down – no – was *already* in pieces. And this was all his fault. All he could do now was find some sort of redemption. He owed that to his dead daughter and his grieving wife. By protecting their reputation. By keeping his secrets.

He heard the front door open and took a deep breath. He couldn't tell Claire about the call either – she'd ring that irritating police officer immediately. God knows what it would do to her already fragile state of mind too. She walked into the room and he smiled sadly at her.

'Hey . . .' he said, but the next words died in his throat as he saw the look on her face. She didn't waste any time going for the jugular.

'What I can't get my head around – and there's a lot I can't get my head around – is that you keep defending what you did.'

'That's not fair, I'm not defending it. All I've done is try to explain. If I could go back and do it differently, I swear to God, I would.'

'Really? Because all I'm hearing is how it "made sense" in the moment. That Leah "wanted" you to leave her alone with some psycho carrying a knife.'

'Because that's what happened—'

'And don't you tell me I "wasn't there". I keep putting myself in your shoes, and every time I think it through, there's no version of it where I abandon my daughter.'

'I can't change what happened, Claire.'

'And the other thing I keep thinking about is why this person killed her. Why did he tell you otherwise? Why did you fall for it? How could you be so stupid? Why didn't *you* attack him – give Leah a chance to run?' She was shouting now, the questions tumbling out. He tried to answer her but she shouted over him. 'I'll tell you why – because you would have got hurt . . . and you weren't prepared to do that for her.'

He shook his head.

'You don't understand . . . it all happened so fast—'

'Oh, give it a rest. I don't want to hear it. You've spent a career thinking on your feet. But when it really mattered, "it all happened so fast".' Her mocking impression of him hung in the air. 'Are you sure you don't know who this was? I'm not the police – I'm talking to you as your wife of twenty-four years, the mother of your child. Are you *sure* you don't know? Because we both know some of the things you've done . . .'

He was already shaking his head.

'I promise you – I don't who this guy was. Why he did this to us . . .'

His phone vibrated in his pocket and he felt his heart miss a beat.

'We'll see, won't we? When they eventually catch this guy. It'll all come out then, and I'll remind you of this conversation. I hope for your sake you're not lying to me.'

She looked at him with contempt, turned and walked into the kitchen. He waited for her to go, and pulled the handset from his pocket. He'd been sent a picture – it was of Leah, dark and blurry, her dead eyes bulging from their sockets, blood pouring from a huge gash in her throat. Karl felt the vomit rising in his throat. Underneath the image was an emoji:

8

Paulsen was in her car when Finn called. She turned down the loud music she'd been listening to and put him on hands-free.

'Where are you?'

'On my way to the Sulemans – what's up?'

'Do they know about that piece on the *Mail*'s website?'

'They do, I talked to them before I left. Claire's okay, I think, but Karl's pretty upset. Blames us for leaking it.'

'Too late now, the genie's out of the bottle. Have you warned them the rest of the media's now likely to show an interest?'

'Yes – I'm not sure it registered though. I'll have another word when I get there.'

'There's something else. I've just been talking to Phil Wadham. He reckons Karl has a bit of a taste for coke.'

'That puts a different spin on things. Maybe that's why he was in the park last night? Was all this a deal that went south?'

'Perhaps. Or it could just be bollocks from a bloke with a good reason to slag him off. He's never actually seen him using. And would Karl really have taken his daughter with him to do that?'

'I don't know, might all be part of their Friday night tradition.'

'Do we know any more about her yet?'

'Uniform have spoken to her work colleagues and flatmates. DS Ojo was making calls about this guy on the dating app and her ex-boyfriend when I left. Nothing's come up about drugs so far though.'

'Work it in when you talk to him about the photo – see how he responds. If this is about drugs, then it certainly fills in some of the missing gaps. They'll need handling carefully, though.'

Paulsen glared at the handset, repressing the urge to respond with 'No shit, Sherlock'. 'Of course,' she said instead. 'I'll see you later.'

When she arrived at the Sulemans' house, a young woman in a long coat with short black hair was standing in the doorway of the property opposite. The front door was open and she was deep in conversation with an elderly man. The woman kept her eyes on Paulsen while she parked up. Paulsen returned her interest with a long look of her own. As she got out of the car, the woman finished her conversation and came straight over. She brandished a laminated blue press card.

'Hi – Nicky Paige, Sky News. Do you live around here?'

Paulsen produced her own card and introduced herself.

'I take it you're here to see the Sulemans? Is there an update on the investigation you can give me?' said Paige, not remotely deterred.

'Everything's coming from our media office. If you call them, they'll send you the latest lines,' said Paulsen. She turned and headed for the Sulemans' front door. She could see Karl watching the exchange from the window of the living room.

'Can you confirm the story the *Mail* are running?' Paige called out.

'We're asking the media to respect the family's privacy. I'm sure you understand,' Paulsen shouted back. She turned and rang the bell.

'Is it true Karl left his daughter to die?'

The words rang out just as Karl opened the front door. Paulsen failed to hide a wince of irritation. Karl simply stood and stared out at Paige.

'Ignore her. Come on, let's go inside,' said Paulsen, the arm she put around his shoulder more a gentle restraint than a show of sympathy. She guided him in and shut the door behind her.

'This is your fault,' he said.

'I'm sorry. As I said on the phone, it's unfortunate the press has got hold of this. It's best to simply not engage with them.'

Karl looked like he did want to engage with them. Forcibly and loudly.

'Did she try and talk to you?' asked Paulsen.

'She rang the bell just before you arrived, but we ignored it.' Paulsen nodded.

'That was the right thing to do.'

Claire joined them in the hallway.

'Can't you make them leave us alone? My daughter's not even in the ground yet.'

'I'm sorry – but they're not breaking any laws. We've asked them to give you some space. Most of them should respect that.'

'*Most?*' said Karl.

'Some will do their own thing. You may well be offered moncy for exclusivity on your story.'

'Jesus,' he said, turning and walking into the living room. Claire and Paulsen followed him in.

'If it gets too much for you, tell me, and I'll have a word with the reporters concerned,' said Paulsen. Karl was peering out of the window again, and Paulsen could just about see Nicky Paige's silhouette on the pavement.

'Where's that one from?'

65

'Sky.'

'Maybe I should say something to her – put the record straight?'

'It's entirely up to you, but my advice would be to wait a bit. If you want to talk to the media, we can hold a press conference at Cedar House later. It'll give you a bit more control of the situation.'

'And if I don't, that woman will write whatever she wants?'

'There's nothing new to say. All she can do is rehash what the *Mail* are running. Like I say, it's best not to feed it at this point.'

Paulsen was trying hard not to allow her frustration to show. She could see where this might go. An angry Karl shouting at a journalist – and how that might be depicted. The man, already being described as a coward, could be a national bogeyman by the following morning if he wasn't saved from himself. She needed to calm him down and she wasn't just thinking of his welfare. She could well imagine Finn and Skegman's view if she allowed this to escalate.

'There's been a development in the investigation,' she said carefully, and was grateful to see him turn away from the window. 'We've managed to pull an image off the CCTV cameras next to the park.'

She opened her bag, and pulled out the picture. Karl strode across, and took it from her with both hands.

'That's him,' he said. 'No question.'

Claire was looking over his shoulder at the pixelated outline, the individual who'd changed her life forever.

'How does this help us? I mean, you can't really see anything,' she said.

'We were able to track him a little further from this point, so it gives us an idea of which direction he was going. It's not much, but it's something to work with.'

'So you don't know who he is yet?' said Karl.

'No, but there are forensics officers all over this. If there's any DNA or fingerprints and this individual's in the system, it'll be a fairly swift process to find him and bring him in. The post-mortem might help us as well.'

Karl made a sound which could have been a snort of derision. He'd been jumpy since she'd arrived. Given the information Finn relayed on the way, she wondered if he'd taken something to help him through this. Then again, maybe this spikiness was a normal character trait, one that might be easy to confuse with a coke habit.

'I've one more question before I go. I'm sorry to raise this, Karl, but it's something that's come up. Have you ever taken drugs?'

His expression changed instantly, the question clearly throwing him, and his unguarded reaction suggested the answer was a comprehensive yes. Paulsen could see from the disgust on Claire's face that she was thinking the same thing too. He recovered quickly, the anger reasserting itself.

'Of course not. Why would you ask me that?'

'It was suggested to us by a former employee of yours. Again, I have to ask, but were you in the park last night to buy drugs?'

'A former employee? There's a few ... but I'm guessing you mean Phil Wadham? You're listening to him? Seriously? That's the pot calling the kettle black.'

Paulsen didn't answer, and waited for a reply to her question instead. Karl smiled narrowly, baring his teeth.

'No, I was not in the park to buy drugs. Neither was my daughter. *Now get out.*' Paulsen looked over at Claire, but she was looking hard at her husband.

Paulsen could feel this starting to run away from her. She'd been hoping to build a relationship with the Sulemans, establish some mutual trust, but it wasn't happening. If anything, her presence seemed to be making things worse.

'Of course if you need space, I'll respect that. If there's anything urgent, I can call instead.'

'No, I'm more than happy for you to come round. In fact, I'd prefer it,' said Claire. She was barely attempting to hide her disgust for her husband. Whatever anger he'd been directing at the police officer was being scorched away by his wife's contempt. Paulsen made her excuses and left.

As she stepped outside the blast of fresh air that hit her was welcome. There was no sign of Nicky Paige. Either she'd found another neighbour to talk to or had decided she'd got as much as she was going to for the moment. It was a relief, frankly, given the tinderbox behind that front door. Paulsen climbed into the front seat of her car, glancing across at the Sulemans' living room window, wondering exactly what was going on in there now. *Nice one, Mattie*, she thought – two for the price of one. You're screwing up their marriage when they most need each other, and destroying any trust you'd hoped to build at the same time.

'Fuck,' she said out loud, to nobody in particular.

9

'You understand what you have to do?'

The terrified boy tried to nod but couldn't even manage that. They were standing on a narrow thoroughfare on the ninth floor of Ashbank Tower, one of the three main blocks of flats that overlooked the Hope Estate. Two figures stood in front of him. The first was Andy Forbes, a short white man wearing a Canada Goose jacket. He reached out and slapped the boy's face with an open palm.

'I said, do you understand?'

'Yeah.'

'So tell me what you have to do?'

The boy swallowed and tried to focus.

'I get the train . . .'

'With what?'

'. . . with the ticket you gave me.'

'Show me.'

Panic-stricken, the youngster fumbled in his pocket, finally holding up the rectangular orange card like a tribute at an altar.

'And then what?'

'I go . . . I go . . .' he faltered, desperately trying to remember the instructions he'd only just been given.

'*Then what?*'

'I . . .'

'Fuck's sake.' Andy pulled a knife from his pocket, and in

one swift movement pushed the end of the blade up in front of the boy's face. 'Try again.'

'Andy,' said the second figure. 'He's twelve years old . . .'

Hayden Simms turned to face his friend. They were both in their early twenties. Hayden – tall, black and muscular – might have been good-looking if it wasn't for the long ugly scar that ran down his left cheek. He wore a black jacket over a grey T-shirt, dark jeans and red trainers.

'I don't care. He needs to understand, because we're giving him that.' He pointed at a navy blue backpack on the ground. 'Do you know how much shit there is in that bag?'

Hayden knew exactly how much 'shit' there was in the bag. Roughly four thousand pounds' worth of heroin, crack cocaine and amphetamines. He knew, because he'd packed it himself.

'You'll be alright. Won't you?' he said to the youngster.

The boy nodded furiously. Hayden watched him like a mechanic assessing an engine, judging whether it was fit for purpose. The boy didn't know and certainly didn't understand, but that was exactly what he was: a component in the smooth running of something bigger. Hayden leant in and when he spoke, it was quiet and encouraging.

'Come on, we've been through this. You're going on a ride, aren't you? Where are you going?'

'Swindon. I'm going to Swindon.'

'And what are you going to do when you get there?'

'Meet your friend. Go with him – give him the bag.'

Hayden looked round at Andy.

'See? All good,' said Hayden. He gestured at the boy to get moving, and the youngster gratefully grabbed the backpack and strapped it on. The two men watched as he headed away, stooping slightly under the weight of the bag. He turned a corner and disappeared from view.

'You shouldn't scare them so much,' Hayden said to Andy. 'If they're too frightened they make mistakes.'

Andy shook his head.

'That's exactly why you have to be hard with them – so they *don't* make mistakes.'

'Doesn't sit right,' said Hayden. 'My little brother's about that age.'

Andy grinned.

'You always were a big doughnut. Soft and full of jam.'

Hayden wasn't smiling though. He looked at Andy searchingly.

'Are we doing the right thing?'

'What do you mean?'

'You and me – we're not gangsters, never have been.'

'Of course we're doing the right thing. This is an opportunity, and if it means pushing a few kids around to make a bit of money, that's fine by me.'

Hayden frowned. He and Andy were lifelong friends who'd grown up on the estate together. In recent years they'd lived on the periphery of the gangs who frequented the area, more intent on staying under the radar than being noticed. But after the police raids earlier in the year, there was a power vacuum and it'd been Andy's idea to try and fill it. There were people out in the regions who were keen to see their drug supply from London resume, and were offering eye-watering sums of money. All of a sudden he and Andy were packing off twelve-year-old kids with bags full of drugs and it made Hayden feel uncomfortable. It felt like he'd slid into something that might not be as easy to step out of again.

'Don't you want to make some money?' said Andy. 'Proper money, I mean. Think what you could do with it.'

Hayden looked at him uncertainly.

'How do you mean?'

'You could look after your brother. Make sure he doesn't have to grow up like we did.' He shrugged. 'Never has to do shit like this.'

Hayden considered it.

'Maybe. I just don't want to end up bleeding out on a street corner, that's all.' His hand went instinctively to the scar on his cheek.

'You won't. Because we're not stupid enough to get caught out like that.'

'Did you see what happened in the park last night?'

Andy's face creased into a frown.

'Yeah . . . who did that then?'

'Thought you might have heard something.'

'Nothing to do with us, or our business, or I'd know. Probably just a mugger. Last thing we need though, don't need any extra feds in the area.'

Hayden looked at Andy unconvinced.

'Stop worrying, H. Everything's good – I'll tell Swindon there's a package on its way. This time next week we'll be laughing.'

Andy grinned again then stopped, something catching his eye. Hayden turned to follow his stare. A tall man in a billowing raincoat was striding across the concourse at the centre of the estate.

'Who's that?' said Hayden. 'Looks like he thinks he owns the place.'

'Police. I've seen him before. When the raids happened.'

They both continued to watch Finn. He was being greeted by a middle-aged man in blue overalls, the pair now shaking hands.

'That's your dad. What's he want with him?' said Andy.

'Nothing we need to worry about,' said Hayden. But his expression was hardening.

72

'You sure?'

'You know what my dad's like – probably some project he's got going on. Some anti-knife-crime thing. He's not a grass. Whatever else he is . . .'

'I know.' Andy put a hand on Hayden's shoulder. 'I've got to run. Let me know when our delivery arrives in Swindon, yeah? I'll call you later.' Hayden nodded, but as Andy left, his focus remained on the two men below.

Hayden hadn't properly spoken to his father since the death of his mother, five years earlier. Her cancer had become their cancer, infecting and destroying their relationship from the inside out. It was in the aftermath of her death he'd left home. To make ends meet Hayden had done some low-level dealing, even carried a knife himself for a while. For Isiah, to see his son folding into a world he'd railed against for so long – it was a betrayal. For a grief-stricken teenager, the cold, withdrawn figure his father had become was an abandonment he couldn't forgive. It was why the schism between them had become so pronounced with each passing year.

Both felt the moral high ground was theirs; both felt any attempt to build bridges should come from the other. Father and son haunted each other from afar, their mutual contempt perfectly weighted. The fly in the ointment was Isiah's other son, Michael. The boy lived with his father, and though Isiah didn't like it, often spent time with his brother too.

Hayden's phone rang, distracting him from the conversation on the concourse. A picture of an attractive girl in her early twenties, with long hair, big earrings and a broad smile, beamed up at him from the display. He glanced along the narrow thoroughfare to check he was alone and his expression softened as he answered.

'Jade . . .'

'Hey baby,' said the voice on the other end. 'What are you doing?'

'Not much, why?'

'Wanna meet up?'

He looked at the time, feeling his irritation with his father dissipating.

'Yeah. Come to mine. I'm starving – bring fries.'

He heard her laugh and smiled, but his eyes remained cold, focusing again on the two men talking nine floors below.

Isiah Simms was exactly as Finn remembered him: in his mid-fifties, softly spoken, with a puppy-dog friendliness about him. They'd first met when the son of a friend of Isiah's was stabbed a couple of years before. He'd also been of great help in the aftermath of the recent raids. He'd calmed some of the tensions on the estate, getting through to people in a way the police couldn't. Isiah wasn't someone who'd be comfortable being called a community leader or an activist. They were labels other people ascribed. But Finn was in no doubt that's what he was. The estate mattered to him, an old-fashioned man who strongly believed in the concept of community.

Before the raids, there'd been two separate worlds co-existing on the Hope Estate. There were the gangs with their dealers, and a county lines operation worth tens of thousands of pounds. And there were the residents, the people who called the estate home, who met regularly, plotting and planning to make it a place they could take some pride in. As long as one faction didn't intrude on the other, an unspoken pact of non-aggression existed between them. And it felt to Finn that Isiah was almost the fulcrum in the middle of that. Someone able to communicate with both sides.

'I'm sorry,' said Finn. 'I hope I'm not making you late.' He nodded at the toolkit Isiah was setting down on the ground next to him.

'No, no, no. This isn't work. I promised Maureen ... ah ...' He struggled for a moment to place the surname. 'Maureen, anyway.' He pointed in the general direction of Ashbank Tower. 'Flat 31. I said I'd take a look at her boiler. It's been playing up.'

'I'll try not to keep you.'

Finn explained why he was there and began by showing him a copy of the image they'd pulled off the CCTV in Crystal Palace. Isiah studied it intently for a moment.

'Sorry, it's too blurry. It could be anyone.'

'You've not heard anything about it?'

He shook his head.

'Who was the victim?'

'A twenty-three-year-old girl, out with her dad.'

'Black? White? Middle class? Working class?'

'White middle-class family from Dulwich.'

Isiah raised an eyebrow and Finn knew why. The simple, sad truth of it was that Leah didn't fit the profile of the usual stab victims in London.

'Interesting. What was it then, a mugging gone wrong?'

'We don't know. Nothing was stolen.'

Isiah processed this for a moment, then shook his head.

'Usually when something like this happens, if it's gang related – you hear something. And you can tell by their body language ...' He gestured at the concourse. 'Around the place, you can see when something's up. But it's not been like that this morning. I'll ask around though.'

'Thank you, I appreciate that. How have things been since the raids?'

Isiah took a breath and screwed up his eyes as if trying to place a flavour or a smell.

'It's been a funny atmosphere. Different, certainly. Try and think of it like Iraq.'

Finn raised an eyebrow. 'Come on, that's a bit melodramatic, isn't it?'

'You misunderstood me. When you have a leader – or in this case, *leaders* – who've been around for a while – however bad they might be, people get used to them. Get used to how they do things. They start working round that, and it becomes the new normal. So when you take those leaders away, there's change. And with change comes uncertainty.'

Finn nodded, understanding.

'It'll calm down. A *new* new normal.'

'Maybe. But I know one thing – there's a vacuum, and you know what Mother Nature thinks of those . . .'

'We're aware and we're watching. If the head grows back on the serpent, we'll come back and cut it off again.'

Isiah nodded, and Finn knew better than to ask him if he'd noticed anything like that developing. It was one thing protecting his community, another to effectively become a police informant. It was a tricky balancing act he was walking, and Finn knew better than to cross those lines.

'How's your son?' said Finn, changing the subject.

'Mikey's good. Though he's got a smart mouth on him these days.'

Finn smiled, deciding against inquiring about Isiah's other boy. Hayden Simms hadn't ever got into serious trouble with the police, but Finn was aware of who he was. He'd never really had the conversation with Isiah – children weren't exactly his speciality.

'Do you have kids yourself?' asked Isiah, as if reading his mind. Finn shook his head. 'That'll be why I have more worry lines than you.'

Finn smiled.

'It can't be easy raising Michael on your own,' he said.

'He's a good kid. But my job's to make sure he stays that way. Dawn was better at all that stuff than me. She knew how to talk to them. I just end up barking all the time.'

Something in Isiah's tone, the look on his face, felt very familiar. It'd been five years since Dawn Simms died, just the one since Karin's death. And for a moment Finn shivered. He didn't know whether Isiah was in a new relationship, but instinct told him not. He wondered whether people would look at him in the years to come and reach that conclusion too.

'I'm sure you're doing a brilliant job.'

Isiah smiled wistfully.

'We'll see. They drive you crazy, but you'd do anything for them.' Finn could only speculate if that comment extended to his other son. Isiah sighed. 'I'd better get on – if I hear anything about your stabbing, I'll let you know.'

He watched Isiah pick up his toolkit and walk away, and wondered how he lived with those conflicting feelings about his children. Some choices, he thought, didn't necessarily come at the end of a blade, but cut just as deep.

10

Karl was listening to the radio when the next message arrived. The comforting voices on *5 Live*, which he was used to hearing talk about football or films, were inviting phone calls instead about him. 'Would you leave your child,' they were asking, 'if you thought it was the only way to save them?' Wanda from Moseley thought Karl was a monster. Jim from Stirling had a lot of sympathy for him and believed he'd done the right thing. Lorna from Plymouth thought Leah's mother would probably have been braver in that situation. He turned the radio off and glanced at his phone. He recognised the picture on the screen straight away – the knife used to murder his daughter, still stained with her blood. An emoji of a little waving hand followed, then the words.

Pissed your pants yet, Karl?

He swallowed. He should take this to the police, he knew that. Instinctively he still didn't *want* to tell them, and felt ashamed now after listening to those radio calls. He glanced back at the image, a small rivulet of blood on one of the blade's teeth catching his eye. He felt hot and his heart began to pound. He was a man used to being in control and in the last twenty-four hours he'd lost his grip on just about everything. Normally he hated people who looked back, crying over the spilt milk of their mistakes. But he knew now the rest of his life would be spent doing just that, forever caught in the moment of that choice.

Claire was in the kitchen, finding distraction by making some dinner. He was actively scared of going to bed later, happy to delay that for as long as possible. Neither of them had a hope in hell of sleeping and there was the dreadful prospect of six, seven hours lying on a mattress marinating in their own torment. She came through the door holding a couple of plates. Nothing elaborate, just scrambled eggs on toast. Functional food to fill a gap.

She put the plates on the table, sat down and began eating without waiting for him. He rose from the sofa and joined her, trying to disguise his feelings. The silence was filled by the click-clack of their cutlery. He watched his wife eating, her eyes carefully pointing anywhere except at him, contempt screaming from every pore.

'What is it?' he said finally. She carried on shovelling the food in, clearly keen to get the whole process over with as fast as possible. 'Since that policewoman left you've hardly said a word. Please . . .'

She looked up at him as if he was being a bit slow.

'How long have you been taking drugs, Karl?'

'Oh come on – like that's the most important thing right now.'

'So it's true?'

'Does it matter?'

'Coke, I'm guessing – it certainly explains a few things about your temper.'

'Occasionally. Very occasionally.'

She stared at him in disbelief.

'Here? In this house? There's cocaine in my home, right now?'

'No, of course not. It's at work – a few lines to keep me sharp, that's all.'

She forked some more food in her mouth and looked away again. He surrendered on his own plate and tossed his fork into the centre of it with a clatter.

'Can't we at least have an adult conversation about this?'

'You want to talk about being an adult? When you're sticking coke up your nose like a twenty-something City boy trying to look clever?'

'You don't get it. It helps me work. Helps pay for all this.'

'No, I don't get it. But you're full of secrets, aren't you? I've even kept some of them for you over the years. And now we're paying the price, aren't we?'

'You're being ridiculous.'

'I'm being ridiculous? *You* left our daughter—'

'And there it is. Finally. Go on, say it. You know you want to . . .'

And so she did.

'It's your fault she's dead.'

The words reverberated around the room. The impact stunned them both. Claire recovered the quickest.

'What kind of man leaves his child? She must have been terrified, and you ran away while she lay dying in the mud. I'll *never* forgive you for it.'

She put her hand to her mouth, in too much pain to even cry. He tried to respond, but this time couldn't find the words.

As she made her way home from Cedar House that night, Mattie Paulsen couldn't shake the Sulemans from her mind. Karl in particular was nagging at her. She now regretted her initial snap judgement of the choice he'd made, having seen the toll it was taking on him. It wasn't so much cowardice, she thought, as a misjudgement; a gamble he'd taken and appallingly lost. It was hard not to think of him running back through the half-light, listening to his daughter's dying scream. Helpless and alone.

'There's no fucking way I would have left you,' said Nancy later.

She was laying the table in their small kitchen diner for three people. They'd managed to reschedule the meal with Mattie's brother Jonas. Nancy was cooking while Mattie attempted to get the flat into a state that at least partly resembled tidiness.

'But if you thought that was the only way we'd both walk away ...' said Mattie, fiddling with the head of the hoover. 'Wouldn't you?'

'No, I sodding wouldn't. Whatever shit was going down, we'd do it together.'

'Do you know what a zombie knife does?'

'Makes little boys with small penises feel very well endowed?'

'It guts you from the inside. It's designed to cause the maximum pain possible.'

Nancy said nothing, fetched some vegetables from the fridge and went over to the kitchen counter to chop them. Mattie watched her pick up a large kitchen knife and lift an eyebrow.

'Well, I still wouldn't have done it,' said Nancy. 'I wouldn't have taken the risk – why did he think some low-life piece of shit holding a thing like that was going to keep their word?' Nancy was waving the knife illustratively as she spoke.

Mattie put the hoover head down and reached for her glass of wine.

'Because you haven't got time to think in those situations. You make a decision in the heat of the moment and you hope it's the right one.'

'And how's that sitting with your guy now? From what you're telling me, it's not, is it? Sounds like he's no angel anyway. I worked with men like that when I was temping.

81

Coke-fuelled tantrums because you forgot to post a letter or something. They always think they know better. Even now, with you. And you're just there to help him, aren't you?'

'I can forgive him that. It's hard to take it personally in the circumstances. You can see it in his eyes – there's something broken in there. I'm not sure it'll ever get fixed either.'

Mattie shivered. Think about Karl too much, and it kind of crept into your head – the aching pain, the pervading guilt. She'd felt it in his house and could still feel it now, even see Nancy was getting a sense of it too. She drained her glass and turned the hoover on, looking for a distraction.

Her thoughts turned to her brother Jonas, glad they were finally having a chance to catch up. He was older than her by two years, but often felt more like a little brother. Like Mattie, he possessed a quiet seriousness about him, but none of the suppressed anger she often carried. He was a teacher at an inner-city school in east London, and despite their proximity they tended to lead separate lives. It wasn't deliberate, but the annual New Year's resolution to see more of one another never seemed to happen. In recent months there'd been a slight undercurrent to their relationship. For a while he'd been raising some concerns about their father, concerns she'd swept under the carpet. The way you do when you really know you shouldn't.

Christer Paulsen lived with his wife Evelyn, Mattie and Jonas's mother, in Norfolk. Christer came over to England from his home city of Gothenburg in search of work in the mid-seventies, while Evelyn was the daughter of a nurse who'd come to Britain in the mid-fifties after growing up in Trinidad. The pair had met through their work, scientists working on a research project at a laboratory in Croydon. They'd settled in the area, raising Mattie and Jonas in south London, before choosing to retire in the English countryside.

Over the last year that precise mind her father possessed seemed to be failing him. At first Mattie hadn't taken Jonas's warnings as seriously as she should have done. Christer, like many brilliant people, had always been a little scatter-brained. Taking her brother's advice, she'd spent more time visiting them recently. She still wasn't sure there was anything more to it though. Neither Christer nor Evelyn seemed keen on investigating the issue further, and her brother's view was that they were burying their heads in the sand.

When he arrived he seemed determined to make the atmosphere bright and breezy. Jonas Paulsen shared some of his sister's physical attributes: the jet-black hair, the Roman nose and the Scandinavian inflection in his voice. He was as direct as her too, and it didn't take long for the conversation to turn to their parents.

'I don't see how you can have gone up there and not seen it,' he said.

'He's just getting old, they both are.'

'How much time have you actually spent with them?'

'A few weekends – enough.'

'A *few* weekends – how many? Two or three in six months? Fuck's sake, Mat . . .'

'Jonas—'

'There's a reason I wanted to see you tonight.'

'No shit.'

He gave her a withering look.

'I've finally persuaded them he needs to see a doctor, to get himself properly tested. We'll know definitively if something's wrong then. I thought you should know – have some warning so it doesn't come as a bolt from the blue.'

'You're that certain?' said Mattie.

He nodded, his chestnut brown eyes locked on hers, genuine concern now on her face.

'Maybe we should go up and visit them next weekend,' said Nancy carefully.

'I think that's a brilliant idea,' said Jonas.

Mattie held her hands up. 'Okay, I surrender. Now will you get off my case?'

It was after they'd eaten and were on the coffees that Nancy brought the conversation back round to Karl Suleman. She seemed fascinated by the choice he'd been ask to make, and was clearly still thinking about it.

'I'd have gone – no question about it. Christ, if it was me or you, Mat, there'd have been a dust cloud after me,' said Jonas. He grinned at his sister, who responded with a slow, methodical raising of her middle finger.

'Seriously,' said Nancy.

'I am being serious. No point both of you dying. He did the right thing. I mean . . . I'd have probably told the other person to leave, then tried to talk my way out of it.'

'Yeah, because that would *really* have worked,' said Mattie. Jonas made a face at her.

'Surely the question's not what you would do, it's why would you ask the question in the first place,' said Nancy, who always enjoyed playing amateur detective on her partner's investigations.

'It's obvious, I'd have thought?' said Jonas. They both looked at him. 'It's what he wanted the survivor to *feel*, isn't it?'

'Powerless,' said Mattie, almost to herself.

II

As was his habit, Finn was flicking through the news headlines on his phone while he ate breakfast. He was dismayed to
see the Sulemans were everywhere. The reporting, while
generally accurate about the broad sequence of events, subtly
continued the *Mail*'s insinuation that a cowardly man lost his
nerve, ran away and left his daughter to a monster. It felt like
a national debate was unfolding; the *Sun* even dug up a
psychologist to give some quotes on 'fight or flight' response.
Social media was predictably brutal, with everyone and their
mother chipping in on Twitter. There was the odd voice
defending Karl, pointing out he'd just lost a child, but most
were angry and judgemental.

One sentiment repeated itself over and over – 'no parent leaves
their child' – but Finn knew differently. He'd arrested men and
women for murdering their children, abusing them, neglecting
them. Karl's crime was something altogether different and argu-
ably more tragic. A decision made at speed, with the best of
intentions and the worst of outcomes. On top of dealing with the
loss of their daughter, the Sulemans were now in the eye of a
media storm. He made a mental note to check in with Paulsen on
how they were coping – and to see how she was coping too.

His phone buzzed with an incoming text and he knew
instinctively who it was from.

I'm not going away, you know . . .

Why did she do this in the mornings? Did Cally Hunter sit there over her corn flakes thinking it was the best time of day to nag him? He considered his options. He could ignore her again, or he could put her off for a bit. Or he could promise to see her, then find reasons to cancel until she got the message. Or God help him, he could actually agree to meet her.

'Finally ...' said Karin. For a moment he could see her, sitting in her dressing gown, fingers interlaced around a mug on the opposite side of the table. He closed his eyes, opened them, and she was gone. He picked up the phone and tapped out a text.

Alright – tell me when's good?

The reply came instantly.

Tomorrow night?

He sighed.

The waiting room outside the hospital morgue was a small unassuming space, not entirely different to the sort you might find at a doctor's surgery. The simplicity of the room was at odds with the great sadness that passed through it on a regular basis, and Paulsen wondered what stories the wooden chairs that lined it would tell if they could speak.

The Sulemans were due shortly, and this wasn't going to be easy. Leah's post-mortem had now been completed. She'd been stabbed seven times in total. The nature of the murder weapon meant there was no surgical precision to it; the ridges of the knife had torn through her like the teeth of a wild animal. There was confirmation too that she hadn't been sexually assaulted, and the toxicology report showed no signs of drugs in her system. Critically, traces of DNA, most likely the killer's, had been found under her fingernails. It was something, and Paulsen hoped the results would bring Leah's parents at least some consolation.

When the Sulemans arrived, the atmosphere between them was chillier than the morgue itself. It wasn't hard to figure out why. They were being confronted with the details of their own tragedy wherever they turned – whether they looked online, turned on the radio or switched on the television. It was bound to have an effect. Karl was deferring to his wife, looking for the smallest scrap of *something* from her, while in return she seemed barely able to acknowledge his existence. Paulsen couldn't help but feel some sympathy for the man. Whatever the wisdom of his choice, he was certainly paying a terrible price for it. She could also sense now why he hadn't connected particularly well with her so far. Mattie was only a few years older than his daughter. Without meaning to be, she was a reminder. His angry tone with her was probably the same as he'd used with Leah once.

She could see the dread in their eyes, understanding immediately the dilemma they faced. The prospect of seeing their daughter's corpse would be almost too painful to bear; the opportunity of seeing her one last time equally impossible to resist. Paulsen left them briefly to tell the mortuary staff they were ready, before leading them into the morgue itself. Leah lay on the mortuary table covered in a sheet up to her neck, except for one hand which lay in the open beside her. There was a faint hint of a Mona Lisa smile on her lips. Paulsen recognised it from the photographs on the walls of the Sulemans' living room. She guessed her resting face always carried it. She could only wonder how it felt to see such a familiar expression in death. Karl looked over at Paulsen and nodded his confirmation of her identity.

'You can hold her hand if you want,' she whispered. Both the Sulemans looked unsure. 'If you'd find it comforting. It's okay.'

Claire tentatively walked over, reached out and took the hand, clasping it, the tears coming freely now. Karl moved to join her, but she held up her other hand sharply, a clear gesture to stay back. The hurt look in his eyes would stay with Paulsen later.

'Thank you, I know that was difficult,' said Paulsen as she accompanied them out.

'Do you mind if I use the toilet?' asked Claire, following the signed directions without waiting for an answer. Paulsen guessed she needed a few moments to pull herself together. Karl stood alone looking self-consciously at the grey tiled floor. In the short space of time she'd known him, she'd already seen so many sides of his personality. The haunted victim in the interview room, the angry man who'd all but thrown her out of his house. And now something else – a lost little boy, humiliated and broken. It was hard to believe this was also the CEO of a major London ad agency. She hadn't yet seen that version of him. Not for the first time it struck her how easily people judged others, gave them simple one-line descriptions, when in truth nobody could be defined so easily.

'There's something I need to tell you,' he said, looking up suddenly. 'I should have told you before – I'm sorry. The man who killed Leah . . . He's been . . . in touch with me.'

It took a second for the words to fully register with Paulsen.

'What do you mean, "in touch"?'

'I haven't told Claire. I thought it would upset her.'

He told her about the call he'd received, and showed her the subsequent messages he'd been sent. Paulsen bit her tongue as she took it all in. She wanted to scream at him. They now had a picture of the murder weapon. More than that – evidence that could be used in court if they ever managed to find and arrest whoever sent this.

'You should have told me about this immediately – it's evidence. How did he get your number?'

'It's on my agency's website. I'm guessing he must have Googled me.'

'This wasn't a random attack, was it? Why else would he be following it up?' Karl shrugged at her helplessly. 'That's not good enough, Karl – you must have some idea who this is. It's personal, isn't it?'

Before he could reply they heard Claire's footsteps coming back down the corridor.

'Please . . . I want to tell Claire about this in my own way. She should hear it from me – and definitely not here.'

Paulsen saw Claire walking towards them and nodded.

'I'm going to have to take the phone,' she said quickly, 'and we're going to need to talk to you again – do you understand?' He gave his assent with his eyes as Claire re-joined them. Paulsen pocketed the phone discreetly.

'Are there any other questions I can help you with?' she said, and Karl shook his head. He looked over at his wife, who also declined, and they all headed for the double doors that led out on to the street.

As they stepped through, a burly man in a denim jacket held up a large camera and pointed it at them. There was another photographer next to him and they seemed to be moving in tandem.

'Jesus,' said Paulsen. 'Where are you parked?'

'Other side of the road,' said Karl, pointing at a row of cars.

'Go. I'll deal with this,' said Paulsen.

She strode over to the two photographers, who were now jogging to keep pace with the Sulemans.

'DC Paulsen, Metropolitan Police.' She stepped into their path, blocking their line of sight. The first one grimaced at her, but she held her ground. 'You got a problem, or do you want one?' she said.

'What's he not telling us?' said Finn later in the incident room.

'He's still claiming he doesn't know who's behind this,' said Paulsen.

'And you believe him?' said Ojo, the look on her face the same as earlier when she'd trodden in something unpleasant. Paulsen held out her hands.

'Who knows – I didn't really have a chance to talk to him about it before Claire came back, and I agreed it was best to give them a bit of time together before we had that conversation. They'd just seen their dead daughter on the slab and that was before they were ambushed by the press.'

'How did they even know you were there?' said Finn.

'Someone must have leaked it,' said Ojo.

'Well, hopefully the DNA they found under Leah's fingernails will give us something concrete,' said Finn.

'Karl's phone's with digital forensics, though I'm guessing the messages were sent from a burner phone,' said Paulsen.

'This can't be a stranger,' said Finn.

'Unless it's just some little sadist doing it for kicks,' said Ojo.

'Possibly. But while we're waiting on the lab to come back on that DNA, I think our next step is to look a lot more closely at Karl.'

'I've found nothing on Leah,' said Ojo. 'I spoke on the phone to the guy she was dating. He's a finance lawyer straight out of university. Has an alibi for last Friday, and is pretty shaken up. The ex-boyfriend in Scotland checked out as well. He's in a new relationship, and had lost contact with her. Again, pretty devastated by it. They all spoke very highly of her.'

'Anything off the dating apps?'

'Doesn't look like she'd been using them for long. This lawyer was the only one it looks like she actually met.'

'So how do you want to proceed?' said Paulsen. Finn considered it for a moment.

'Let's push harder on the drug angle.'

'Karl denied using when I asked him, but I don't believe him,' said Paulsen.

'Exactly. In front of his wife, he probably would deny it,' said Finn. 'If he is using, where's he getting it from – who's his dealer? And is it just a dabble? We know he's wealthy, runs a business, owns a big house – it might be more than just a bit of coke he has a liking for.'

'I'll have a look into his finances, see if there's anything unusual there,' said Ojo.

'Talk to some of the other people who work for him too, Jacks. Wadham was bitter because he'd been laid off – see what his employees have to say. If there's something hidden there, I want to make sure we find out before the press do,' said Finn.

'When do you want to have this conversation with Karl? He's pretty raw right now, they both are. They're not coping well with this media intrusion,' said Paulsen.

Finn nodded.

'Do we need to be concerned?'

Paulsen thought about it for a moment.

'If you're referring to the VAF – no. At least not now. They're certainly traumatised and their relationship is under intense pressure, but it's no more than you'd expect in the circumstances.'

'You're sure it's nothing more?' he said, and she nodded.

The VAF was the vulnerability assessment framework, used by officers to identify potential mental health issues in the victims of serious crime. A combination of factors such as appearance, behaviour and communication skills were all used to determine whether someone should be deemed vulnerable. If, by Paulsen's judgement, Karl or Claire fell into that category, then a Merlin report would be drawn up and entered into the Met's intelligence systems. An appropriate safeguarding response would then be initiated with multi-agency support. Like all protections, it wasn't foolproof, but it was an important vanguard for the deeper, more powerful help victims often needed. It was a standard part of every officer's foundation training and Paulsen knew what signs to look for.

'Still, we need to tread carefully,' said Finn. 'I don't want to break the guy, and I'm aware he's living with a lot right now. Put a uniform outside their front door. It'll send a message to any press who fancy turning up uninvited, and it might make them feel a bit safer too. If the killer knows his phone number, he might know where they live as well.'

'Do we need to protect them?'

Finn mulled it. There was a range of options open to them, from securing the Sulemans' home, to installing cameras and alarms if necessary.

'Run through the choices with them. We'll increase the number of patrols in the area as well.' He shook his head. 'Go in softly – but one way or another, he needs to start giving us some answers. And make sure he understands not to tell the media about those messages. I want to keep that contained for the moment.'

Paulsen nodded and Finn indicated the meeting was over. Ojo headed back to her desk, and as Paulsen started to move towards hers, Finn called out to her.

'Wait a second, Mattie.' She came over and joined him. 'How are *you* getting on? I'm aware this investigation's become more complicated with all this press interest.'

She scowled at him. She hated questions like that, largely because she was sure he never queried anyone else in the same way.

'You drop me into this role – now you think I'm not up to it?'

'I didn't "drop you" in it, I asked if you'd do it, and you accepted. When I ask how things are, it's not because I'm making conversation, it's because it's my job to know.'

'I'm fine, thanks for asking.'

'Really? You're supposed to be paired with Sami, but you seem to be doing all this on your own. Are you getting enough support?'

'Sami's up to his eyes. He's been helping though – doing a lot of the legwork back here while I build the relationship with Karl and Claire.'

Finn frowned. That wasn't quite how he'd seen it working when he volunteered her for the role. He knew Dattani was busy, but hadn't anticipated Paulsen being left quite so exposed.

'And how is that relationship?'

'Karl trusted me enough to tell me about those messages. It's taken a while, but I think we've managed to build an understanding. So yes, I think it's going okay.'

'I'll have a word with Sami. Don't forget the Occupational Health Unit are there if you need them and there's support here – from me and Jacks as well – if you want to talk.'

'Good. But I hope that works both ways . . .'

Finn looked confused.

'What do you mean?'

'I hope the job provides the same support to its senior officers too. The ones that need it, that is.'

She looked him in the eye long enough to ensure her point had registered, then turned and walked away.

12

There were three of them and they said nothing. Hayden and Andy heard the car first, then saw it screeching around a corner, skidding to a halt. The youths jumped out, each brandishing a knife. Hayden wasn't surprised, he'd been expecting something like this. He was carrying a knife for protection and these three were the reason why. The county lines operation Andy was hoping to make theirs was lucrative. No one was simply going to let them take it. Andy stood his ground, clasping his own blade tightly by its handle.

'Come on then . . .'

They charged at the trio. One of them came for Hayden, who'd been anticipating the move, and easily sidestepped him. He brought his hand straight down, bringing the tip of his knife straight through the centre of his assailant's flailing palm. The youth screamed in pain, blood squirting out of the wound, and dropped his own weapon. The other two were momentarily distracted and Andy smashed a fist into the nearest one's face, his nose exploding in a spray of crimson. He followed it up with a second punch, putting him down, then stamped on the hand holding the knife. The third was suddenly outnumbered. His nerve broke and he turned and ran back to the car, screaming at his two wounded comrades to retreat. They all dived into the still-open doors, and the car skidded away.

Hayden watched them go and looked over at Andy, both of them still wearing their game faces. They stood panting for a moment, the street quiet again. Andy burst out laughing.

'Fucking brilliant.'

Hayden shook his head, struggling to see what was funny.

'We were lucky. Next time we might not be.'

'Don't be stupid. We've just sent a message out – this estate is ours.'

An exultant grin spread across his face. Hayden rolled his eyes. Andy was the bloke he played FIFA with – they weren't warriors and they'd been lucky.

'Or maybe they'll just wait until one of us is on our own. Then what?' Hayden looked at the splashes of blood on the pavement. 'That could be ours next time – I don't know if I want to do this. This isn't who we are.'

Andy put his hands on Hayden's shoulders, looked him in the eye.

'It's absolutely who we are. Don't bottle it now. We're building something, you and me. You want to look after your brother? How else are you going to make *real* money?' Hayden didn't have an answer. 'There you go. We stick to the plan, do this for a few months, then get out – after that you can do whatever you want.'

Hayden looked unconvinced. He stared at the knife he was still holding.

'I suppose . . .'

Andy pointed at the blood on the ground.

'You want to achieve anything – that's the price.'

Hayden walked through the front door of his flat. The adrenaline surge from earlier was wearing off, and he felt tired and nauseous. Some gangster he was – all he wanted was to have a shower, eat and get some much-needed sleep.

His flat was functional and basic, but he took a pride of sorts in it. Though it could always use a clean, he didn't like letting mess gather. The living room was dominated by a large wall with a huge canvas of Donald Duck above the slightly tatty sofa. It always drew his gaze and he found the bright cartoon bird a strangely comforting presence in times of stress.

His little brother Michael was sitting beneath Donald as he entered, feet up, head in phone. He'd made himself comfortable by the looks of things, an open bottle of beer next to him, one hand buried in a bumper bag of crisps. Thirteen years old, he possessed an attitude as cheeky as his smile.

'What are you doing here?' said Hayden.

The boy looked up from the screen, not expecting the terse tone.

'You said I could come round.'

'Jade's coming over, you need to get going. It's late, Dad will be wondering where you are.'

Mikey didn't answer. Instead, he was looking at the still-wet bloodstains on Hayden's clothes.

'What's that?'

'Nothing you need to worry about.'

Mikey looked at him uncertainly.

'Friend of mine cut himself,' said Hayden. They both knew he was lying, but the expression on his face dared the boy to push the point. He reached down and touched the wet, dark patch, glanced at his fingers and wiped the sticky liquid away on his sleeve.

Mikey was watching, almost hypnotised.

'Look, mate, I don't mind you coming round. I like seeing you – but you've got to give me some warning. You can't just turn up like this.'

He took off his bloodied T-shirt, revealing a heavily tattooed, muscular body beneath. He walked through to the small kitchen area and chucked the top into the washing machine.

96

'Worried I might catch you and your new girlfriend going at it?' shouted Mikey after him. That was the least of Hayden's worries. What he didn't want was his little brother coming to any harm. The events of the last few hours showed he was right to be concerned.

'Mikey . . .'

Before he could continue there was a knock at the front door. The boy grinned again.

'I'll leave you to it then . . .'

Hayden smiled back, despite himself.

'Where are you going to tell Dad you've been?'

'That I was out with my mates. He always believes me.'

'Bet he does. We all fall for your bullshit, don't we? Go to the bathroom and use the mouthwash – you don't want him smelling beer on your breath.'

Hayden picked up Mikey's unfinished bottle, took a large swig, then went to the front door and opened it to find Jade waiting outside. A trainee beautician in nearby West Norwood, she never looked anything less than immaculate. It matched her temperament – calm, without any of the drama he was used to from some of his exes. Mikey re-emerged from the bathroom suspiciously quickly. He smirked at them both, and raced past.

'Call me next time,' Hayden shouted after him. Jade looked at him suspiciously.

'What was that about?'

'Don't ask.'

He ushered her in, taking just a moment to discreetly check the walkways either side of the front door were clear.

'What's with the topless look, baby – you starting without me?' she said coyly. Then she noticed the dried blood on his stomach, and her expression changed to one of concern. 'What happened?'

He looked down awkwardly.

'It's not my blood. Me and Andy – we were ambushed.' He saw the alarm on her face. 'It's okay, we're both fine.'

'What about the people who attacked you?'

'No one got hurt.'

'Really? So where's that blood come from?'

'No one got *seriously* hurt.'

She didn't look convinced.

'Do you want something to eat?' he said. She shook her head, and he sighed wearily. 'Well, I do.'

He walked through the flat and opened up the freezer compartment of the fridge, rummaging inside until he found a packet of fish fingers and a bag of oven chips. She followed him in and sat on a bar stool by the door.

'Are you going to tell me what happened or aren't you?'

'Come on, Jade. You know what I'm involved in at the moment.'

He switched on the oven and tipped a handful of fish fingers out on to a baking tray, burying them under a pile of chips.

'I still don't understand why you're doing it. It's Andy – you just do what he says all the time. He's a bad influence on you.'

Hayden turned to face her and frowned.

'Bullshit.'

It was a conversation they'd had before. Though the relationship was relatively new, and she'd only met Andy briefly, she hadn't taken to him. But one thing he'd already learnt about her was that she didn't let things drop easily.

'Didn't you see what happened in the park the other night? That girl who got murdered? What makes you think you're immune?' she said.

'You think I'd run away like that bloke did?'

He'd seen the story in the papers. Some rich guy out of his depth, shitting himself.

'They were talking about it on the radio this morning. What would you have done if you'd been him?' she said.

'If it was you? Or Mikey? I wouldn't need a knife. I'd tear the guy apart with my bare hands.'

If that was meant to reassure her, it didn't.

'So you'd be happy to kill someone then?'

'Fuck's sake, Jade – what is this? Give me a break. I've never killed someone, never will either.'

'I don't like it.'

He leant forwards and kissed her gently.

'Neither do I. But I'm not going to do this for long. It's like Andy says, it's just a chance to make some money. Listen, I'm not sure you should come over for a bit. What just happened . . . might stir things up. Doesn't mean we can't see each other, but I don't want you getting caught up in anything.' She looked up, alarmed. 'No one's going to hurt you. It's just for a bit.'

She looked at him uncertainly.

'Hayden . . .'

She was staring now, something disturbing her.

'What is it?'

'Your hand . . .'

She pointed down at his side and he saw what had caught her attention. He was shivering, shaking violently, his right hand trembling like an old man's, and to his own shock he hadn't even noticed.

99

13

A sheepish Sami Dattani finally found Paulsen for a catch-up about the Sulemans. He apologised for his absence, but she brushed his concerns aside. She liked Sami – there was something of the fresh-faced schoolboy about him, which masked a deceptively shrewd streak. There weren't any sides to him either, and she appreciated that. Although he hadn't spent as much time with Karl and Claire as she had, he'd done a lot of the hard yards in the office taking care of the paperwork. It had saved valuable time and in turn enabled her to focus on the couple themselves. His advice was to leave the Sulemans alone for twenty-four hours. They needed space after their visit to the morgue that morning, and Paulsen could see the sense in that.

But the following morning, Paulsen walked into a deluge of emails from the media team. Interview requests were flying in – Sky News, BBC News, ITN, local and national radio stations, and most of the print media too. They all wanted Karl's story. And these were just the organisations going through the correct channels. She was in no doubt the Sulemans would be receiving direct offers as well, and some of those would be eye-wateringly lucrative.

She found Finn at his desk watching one of the news channels. A tear-stained woman with a northern accent was describing how she'd abandoned her baby years before, during a mugging. The now grown-up child was sat beside her nodding sagely as her mother relived the ordeal. The strapline running across the screen said: 'I left my baby to save myself'. Even in the absence of the Sulemans, the story wasn't going away. It wouldn't until Karl spoke, and that was something Paulsen didn't think would be a good idea at all. He didn't come across well – wealthy, spiky, defensive – none of which helped when the narrative being pushed was a collective 'How could you?'. She was fairly certain that, in the court of public opinion, he'd only damn himself further.

Finn turned to greet her as she took off her coat. If he'd enjoyed a relaxing evening off and a decent night's sleep, it wasn't showing. His complexion was pale, his eyes lined and red. There was no welcoming smile either; it was as if he hadn't moved from his chair since she'd seen him last.

'I want to talk to Karl, as soon as,' he said.

'I'll give them a call, see how they're doing. What are we going to do about this lot?' she said, gesturing at the TV screen.

'We need to throw them a bone. I've decided against releasing the picture of the murder weapon – it raises too many awkward questions about where it came from. I've asked the media team to find a picture of a similar knife and issue a press release with that, together with a request for information.'

'That won't keep them quiet for long.'

'No – it's Karl they want, he's the eye of the storm. Maybe we should go ahead with a press conference.'

Paulsen blew through her teeth.

'It's risky; they're falling over themselves to depict him as a coward. They'll push him hard, and I'm not sure he's strong enough to take it.'

'How do you think he'd respond?'

'Aggressively . . . and that's not a good look. Trust me, I've seen it.'

'We haven't told the media the full detail of what we think happened. Partly because I don't want to jeopardise the investigation. The only other person who knows all of it is the killer. But I'm thinking it may help the Sulemans if there was a bit more detail out there. Let Karl give his side of the story – he's being rinsed right now.'

He nodded at the screen, where the daughter was being asked if she'd ever been able to forgive her mother.

'Maybe,' said Paulsen, not hiding her lack of enthusiasm.

'Obviously we'd have to talk about how much information we can give out, find the right balance. But we have a duty of care, and I don't like the narrative that's being written here.'

'We still don't know *what* happened. We've only got Karl's word for it. For all we know he's lying out of his arse and he *did* run at the first sight of this guy. All this talk of a choice might just be a cover for his own cowardice.'

She didn't for one second believe that. But her point was well made – until they possessed more information they simply couldn't be sure what had actually taken place. Finn's jaw tightened, a familiar tell that he was either concentrating or irritated.

'Nevertheless we have to make a decision about the press. The more Karl keeps his head down, the worse it makes him look. He deserves a chance to explain himself, and I'd rather he did it here, sat next to me, than in some one-to-one with a journalist.'

Before Paulsen could respond, Ojo entered the room and came straight over to join them.

'I've got the results from the lab on the DNA they found under Leah's fingernails. It's bad news – it doesn't match with anyone on the database.'

It was a blow and they all knew it, because they'd been privately confident it would give them something. The savagery of the killing, the taunting – it all pointed at someone who wasn't nervously finding their way. As was his way, Finn tried to interpret what the information meant, rather than what it didn't mean.

'This brings it back to someone with a grudge, not someone with a criminal record.' He turned to Ojo. 'What have you managed to find on Karl?'

'I spoke to a few of his employees. You know that adage, "if you can't say something nice, don't say anything at all"? They were all a bit like that.'

Finn smiled grimly.

'Any enemies?'

'Plenty. Karl's got a policy of not paying his bills until the demand comes in red with big capital letters. Always settles in the end but he's left quite a few small businesses in the shit.'

'Did you talk to any of them?'

'Yes – and here's the problem. There's a consensus he's a bit of an arsehole, but nothing more. I didn't find evidence of anything past or present that could have prompted what happened in the park. Nobody hates him *that* much.'

'Nobody we know about,' said Finn.

Paulsen was grateful when it was Claire who answered her call, rather than her husband. She told her they needed to speak with Karl again, and Claire agreed on his behalf. Paulsen decided to take that on face value. If he was resistant to the idea, they'd know soon enough.

Just as Paulsen was about to finish the call, Claire spoke suddenly. 'I know about the messages. He told me last night. That uniform officer outside isn't just to keep the press away, is he?'

Paulsen reassured her that they didn't believe there was any threat, but she couldn't help but wonder how that conversation with Karl had gone. And when Claire asked if Paulsen and Finn could wait a couple of hours before visiting the house, as she and Karl had 'something they needed to take care of first', Paulsen's suspicions were further heightened. When she and Finn finally arrived, it became immediately obvious what that 'something' was.

Nicky Paige, a smug look of satisfaction on her face, was in the process of leaving the house. Two men were following her out – one carrying a television camera, the second with a long boom mic. They brushed past the uniform officer standing on the pavement as if he wasn't there.

'This isn't good,' said Paulsen as they got out of the car. She and Finn watched as the trio headed for a saloon parked on the double yellow lines directly in front of the house and began loading up.

Paulsen was steaming. Paige must have persuaded Karl to talk, then called a crew at short notice.

'Claire should have said that's what they were doing – I'd have told her not to.'

'Come on, let's see what the damage is,' said Finn, as they watched the saloon car roar away. It wouldn't take long for the video to appear on screen and online. The audio would be filleted for radio bulletins, the words transcribed into lurid headlines for the late editions of the *London Evening Standard*. And all of that just the warm-up for the morning's papers.

As they walked into the Sulemans' front room, Karl was looking bullish. It made Paulsen's heart sink even further.

'What did you tell them?' asked Finn carefully.

'The truth. My side of it – what really happened last Friday. It should put an end to all the rumours so we don't have to put up with any more of this shit.'

'Why that journalist?' Again, Finn's tone was neutral, betraying no judgement.

'She wasn't offering money, if that's what you're thinking. We've turned down offers like that.'

'*You* turned them down,' said Claire.

Karl looked surprised.

'You said the money didn't matter?'

'It doesn't, but I'd like to have been consulted,' she replied, the ice dripping across the carpet.

'It's not you they're telling lies about,' Karl retorted. He turned back to Finn. 'She also convinced me that she'd tell my story truthfully. And that mattered.'

Finn nodded without comment. He knew full well how this could turn out. Paulsen was biting her tongue so hard she wondered if the blood was dripping down her chin yet.

'Did you mention the messages you'd received?' said Finn.

'No. DC Paulsen warned me yesterday not to, so I didn't.'

That much at least was good news. Whatever Karl had said on camera would reveal itself in due course. Right now there were other questions to ask. They all sat down and Paulsen was grateful Finn was there to experience first-hand what she'd been dealing with: the oppressive claustrophobia of the room, the seething tension bubbling between Karl and Claire.

'I'm sorry I can't bring you news of an arrest yet. We're still following a number of lines of enquiry. But I need to ask you about those messages you received,' said Finn. 'I gather this began with a phone call – in my experience that's unprecedented in a stranger attack.'

'What are you saying?' said Claire.

'I'm not saying anything, but I am asking: are you concealing anything else from us, Karl? I can't stress enough how important it is you tell us everything you know.'

'Why would I hold anything back? Nobody wants this bastard caught more than me,' said Karl.

'Why do you think he made contact with you?'

'I don't know. Maybe he's enjoying the notoriety. It's every-where, the whole country knows my name. I didn't ask for that. I didn't ask for any of this.'

He was going on the offensive again, Paulsen noticed. She wondered if it was a stock response to any kind of intense scrutiny.

'Can I ask if there's anything in your private life? Are you having – or have you had – an affair, for example?'

'*Seriously?*'

'Karl, just answer the question,' said Claire.

'No. I have not.'

'And in your social life, your circle of friends – is there anyone you've fallen out with?'

'No.'

'And at work?'

'You've already asked me that, and I know you've been snooping about the office. The answer's still no. I piss people off, yes, but not to this extent. Do me a favour – stop looking at me and do your jobs properly, then you might find whoever did this.'

There was a steel in his voice – there, thought Paulsen, as he turned the conversation around – a glimpse of the busi-nessman who ran the ad agency. Finn ignored it.

'I'm going to ask you one more time, so we're clear. Do you have any idea who this might be, and why they might be doing this to you?'

Just for a brief second, husband and wife exchanged a look. The kind only two people who knew everything about one another did. Paulsen caught it, and saw that Finn had too. Karl looked him in the eye.

'No.'

*　　*　　*

'You should have told him,' Claire said later, after the two detectives had left. She was sat at the kitchen table. Karl was stood by the window again, his back to her.

'Told him what? There's nothing to tell. Some things should stay in the past.'

'And what if the press start digging?'

'They won't. I've given them what they wanted now; they've heard my side of it. They'll move on to something else.'

'I hope you're right about that.'

'Can't we just park all of this? We've got a funeral to plan. Do you think Leah would want us to be fighting now?'

'Don't you tell me what Leah would have wanted. Don't you put words in her mouth. Don't you dare – she trusted you . . .'

He swivelled round.

'Claire, please. Don't make me beg. I *need* you.'

His voice cracked but she didn't reply, the contempt of her words matched only by the disgust in her eyes.

14

'Do you know what Karin always used to say about you?' said Cally. Finn was back in the wine bar in Clapham, feeling more like he was in the dentist's waiting room. A long boring delay before things got painful, the only goal to get to the end of it and out the door. One thing he'd never clocked about Cally before was how wearing she could be. After ten minutes, he was already finding the constant verbal sparring tiring. He smiled pleasantly.

'No, but I'm sure you're going to tell me.'

'That you were the man who ran away from the circus to become an accountant.'

He hadn't been expecting that. He could easily hear the words coming out of Karin's mouth though – it sounded like her.

'What's that supposed to mean?'

'Christ, you're the detective. I hope your deductive skills are better than that on the job. What do you think it means?'

'Well . . . the stereotype is someone running away from their boring life to join the circus. So, I guess she meant I ran away from something interesting to do something boring. Which doesn't really make much sense, because my life's always been as vanilla as they come.'

'You're close.'

He shrugged. 'You tell me, then.'

'Whenever I *frequently* told her how starchy I thought you were, that was her way of telling me not to judge a book by its cover. That despite the middle-aged-man-from-M&S exterior, there was something a bit more colourful going on in there. I've never seen that side of you, but I've always been curious.'

'What do you want me to do, start juggling?'

She smiled with genuine warmth.

'She knew you better than I do and was an impeccable judge of character – so I'd take it as a compliment.'

'Can't say I feel like Mr Jazz Hands most days of the week. There isn't the time. Must be the same in your line of work, I'd have thought?'

He drained the last of his whisky, and brought the empty glass down with just enough of an emphatic thud to suggest he was ready to bring things to a close.

'Fancy a refill?' asked Cally.

'Better not – trouble with my job is you're always on call.'

'When was the last time you had a night off, got drunk? And I'm not talking about post-bereavement drinking on your own . . .'

He sighed at the dig, but she wasn't wrong.

'With Karin probably.'

His jaw reflexed suddenly into a yawn, which he failed to stifle in time.

'Keeping you up, am I?'

'No, I'm sorry, it's just been a long day.'

'I bet it has.' She sized him up. 'I know what a man who throws himself into his work looks like.'

He smiled at her, without a great deal of mirth.

'Alright, you win – I'll take that refill,' he said, more to change the subject than anything.

'You sure?'

'Yes, there's other people who can cover for me if anything does come up.'

That was true enough, though Jackie Ojo wouldn't thank him for it. He knew he shouldn't, but to his own surprise he realised he was gasping for another.

Mattie Paulsen spent her evening driving to her parents' home in Norfolk. Finn had approved her request for some time off and after some discussion, she and Nancy agreed it would be best if she travelled solo. Sami was available for the Sulemans, and Mattie was grateful to temporarily give her brain a distraction. Her parents lived in a small cottage in the market town of Holt, not far from the Cromer coast. There were no railway stations close by, so it was up the M11 before hitting the A roads into the countryside, crawling behind the endless tractors which ambled their way around the county.

The journey at least gave her a chance to think. It was hard not to feel like she was deserting the Sulemans. Sky News were trumpeting an exclusive interview with Karl, at 9 p.m. that evening. At about five-to she switched off the music she hadn't been listening to and found a talk station on the radio. Although Sky were claiming an exclusive, releasing a few short clips to other media outlets was standard practice – all publicity being good publicity. Thirty seconds into the news bulletin which followed, her worst fears began to materialise.

Finn waited for Cally to go to the toilet before quickly checking the Sky News website on his phone. The headline above the video clip didn't bode well:

'I'm no coward,' says father who left daughter to die

Finn watched the first thirty seconds or so. The camera stayed close in on Karl's face. There was no aggression; it was more the little-boy-lost version of the man, sweaty and stumbling as he tried to explain himself.

'You were given a choice, but you chose to run – is that what you're saying?' asked Paige out of view, as if puncturing the logic of a floundering MP. In every sense of the word, Karl looked pathetic. Finn decided he'd seen enough and stopped the video. He'd watch the whole thing later when he was in the right frame of mind. He dreaded to think what the early editions would look like tomorrow. Cally returned and he closed the page down, though not quite fast enough to prevent her from seeing what he'd been watching.

'I was going to ask you about him – I thought that was on your patch. It's everywhere, isn't it? Poor bloke.'

'That's more sympathetic than a lot of people have been.'

'Idiots – I can only imagine how he's feeling. He's got to live with what he did for the rest of his life now, hasn't he?'

'What would you have done in that situation?' asked Finn, curious. The more people he asked, the more he felt he would understand what had happened to Karl. Her eyes widened briefly as she contemplated it.

'Say it was your husband,' he added.

She pulled a face.

'Run for the fucking hills and leave him to it,' she replied with unexpected ferocity. Finn was surprised. It was hard not to like Eric Hunter. He dressed in the blandest clothes, wore sensible glasses and did something dull in the City for a living. Cally looked awkward.

'You clearly haven't heard then? He left me last year.'

Finn's jaw literally dropped.

'There's no need to look at me like that,' said Cally, more amused than offended.

'I'm sorry. I had no idea.'

'Well, of course not, you didn't stay in touch after Karin died, did you?'

That was a bit rich, Finn thought, given Cally herself was only here under his late wife's instruction.

'When did it happen?'

'Just before Christmas. We were hardly seeing each other. The restaurant keeps me extremely busy and he used to work long hours. There wasn't anyone else, but he felt we'd become strangers. I couldn't really argue with that in the end. He was adamant he wanted out.'

Finn didn't know quite how to react. To be blunt, he didn't think the man he'd met possessed the balls to do something like that.

'I'm so sorry,' he said again, automatically.

'You can stop saying that now.'

Out of the tourist season, Holt was quiet on a Monday evening, and the final stretch of the drive was mercifully brief. The single fifteen-second clip on the news of Karl, whiny and pleading, told Paulsen everything she needed to know about the interview. When she returned to London, she wanted a proper sit-down with Finn. They'd need a strategy to manage this now. She checked herself – that sounded like a cry for help, an admission she couldn't handle the Sulemans on her own, and she wasn't going to have that. Not with Finn and Skegman scrutinising her so closely. She'd use the time in Norfolk to work up her own plan. For now though, difficult as it was, she needed to compartmentalise. The Sulemans would have to wait.

It was dark when she pulled in to the drive of the picturesque cottage where her parents lived. Her father came out to greet her first. His thick mane of blond hair, yellowing with age now, combined irresistibly with the stubble on his chin to give the impression of a slightly manic Richard Branson. He smiled and she couldn't help but beam back. His grin was so wonderfully normal, his eyes lucid and clear, his expression so familiar. Jonas was wrong about all of this, he had to be.

'You're late, and your mother's on the warpath,' Christer Paulsen said as they embraced. His Swedish accent hadn't faded in the years he'd spent living in the UK.

'I'm sorry ...' she began, but he cut her off with a raised finger.

'Plenty of time for all that later.'

His voice sounded firm and rich, and as she followed him in, the world was as it should be. It occurred to her that this was probably how Leah Suleman felt when she met with her father in the park.

Evelyn Paulsen was stood with an apron on, stirring a pot on the Aga, which dominated the large rustic kitchen. It was another familiar silhouette, one which went right back to Mattie's childhood in south London. A diminutive figure, the tight curls on her mother's head seemed whiter and greyer than before, though Mattie was sure that was just her own imagination playing tricks. The brief frown on her face melted into a warm smile of recognition.

'You've done something to your hair,' her mother said suspiciously. 'You're always doing things to it.'

'She looks fabulous. Ignore her,' said Christer.

'Like you even noticed her hair,' said Evelyn, and Mattie smiled. She'd grown up to this soundtrack, the light-hearted bickering between them. But there was something about the tone, the rhythm of this that didn't feel quite right. It was only small, but she could detect it; an underlying melancholy.

Mattie watched her father carefully over dinner, looking for signs of something, anything. He was continuing to slightly over-egg the hail-fellow-well-met approach he'd adopted since she'd arrived. Her mother's more frayed expression was the bigger indicator something wasn't right.

She updated them on her life in London, her parents reacting, as usual, as if she lived on Mars. But it was when they got on to the subject of her work that things took a detour. Both her parents were very keen to get the inside track on Karl Suleman.

'We were talking about him over breakfast,' Christer said. 'There's something wrong with the man. You can tell.'

'Dad, it's not that simple.'

'I agree with your father. Something will come out. I think he's done something like this before,' said Evelyn.

It was faintly depressing hearing her parents talk like this – sounding like the same people who'd posted comments beneath the *MailOnline* story. Mattie talked them through the investigation but they seemed even less impressed afterwards.

'So there's a man with a knife threatening to rape this guy's daughter. And he decides the best thing to do is run away? And you're defending him?' said Christer.

'I didn't say that. It's more about trying to understand his reasoning. He's a lot of things, but I don't think he's a coward – I think that's unfair,' said Mattie.

'I'd love to know what . . .' said Christer. He suddenly looked confused. 'What . . .' He looked towards Evelyn for help, but she looked stricken. Mattie felt her heart start to pound. He was concentrating hard, but the words were eluding him.

'What are you trying to say, Dad?'

He frowned, still struggling.

'. . . to know what . . . your brother . . .'

He looked at them helplessly.

'Jonas. His name's Jonas,' said Mattie.

There was a horrible silence and Christer smiled gently, the sadness for the first time visible in his eyes.

'Mattie,' said her mother, 'there's something we need to tell you . . .'

15

They watched it together in silence, Karl's face filling the large HD screen in the corner of the living room. Words that seemed reasonable coming out of his mouth several hours earlier sounded strangely different through the filter of the TV. They'd done something in the editing, Karl thought. He hated how he sounded; his voice reedy and thin when in his mind he'd been fluent and calm.

He'd begun by talking about Leah – explaining who she was, what she was like, and the hole her death had left in their lives. He'd done that deliberately because he wanted people to know how much he'd loved her. Then they'd understand how ridiculous it was to suggest he'd abandoned her. When the conversation turned to her murder, he'd paused, the difficulty in answering genuine. And then he went through it: the man in the mask, the knife, the choice. Anyone reasonable would surely understand. It was a calculation made in a life-or-death situation. One Leah made *with* him. He hadn't run away, he'd gone to find help. The park was usually full of joggers, commuters and dog-walkers. It was his tragic luck the only person he'd happened upon was an elderly woman without a phone.

'What was it like when you saw Leah's body in the mortuary?' asked Paige. 'Did you feel guilty at that point?'

On-screen Karl swallowed before answering.

'No. My emotion – my anger – was directed at the person who'd put her there.'

'So you felt no responsibility at all?'

'No.'

Claire sat in silence, her face giving nothing away. But as he glanced at her, he saw her head shake almost imperceptibly, noticed her knuckles whiten as she gripped the side of the sofa. The interview ended and within seconds there was a jarringly loud advert for some forthcoming action show. Claire turned the TV off and there was silence. He thought he'd feel vindicated, but he didn't. He just felt alone – as if the entire country was watching and blaming him. Claire was still staring at the screen as if there was more to come.

'It was important to do it,' he said. 'Now people know what happened, it should calm some of this down – let us grieve in peace.'

She breathed hard then turned to him.

'Can you not see it?'

'See what? I don't understand.'

'How the world sees you.'

'No, I can't. Can't *you* see it, see what actually happened? I don't care what other people think. In that moment, it was the right decision. I accept I got it wrong – but when it was happening, it was the . . .' he held his hands out helplessly, '*least worst* thing to do.'

'He threatened to rape her, and you turned your back and ran.'

'You know how much I loved her. You know that more than anyone.'

'Those are just words, Karl . . . it's what you *did* that matters.'

This time he couldn't find a response, because it kept coming back to that.

'You came home and she didn't. And I wish it was you who was dead.' She got up and walked out of the room and a second later he heard the front door slam.

117

He sat for a while on the sofa and looked up at his daughter. She smiled down at him from the portrait on the wall. He genuinely believed what he'd told Claire, and what he'd told the police. That he'd done the right thing. But now he was wavering. It felt like he was in a minority of one. The more he tried to explain it, the less anyone seemed to understand. Over and above it all, he just wanted her back. He stared up at Leah again.

Claire was standing in the rain, almost oblivious as it cascaded down her face. She'd been wandering aimlessly, just grateful to have some space. She knew she'd gone too far, but it was almost as if she couldn't stop herself. Deep down she *did* understand his reasoning. But there was something so cold-blooded about it – the equation he'd worked out while a man threatened their daughter. She checked herself, remembered – again – that it was her idea they should meet for the damned meal in the first place. The truth was, unloading on Karl made her feel better. He'd become the focal point for all her grief and rage and that was unfair. There was a lot in the immediate future they needed to deal with – a funeral to plan, this media onslaught to weather. She couldn't forgive him for what he'd done, but she knew things couldn't go on like this either. One way or another they needed to have a conversation, and she would have to change her approach.

By the time she arrived home she'd already composed in her head what she wanted to say. She put the key in the door and felt the warmth of the house as she stepped back inside.

The first thing she noticed were the shoes. A pair of brown brogues floating above the stairs. They were swaying gently like a bauble on a Christmas tree. When she looked up she could see a sheet tied around her husband's neck, the other end wrapped around the bannister at the top of the stairs. The tip of his tongue was poking out beneath narrow, hooded eyes. Later there'd be anger, this second act of cowardice confirming the first in her mind. But right there and then, her most immediate thought was that she'd all but told him to do it.

16

Jo Corcoran's feet hurt. It was hardly surprising – she'd been on them for twelve hours solid. An A&E nurse at St Thomas's Hospital, she was used to the feeling. It hadn't even been a particularly bad day, not compared to some, but she was exhausted nonetheless. She could have done without the extended shift handover, one of her colleagues managing to miss a bus and keeping her back an extra half hour. Now, as she trudged home, her thoughts were turning to food, reality TV and a much-needed glass of wine. Arriving at the front door of the small terraced house where she lived, she paused for a moment – a strange sense someone was standing nearby. She looked down the deserted street, shook her head and went inside. Tiredness did odd things to you.

Her partner Jamie was sitting in the living room, watching TV with a can of beer in one hand. He gave her a friendly wave as she bustled in.

'I made a chilli – you just need to warm it up. It's still in the pan. There's a packet of rice next to it.'

'You're an angel,' she replied with her broad Belfast accent. 'Nice and spicy, I hope.'

'What do you think?' he said, grinning. 'I chucked in the last of that pak choi as well. Don't let it put you off.'

'You put pak choi in a chilli? What did you do that for?'

'Didn't want to waste it.'

She shrugged. 'Whatever.' She was too hungry to care.

'How was your shift?'

'Fine, no dramas.'

Actually, that wasn't true. There'd been a nine-year-old with severe burns to his arm after his mother spilt boiling water over him, a drunk with a head injury who'd been almost too difficult to manage, and a ninety-six-year-old man with chest pains who'd given them all a scare. But, as ever when she got through the front door, the memories washed away. A clean slate, before the following day brought a whole new set of people and problems.

'Have you looked in on Mum?' she said. Her elderly mother lived with them, and by this time of night was usually in bed upstairs, out for the count.

'I checked about half an hour ago. She was doing a bit of reading.'

'One of those romantic novels full of shagging?'

Jamie grinned and nodded. Jo rolled her eyes.

'How's your day been?' she asked.

He shrugged. 'Quiet.'

She smiled and headed out into the hallway, deciding to eat first before changing out of her uniform – she was too hungry to wait any longer.

Then she heard it. The knock at the door. It was odd, because usually people rang the bell. And this late on a Monday evening it was rare for anyone to call at all. At first she thought she'd misheard, then it happened again. *Rat-tat-tat*. She frowned in irritation. Who knocks when there's a bell? Already she'd decided they were a pain. Someone trying to earn a crust probably, cold-calling to see if she wanted to switch energy providers. She felt her stomach rumble and was tempted to ignore the knock. But against her better judgement, she flicked the latch open.

Standing in front of her was a short figure in a hooded dark jacket. The person didn't seem to have a face, just a strange mirror-like visage instead. He was holding a heavily ridged knife and slowly put a leather-gloved forefinger to his lips – or at least where his lips should be.

'*Shhh* . . .'

Jo took an involuntarily step backwards. She wanted to cry out to Jamie, sat just a few feet away on the other side of the wall, but the sight of the knife froze her in her tracks. The masked figure held the tip of the blade out and pushed it up against her chest. There was a slight rip as it tore through the fabric of her uniform.

'Call for help and I'll kill you.'

The voice was low, and cold as marble.

'Please, my mum's upstairs. You can have whatever you want.' She kept her voice to a low whisper.

'So which one do you love the most?'

'What?'

'Your mum or your boyfriend?'

Jo was nonplussed by the question, still trying to get her head around what was happening.

'I've got money, I can go and get it for you. There's jewellery upstairs too.'

'I don't want your jewellery.'

She could see the ridges on the blade more clearly in the hallway light. She knew what it was now – a zombie knife. She'd seen at work what these things could do, seen teenagers all but disembowelled by them.

'Please don't hurt us.'

'All I want you to do is take a walk.'

'I don't understand.'

'You're leaving. Then I'm going to kill one of them – your boyfriend or your mother. You decide.'

Jo felt her blood freeze over.

'You can't . . .'

All she could see was her own horrified expression in the strange featureless mask.

'I can and I will – or you *all* die.'

He pushed the knife against her chest again and she felt the point of it through her tunic.

'So choose.'

Something about this was familiar – that guy in Crystal Palace who was all over the papers, the one whose daughter was murdered. It'd been on the news in the staffroom earlier – wasn't he given a choice? 'Imagine leaving your little girl like that,' she'd said to someone. The words came back like a sharp dig to the ribs.

'I can't . . . I *really* can't.'

'Yes, you can,' said the man, stepping forwards. There was a sudden flash of movement, a rush of air past her face. She felt a wasp-sting of pain to her cheek and put up a hand instinctively. She saw blood and whimpered.

'I'm only going to ask you one more time.'

He steadied the knife, pointed it at her now, the intention clear. They stood there locked in silent negotiation for another second more.

And then she gave him an answer.

Slowly she turned, as if body and mind were acting independently of one another, the buzz of white noise in her ears. The figure stood to one side and the night opened out in front of her. She thought again of her mother reading upstairs, Jamie in the room next door. And she began to walk.

17

'He's left me completely on my own.'

Claire Suleman was caught in the nether world where anger and grief collide. Her eyes were red and tear-stained, but her fury was unmistakable. Finn was just hoping his breath didn't smell of whisky. He was furious with himself for drinking with Cally when he knew he shouldn't have. He was also angry at the sense he'd dropped the ball with the Sulemans. Paulsen had explained to him the situation with her father and asked for some time off. He'd judged it a reasonable request in the circumstances, but in hindsight he hadn't thought it through. Yes, other officers were available, but that wasn't really the point. Paulsen was the one who'd built the relationship with Karl and Claire, and she'd been missing when they'd needed her. As with the decision to drink, it was sloppy on his part.

Then there was the interview with Nicky Paige. It'd been broadcast literally minutes before Karl had killed himself, if Claire's version of events was accurate. It was hard not to connect the two things. Finn and his team could and should have done better in helping the Sulemans deal with the media. Paulsen had kept him updated on both Karl and Claire's mental condition on a daily basis. She'd applied the criteria of the vulnerability assessment framework and hadn't believed either of them were a risk – and he'd agreed with that judgement. But the margins in these things were always fine. There was only so much you could do; no system was foolproof. Nevertheless, the body hanging in the hallway was damning.

Finn was sitting with Claire around the large table in the living room at which she'd once shared meals with her husband and daughter. Despite her anger she was surprisingly lucid. It was as if doubling down on the grief numbed it in some way. She'd seen her unshakeable belief in her husband erode day on day since their daughter was murdered. He'd saved the final disappointment for last. There hadn't even been a note, nothing to explain himself. A happy family unit of three reduced to one in less than a week.

The thud of footsteps and the sound of muffled voices filtered through from the hallway. As was the norm in these situations, a detective – Sami Dattani – a uniform sergeant and a solitary crime scene investigator were there to ensure there was nothing suspicious about the death. The coroner's office had been informed and they were now waiting for the body to be transferred to the mortuary.

'I'm sorry to ask, but are there any personal items you'd like removed before the body's taken away?' said Finn. There was a pause as Claire thought about it.

'Yes. His wedding ring – I'd like that, please,' she said finally.

'You'll need to get a medical certificate from the coroner to register the death. They'll then issue you with the documents you need for the funeral.'

Claire smiled tightly.

'It's alright, I'm familiar with the drill now.'

Finn nodded awkwardly.

'Is there somewhere you can go tonight?'

'Yes, my mother lives in Hammersmith. I'm going to stay with her for a bit. Until I know what I'm going to do.' She put her hand to her forehead. 'How could he do this to me? Before Leah's even buried?'

It wasn't that she looked broken, Finn thought, more overwhelmed – punch-drunk from it all.

'Again, I'm sorry to have to ask you this, Claire, but are you happy for us to inform the media? We can hold off for a little bit, if you'd prefer.'

'What's your advice?'

'In my opinion it's better to tell them as soon as possible.'

She nodded wearily. The reality was that Karl's suicide would be taken as an admission of guilt. There'd be little sympathy in the comments sections beneath the reports of his death. Finn wondered whether this was what the person who'd killed Leah wanted all along. Was this why he'd rung and messaged Karl, to ramp up the guilt? In the end he needn't have bothered, because the media had done the job for him. Perhaps that's why there hadn't been any new messages – there hadn't been any need.

Claire slumped in her chair silently, and it took Finn a moment to register what was happening. Her mouth was open, but no sound was coming out. Her whole body seemed to be shaking. Finn always found raw emotion the most difficult thing to deal with. She held her hand up in apology before finally emitting a strangulated cry of grief. As she did, Dattani came in from the hallway. He was holding his phone in one hand, but slowed as he took in what was happening. Finn motioned at him to give them some space, but he came over anyway and whispered urgently.

'Guv, it's Jackie – says it's important.'

Finn took the phone and walked into the kitchen as Dattani discreetly replaced him at the table.

'What have you got, Jacks?' said Finn, closing the door behind him.

'Guv, I'm in Penge. I've got a man in his mid-thirties stabbed to death in his front room. The description of the attacker is identical to the one Karl gave us for his daughter's killer. And there's something else – his partner says the killer made her choose – between her boyfriend and her mother.'

Finn listened impassively, looking through the glass door, his eyes still locked on the sobbing woman at the table.

The uniform sergeant drove him the short journey from Dulwich to Penge. Finn's own car was still parked where he'd left it outside the wine bar in Clapham. He was using the time to get his head around what was happening. If it was the same killer, then everything was up in the air. He'd been working increasingly to the premise that the attack on the Sulemans was targeted. It still might have been, but he hadn't expected a copycat murder. This pushed things back into the territory of simple sadism, and that was the one possibility he feared the most. Random murders without motive didn't leave a pattern, no breadcrumb trail which could be followed – they were every detective's worst nightmare.

They pulled up close to a small terraced house in a street backing on to the railway line. There were a number of police vehicles parked together, with an ambulance also in attendance. Finn could see uniformed officers under the beams of the street lights, already engaging in door-to-door enquiries. Gowned scene of crime officers were working outside the entrance of the house, and in the small front garden area. He jumped out of the car and saw Jackie Ojo in full forensic apparel, talking to a PC in the hallway. She saw Finn approaching and came over to join him, taking a detour via a cardboard box by the front gate. She fished inside it, and brought over a blue plastic overall, latex gloves and disposable overshoes. Finn slipped them on as they talked.

'Her name's Jo Corcoran, she's a nurse at St Thomas's. She'd just come home from work, said the killer knocked on their door at just before nine. He made her choose whether he should kill her mum or her boyfriend – said he'd kill all three of them if she didn't. Mum won the lottery. Jo was walking around the block while her partner was murdered.'

'Just like Karl,' said Finn, the image of a man suspended above the stairs, his tongue poking out of bloated lips, still far too fresh. 'Didn't she try and get any help, go to her neighbours?'

'Banged on a few doors, first people to answer were at number thirty-four. By the sounds of it, she was so hysterical they nearly didn't let her in. By the time she managed to convince them she was serious, it was all over.'

'Were they the ones who called it in?'

Ojo nodded.

'And where is she now?'

'With her mother in the ambulance. When I left her she was in full-on nurse mode; I think it's helping to distract her.'

'That won't last. What's happened to the mother?'

'Nothing physical – but she's in deep shock and refusing to go. They're just trying to calm her down.'

Ojo turned and led Finn into the house. He tiptoed past the forensic officers in the narrow hallway and entered the living room. It was clear the victim had put up a fight. A lamp was shattered on the floor, a chair was on its side and there were cushions and magazines scattered about. And everything seemed to be soaked in blood. It was puddled on the beige carpets, stained across the furniture, spattered on the walls. Lying on the floor was the body of slightly pot-bellied man in his mid-thirties. At first Finn thought he was wearing a purple shirt, until he realised it was sky blue but soaked through with blood. His face was frozen in an odd expression of mild discomfort, at odds with the multiple slashes and slices that were visible across his midriff and arms. Scene of crime officers were at work in here too, checking for fingerprints, taking DNA samples and looking for footprints in the sopping floor.

'Any sign of a murder weapon?' asked Finn, and Ojo shook her head.

'So we've got a killer, with no previous, targeting people with a very specific MO. What do we know about the victim?'

'His name's Jamie Baker. He was a self-employed electrician. He'd done three jobs today – we've pulled the details from his phone.'

'What about the mother?'

'Maeve Corcoran, seventy-six years old. Slept through the whole thing, then found the body when she came down to make a cup of tea.'

Finn shook his head.

'Any idea if anything's been stolen?'

'It's been hard to get much detail out of Jo, but it doesn't look like it.'

'Okay. We need to know about the victim. See if he was known to the Sulemans. And follow up on those jobs he did, just in case there's anything unusual. Same goes for Jo – I want to know who these people are and what on earth they might have done to provoke this.'

Ojo nodded, and Finn turned and went back outside. As he approached the open back door of the ambulance he could see an elderly woman lying in the back with a blanket over her. A paramedic was sat with her, talking gently. It wasn't hard to identify Jo Corcoran. She was standing outside, still wearing her uniform. As he got closer he could see blood all over the front of it. She didn't seem to be hurt, so Finn guessed that when she'd returned to the house she'd tried to help Jamie. He wondered what had gone through her mind as she'd left the house, and how long had she given it before returning? How do you measure such things? He was distracted by the detail of it. One thing he knew already was that whoever this woman was, and for whatever reason this had been done, he wasn't going to let her story end the same way as the man he'd just left.

He introduced himself to Jo, who turned and greeted him with lifeless eyes. It was an expression he'd seen far too much of recently – on Claire's face less than an hour ago, on Karl's in an interview room three days before.

'How's your mother?' he asked gently.

'She's . . . she doesn't understand it. She thinks he's coming back.'

It wasn't clear whether she meant Jamie or the killer, but now that she was facing him, Finn could see she wasn't just trembling, she was shaking hard in deep shock. He signalled to one of the paramedics, who brought over a blanket and wrapped it around her.

'We should get her to hospital. They'll sedate her.' As the words came out of his mouth he was aware that Jo probably knew this better than anyone.

'Let me talk to her. She hates hospitals. Had a bad experience in one recently.'

The words came out with a judder. Her complexion was pea green. She pulled the blanket around herself. He wouldn't be getting a statement from her tonight, that much was clear. He felt an unexpected surge of *something* himself, and it caught him out. Twice in the same evening he'd seen crushing bereavement, and he could feel it pulling at the frayed edges of his own loss. He needed to get a grip, stay professional and deal with his own fallout later.

'Guv.'

He turned and saw Ojo standing a short distance away. He made his apologies to Jo, and went over to join her.

'I've just had word from base – there's been a stabbing on the Hope Estate tonight. A teenager, a dealer by the sounds of it. He's been taken to a hospital in a critical condition.' Finn rolled his eyes.

'When it rains . . .'

His wondered immediately whether the two stabbings were linked. He could see Ojo was thinking the same.

'When did it happen?'

'Not clear yet. But there's a suggestion it was a reprisal for something that happened yesterday afternoon. A resident said he saw some sort of ambush.'

'Nothing was called in though?'

Ojo shook her head. It was hardly an unusual occurrence in these situations. Most witnesses to these sort of incidents preferred the hear-no-evil-see-no-evil approach.

'Alright, let's see what CID turns up overnight and we can compare notes in the morning. I'm about dead-bodied out.'

Ojo nodded and turned to go back in the house, a look of vague irritation developing on her face. Finn knew that look.

'Something bothering you, Jacks?'

'Yeah . . . If you don't mind me asking, where's Paulsen? We're really stretched.'

'Dealing with a family emergency,' said Finn.

'Let's hope she gets over it quick then,' she said. Before Finn could reply, he heard a low moan behind him. He turned and saw Jo struggling for air. The paramedic caught her just as her legs buckled. Carefully he escorted her towards the ambulance. He watched as she was helped inside. He'd spent the night with three different women: Cally Hunter, Claire Suleman and Jo Corcoran. Each of them had tugged at him in different ways. The faint taste of whisky was still in the back of his throat, and all he could think was that he could murder another.

18

Mattie Paulsen breathed in hard, felt her lungs strain and relished the feeling. She was taking an early morning run. In London it often felt like a chore, but not here. At half past six in the morning the old Georgian town was gloriously empty. She jogged through the maze of narrow backstreets, past the green carpet sports fields of Gresham's School, and out into the countryside. She was still processing the conversation with her parents from the previous evening. There was no hiding from it now, no pretending the problem didn't exist; her father had Alzheimer's.

It was her mother who'd laid it out. She'd used the same gentle tones she might have deployed to describe a recipe for a nice Victoria sponge. She apologised for not telling Mattie sooner, and explained why. They'd misled Jonas deliberately, told him the doctor's appointment was the following week when in fact it'd been the previous one. Evelyn and Christer, wanting to deal with things alone for a while, had ring-fenced themselves as they tried to make sense of the new reality. The future was now timetabled, a clock formally ticking. They'd called Jonas with the news while Mattie was driving up, and now the whole family was up to speed.

'Are you alright?' Evelyn had asked after she'd finished talking.

'Yes, I think so,' came the reply finally.

'It's okay if you're not,' said her father.

'Jonas did warn me. I kind of knew it was coming, I think. Honestly, I'm fine.'

She was lying. Her mind was already racing to the bottom, conjuring up the worst-case scenarios she'd kept at bay since the spectre was first raised.

'How are you both coping?' she'd said.

'Ingen ko på isen,' Christer had said with a shrug. He'd been saying that for as long as she could remember. It was a collo- quialism Swedes used instead of 'no worries', the expression literally translating as 'there is no cow on the ice'. On this occasion he was wrong though. There was a damned herd, and the ice was cracking.

Evelyn didn't dwell on herself, instead running through what she'd been told by the doctor. She explained the likely timetable of what was ahead. Christer was already reaching the end of the beginning. There were seven stages in total and the doctor estimated he was somewhere between three and four, a state of mild-to-moderate decline. Mattie had listened patiently, but you didn't need to be an expert to know what stages five to seven entailed.

In the same gentle way, Evelyn had explained what was likely to decline – memory, reasoning, judgement. The ability to speak, to express himself, to solve problems. Christer simply listened without emotion as she spoke.

'Right now your father's still the same man, Mattie. You need to treasure him while you've still got him.'

A night's sleep and some exercise made her feel a little more at ease. After showering she checked her phone. She'd deliberately kept it switched off since she'd arrived, not wanting to be distracted by work. There was a missed call from Finn, followed by a text asking her to call him back. There was no hint of what it was about and she shook her head in irritation. The man possessed an allergy to leaving voicemails – as if he didn't have any faith they'd ever be picked up.

It was now approaching 7.30 a.m. – fair game to call. He answered immediately and told her about the events of the previous evening: the new murder investigation in Penge, the stabbing on the Hope Estate and Karl Suleman's suicide. She sat slowly down on her bed and looked out of the window into the mud-brown fields beyond.

'I can't believe it,' she said finally. He knew immediately which of the three developments she was referring to.

'I'm sorry, Mattie. I hate to ask . . .'

She'd already anticipated the question.

'There was nothing in the VAF – in my judgement – that suggested he was suicidal.'

'Are you sure?'

She took a deep breath, weighed it up. He'd been angry, distraught, traumatised. But she hadn't seen a man ready to end things yet, more someone determined to get justice – keen to clear his own name.

'Have you spoken to Sami?' she asked Finn.

'Yes, his assessment's the same as yours. But you spent the lion's share of time with them.'

She said nothing, her breathing heavy down the line as she remembered. There were protocols that would now follow. The death would be referred to the Independent Office for Police Conduct as a matter of course, and her family liaison log would be examined too.

'I'm sure,' she said.

'I believe you and I'm not apportioning blame. I think events must have moved pretty quickly after that interview. I'm not sure what we could have done.'

Paulsen bit her lip. Doubt was starting to seep in now; had she underestimated how damaged he was? Could she have done more? The significance of the other information Finn had shared suddenly penetrated too.

'And you think this murder in Penge could have been the same killer?' she said.

'The description's the same. The choice the victim's partner was given was very similar to the one Karl and Leah were offered in the park. It might be this is some fucked-up new tactic we're seeing. But the location, the description . . . it all suggests the same person.'

'Oh God, Claire . . .' Paulsen heard herself say as the implication dawned.

'Don't worry, she's gone to stay with her mother. Sami's keeping an eye on her. How are things with your parents?' said Finn quickly.

'Not good. They need me. I thought I was doing the right thing coming here. I honestly didn't see this coming with Karl though.'

'You couldn't have known. I wouldn't have let you go if I'd thought this was on the cards. If there's any blame it should go to me.' She appreciated the sentiment, but it did little to help. She could feel a flicker of self-loathing inside, like an old friend waking from a sleep.

'Sorry Mattie, but are you able to come back today? As you can imagine, we're stretched.'

She pondered it for a moment. The guilt about Karl was creeping over her now like a dark shadow. She was getting angry too – a familiar step on from self-loathing. She didn't want to leave her parents but the big conversation had now taken place. They could probably all do with a bit of time and space to let it sink in. Instinctively she wanted to occupy herself as well. Another familiar feeling – the sense of fighting things that couldn't be fought.

'Yes. I'll be back by mid-morning,' she said. The smell of

fresh coffee was working its way up through the house. She'd been hungry after her run, ready for breakfast. Now she just felt sick.

Finn sighed. It was easy to imagine what was going through Paulsen's mind. He'd been careful in what he'd said. He didn't blame her for Karl's death, and didn't want her to feel responsible for it. He knew she would though. God knows she liked carrying a burden on her shoulders, and this possessed the potential to set her back a long way. He felt bad about recalling her and cursed the financial restrictions he was working under. The cuts made a clear difference to how they operated and he'd have that argument with any politician.

Once upon a time he'd have been able to tell her she could take as long with her family as she needed. These days it was different. She certainly wasn't the only officer who'd been forced to choose between work and family in some form. He wondered how long it would be before the law of diminishing returns applied; at what point he'd look across the incident room and see people who'd stopped caring enough to make a difference. At the moment they were running on goodwill and professionalism, but these things had their limits.

He drained the last of his freshly brewed Yirgacheffe, enjoying the sharp caffeine hit. Karin always used to mock his self-indulgent taste in coffee beans, calling it 'poncey' as she pointedly swigged her satanically strong Nescafé. He smiled. It was in the small memories he kept her alive. He swung on his jacket and heard his phone ping with a text. He looked down to see who it was from, then sighed in exasperation when he saw Cally Hunter's name. Another morning, another text.

Hey . . .

'Morning!' he replied with a bonhomie he wasn't feeling. It was going to be a busy day – the media would soon be getting wind of Karl's suicide. A press release was being sent out at 9 a.m. and he expected a shitstorm the moment it was. There was also the new murder investigation. He'd need to talk to Jo Corcoran as a priority, but that would require careful handling. *Very* careful handling, after Karl. He definitely didn't want news of another, similar killing getting out until he was ready, and more importantly, until Jo was ready. And before all of that he wanted to get down to the Hope Estate and visit the crime scene there. In short, he didn't have time for this.

Hope you didn't have to work late last night. Sorry for unloading in the bar. Blame the wine.

'Nothing serious', he tapped out, glancing at the time as he pressed send on the lie. He'd give this two more minutes. Tops.

It really helped to talk.

Finn stared at his phone impotently, unsure what to say.
'Good', he typed after a pause.

We should do it again. Think it's good for both of us.

His fingers hovered over the phone, then he gave up. Cally could wait.

Paulsen was packing when she heard the knock at the bedroom door. Her father entered, a sad smile on his face. Ordinarily that expression made her feel bad; this morning it cleaved her in two.

'Your mother and I understand why you have to leave. It's okay. Life of a policeman, isn't it.' His face clouded for a moment. 'Policewoman? Are you not supposed to say these things any more? It's all very confusing.' He sat down on a wicker chair by the bed.

'Police officer is fine, Dad.'

'I prefer that. Sounds more proper.'

She smiled and his expression clouded over.

'I don't want to forget your smile, Mathilde. Or anything about you, for that matter. How you look, how you dress. The things you say. But I'm going to . . . I can't prevent it. So while I've still got some semblance of who I am, I don't want to waste a second. I want to make sure when the time comes, there's nothing unresolved, nothing unsaid between us. That's the best gift I can give you. Do you understand?'

She looked at his familiar craggy face and nodded.

'Are you okay?' he asked. 'And don't just say yes to palm me off.'

'I'm okay.'

'You're palming me off.'

She smiled again.

'Really, I am.'

Again his expression remained serious.

'You see, that's my concern about you. I've always understood you. You're a mystery to your mother sometimes, but not to me. And I worry when I'm gone – or when I don't know the difference any more – that there won't be anyone left who can read you the way I can.'

There was truth to that. Her relationship with her father was unique, something that was literally irreplaceable. The idea of it slowly eroding before her was almost too much. He stood and opened his arms, and she went over and embraced him – felt his stubble itch against her, smelt the soap on his skin, buried her face into his blond lion's mane of hair, trying to commit every last detail of it to memory. He disengaged.

'So what do you want to do today? We could go to the beach if you like? Brancaster . . . or Blakeney? Pub lunch afterwards, maybe?'

She felt her heart break.

'I can't, Dad. I have to leave.'

'Leave? Whatever for? You've just arrived.'

'I have to go back to work.'

'Oh. Well, that's a shame.'

'Yes,' she said. 'It is.'

19

Finn walked through the Hope Estate and watched the people trudging past, heading off to work. Word of last night's stabbing would probably have got around by now. A few years ago there might have been some concern, a sense of unease about the place. Not any more though; it was just another normal weekday morning. He turned a corner and saw what he'd come here for. A small inconspicuous road adjacent to the estate, cordoned off with police tape, a busy crime scene in place. A police car was parked a few feet away. He could see traces, too, of the drama that had played out the previous night: dark patches of pooled blood still sticky on the tarmac, bandage wraps nearby where they'd been discarded by the paramedics.

Ojo was there talking to a plain-clothed officer he recognised as DS Derek Vincent from Cedar House's CID. They finished up and Vincent ducked back under the tape to speak to one of the SOCOs. Ojo turned, saw Finn approaching and walked over to meet him.

'How's it looking?' he said.

'Depressingly familiar. Uniform got the shout just after half past nine last night. They attended along with London Ambulance Service and just about managed to resuscitate the victim and get him into hospital. He's lucky to be alive.'

'What's his condition?'

'Still critical. His name's Mark Connors. Twenty-one years old. They found crack cocaine and a quantity of cannabis in his pockets.'

'A dealer?'

Ojo nodded.

'We've got an eyewitness who says Connors was hit by a car around half past nine last night. Two men jumped out, beat and stabbed him multiple times. According to Vincent, there were other people who saw what happened – but persuading them to come forward has been like getting blood out of a stone.'

Finn weighed it up. All this was around half an hour or so after Jo Corcoran opened the front door to her partner's murderer. While the two incidents were unlikely to be linked, the timing did work.

'Don't suppose the witness gave a description of the attackers?'

'Yes – neither of them were wearing mirrored masks. I'd be very surprised if it was connected to what happened in Penge. This was probably a tit-for-tat, like most of these are.'

'For this other incident here on Sunday? The one we know next to nothing about?'

'Presumably. We've checked with the local hospitals; they haven't treated anyone with stab wounds apart from this one.'

'Any ideas about who the two groups might be?'

'Vincent's fairly certain one of them are the Thornton Boys.'

As a matter of course Vincent would have run Connors' name through the gang matrix. The database was the Met's attempt to collate, identify and risk-assess gang members across the capital. The Thornton Boys were, as the name suggested, from Thornton Heath, and were well known to Cedar House.

'That's Gary Ritchie's gang, isn't it?' said Finn.

'Yeah. I doubt he was here in person last night, but I'm willing to bet he orchestrated this.'

'Why, though? I thought we'd shut down the county lines operation running out of here?'

'Come on, guv – we lifted up a stone, cleaned out some maggots and put the stone back down again. What do you think happens next?'

'I get that. I just thought it would take a bit longer for things to get organised again. Who's Ritchie after? Did Vincent get any names?'

Ojo nodded. 'You won't like it. Hayden Simms . . .'

'Isiah's son?'

As far as Finn was aware, Hayden was a bit of a waster, someone who'd done a bit of low-level dealing, but wasn't a major player. Or at least hadn't been.

'Has anyone talked to Isiah?'

'Not yet.'

Finn thought about it for a moment.

'The murder in Penge took place around half an hour before this incident. The assailant doesn't match the description of anyone here. The timing fits, but not much more. I agree with you, I think they're probably two separate incidents.'

'So what do you want to do?'

'You stay across this one. I'll go and talk to Isiah and then we'll try and pull all of this together. We've got three separate major investigations, all within the same couple of square miles. It's got the potential to get extremely messy.'

He looked up at Ashbank Tower and sighed. He felt exhausted, and the day hadn't even started yet.

'What are we having for dinner tonight?' said Mikey, grinning at his father across the breakfast table. Isiah slapped his forehead.

143

'I forgot to go shopping. I'll buy something on the way home from work. Bit of fish maybe.' Mikey gave him a look of disgust. 'It's healthy. You need to eat better – too many burgers.' Mikey rolled his eyes.

'I suppose that's what you eat when you're round at Hayden's, too . . .' said Isiah, waiting for his son's reaction.

'I don't go round to Hayden's,' Mikey replied, unconvincingly.

'Liar.' Isiah sighed. 'How is he?'

'Why do you care?'

'I care because you spend time with him.'

The cheeky grin that seemed to permanently adorn Mikey's face turned into something else. His father was on it immediately.

'What is it?'

Michael hesitated, before cracking under his father's gaze.

'The other day, he was being funny. Think he'd been in a fight or something. There was blood. Not his. But he wouldn't tell me whose. Then his girlfriend arrived and he kicked me out.' The grin returned. 'I think they were gonna . . . you know . . .' But Isiah wasn't smiling.

Things hadn't always been this way. It all began when Isiah's wife, Dawn, Hayden and Mikey's mother, was diagnosed with cancer one August day, five years ago. She died less than five weeks later. The speed of it was devastating. Isiah hadn't been remotely prepared for it. By the time he'd got his head around what was happening, he'd already lost her. It was in the aftermath of his wife's death that the schism with Hayden began. It was easy to blame their bereavement. Too easy in hindsight.

The boy drifted away from his education and into a crowd of people Isiah didn't like one little bit. He'd tried talking some sense into him, but the rows became more frequent, louder

144

and uglier. And then he'd caught him carrying a knife. That was the red line, the moment their relationship fractured for good.

Isiah's brother, Hayden's uncle, had died in a knife attack years before. That was nothing to do with gangs or drugs; he'd simply been in the wrong place at the wrong time when a group of drunken racists turned a corner. Both his boys knew the story, and knew how he felt about knives. To see Hayden carrying one was a huge shock and it still burnt all these years later.

'Who's this girlfriend then?'

'Jade? She's nice. I think he *lurves* her,' said Mikey, his grin back again.

'Serious?'

'Think so. Why, do you want them to get married?'

He did, actually. Because deep down, despite everything, Isiah still believed in his other son. He'd just got a little lost. A serious relationship, children – it might be what he needed to get him back on track.

'What does this Jade do?'

'She's a beautician. She's pretty . . .'

Mikey's grin turned leery and Isiah was about chastise him when the doorbell rang. He pointed at his boy instead.

'Don't be late for school.'

Mikey put his blazer on as Isiah went to answer the door. He was surprised to find Finn waiting on the walkway outside.

'Have you got a couple of minutes?' said Finn and Isiah ushered him in. They walked into the compact living room as Mikey was hooking the straps of his sports bag over his shoulder.

'Have a good day,' said Isiah, grabbing a satsuma from a bowl. He lobbed it at the boy, who cupped his hands and caught it. 'And try to eat healthy, yeah?'

Mikey pocketed the satsuma, gave Finn a curious look as he passed him, and headed out.

'Back again, Detective Inspector? What can I do for you now?'

Isiah sat down, as Finn frowned awkwardly.

'I don't know whether you've already heard, but there was a stabbing down here last night.'

Isiah nodded.

'How is the kid?'

'Touch-and-go.'

'I don't know who did it if that's why you're here. The boy was a dealer, but I'm guessing you already know that.'

'We've reason to believe it was a reprisal attack. For something that happened here Sunday afternoon. The officers who've been investigating overnight . . . Hayden's name has come up.'

Mikey's comments about Hayden came back to Isiah: the blood that wasn't his, from a fight. He shook his head.

'He and I . . . don't talk so much these days. I don't know what he's up to, what he's involved in. If Hayden's connected to this in some way, I'd be the last person who'd know.'

There was a mixture of sadness and pain on the older man's face, no question he was telling the truth. Finn sat down on one of the chairs at the kitchen table.

'If he is involved, he might be getting out of his depth. There's a power vacuum on this estate after what happened here earlier this year – you told me that yourself the last time we spoke.'

'And you think Hayden's trying to fill it?'

'I don't know. Like I said, his name's come up. But if he is getting tempted to move up a level . . . he could get hurt.'

Isiah winced at the words.

'What are you trying to say?'

'That maybe you can help him. If you can get past your pride.'

The usually warm and affable expression on Isiah's face gave way to something harder.

Just then Isiah's phone, which was sitting on the table between them, lit up with a text. He read it and stood up.

'That's my boss. I ought to be getting off to work.'

'Of course,' said Finn, standing. His eyes were on the phone and its wallpaper, which was now illuminated: a black-and-white photograph of two little boys laughing with their mother. Isiah saw him staring, but looked more uncomfortable than angry.

'You know where to find me if you need to,' said Finn.

Hayden woke in a cold sweat. After the weirdness with his shaking hand a couple of days ago, he was beginning to think he might have picked up a bug or something. He rubbed absently at the scar on his face, looked over and saw Jade wasn't in bed with him. He heard her moving around in the living room and staggered out of bed to join her.

'Hey baby, want coffee?' she said, greeting him with a smile as he walked in. She was standing in the small kitchen area wearing one of his T-shirts, buttering a slice of toast. He nodded and she went over to put the kettle on.

'What were you dreaming of last night? Better have been me. You were kicking around, talking in your sleep – all sorts.'

'It was nothing.'

He looked embarrassed and slumped down on to the sofa.

The truth was he'd been dreaming of Mikey. In the strange, imprecise way of dreams, he couldn't quite remember it properly, but his brother had been standing just out of reach. Something bad was happening and Hayden was frantically trying to reach him. Pushing, scrabbling, stamping his way through. He couldn't quite retrieve the memory and he shivered, feeling unsettled by it.

Not for the first time there was a strange dislocation, the desire to talk to someone he could trust. Not a friend or even a girlfriend. His mum, he thought. So much for being the bad-ass gangster. Jade joined him on the sofa, passed over a steaming mug and he took a noisy sip. She peered at him, noticing the moisture on his brow.

'Are you okay? You're sweating.'

'I'm fine. Just getting a cold or something.'

He slurped at the coffee again.

'Are you sure?'

She fed him a slice of toast and he took a hungry bite.

'You said I was talking in my sleep? What was I saying?'

'Wasn't really listening – too busy trying to get some zeds of my own.'

He look embarrassed.

'Sorry.'

'Don't be. Think it was something to do with Mikey . . .'

'Can't escape him. Little shit gives me grief even when I'm sleeping.'

'Don't be embarrassed. It's good that you care about him like that.'

Before she could say any more the doorbell rang, someone holding their finger down on it. Jade began to rise, but Hayden was already on his feet.

'No. You wait here.'

Suddenly he was alert. She shouldn't have stayed over, but she'd talked him into it the previous night. He felt jumpy, hated the feeling – was this how things were always going to be now? He went over to the kitchen counter and grabbed the knife Jade had just used to butter her toast. There was no way of seeing who was out there, so he stood by the door and shouted instead.

'Who is it?'

The bell finally stopped ringing.

'Andy. Let me in.'

Hayden opened up and saw the familiar squat figure of his friend.

'What do you want?'

'Didn't you get my texts? Mark Connors got stabbed last night. The fuckers came back.'

'How bad is he?'

'Don't know – but the place is crawling with police.'

'I've just got out of bed and Jade's here. Can't this wait?'

Andy looked at him in astonishment.

'No, mate, it can't.'

Hayden held his hands up, still clutching the butter-streaked knife.

'Alright. Give me half an hour, I'll call you.'

'Make it twenty minutes. I won't be far away.'

Hayden nodded and shut the front door. He felt hot again and leant up against it, taking some deep breaths.

'Hayden?' said Jade.

'I'm okay, don't worry,' he said. But he wasn't. His hand was trembling again and Jade was staring, even as he tried to move it out of sight.

Half a mile away, Michael Simms walked past the site where Mark Connors had been stabbed. He stopped to watch the ongoing police activity. Numbered markers were dotted around within the cordon and various people in blue gowns were on their knees studying the ground as if it held a secret. He could see bloodstains on the pavement and peered at them curiously. After a few seconds he went on his way, pulling the satsuma from his pocket and tossing it casually between his hands. He turned a corner and saw a boy roughly his own age wearing an identical blazer. He threw the satsuma and it caught him square on the side of the head. His victim looked up, startled, then grinned when he saw who'd thrown it.

'Where do you want to go then?' said the boy.

'Let's get a burger, I'm starving,' said Mikey. 'And then we'll see . . .'

20

Paulsen pulled up in the Cedar House car park and realised she couldn't remember a single detail of her three-hour drive from Norfolk. She'd spent much of the journey thinking about her father, and what lay ahead. Instinctively she felt she needed to fashion a response to his illness. She couldn't manage what was happening to him, but she could at least control her own passage through it. That much she'd decided. A small sense of empowerment, however illusory, in a battle that couldn't and wouldn't be won.

Then there was Karl. Aware the news was being released to the media, she'd listened to the radio and heard his death announced in cold, staccato terms. She felt a responsibility, but also plenty of anger at those who'd branded him a coward. Keyboard warriors who'd never accept – but also bore – some of the blame. She'd thought a lot about his final moments and what they must have been like. His daughter dead, his wife with her back turned and the world throwing nothing but contempt at him from every headline, speaker and screen. No one deserved that. But what chilled her the most was the possibility that someone else was now trapped in the same hell. Another victim dealing with a choice made at knifepoint. Whoever was responsible for this needed to pay.

There was a different atmosphere in the incident room as she walked in. It was industrious, busy with two live murder investigations, but the normal hubbub was muted. It was as if there was a cloud of collective failure hanging over them all following Karl's suicide. Finn looked up from his desk, a furrow of concern on his face as he saw her.

'I'm so sorry to have dragged you back, Mattie.'

'It's okay, honest.'

He didn't look convinced, probably because she didn't sound it herself.

'We need a catch-up.' He looked around the room, as if only now becoming aware of the mood. 'Come on, let's grab a coffee.'

Finn, Paulsen and Ojo were sitting at a table in YoYo's, the small cafe situated opposite Cedar House. It was a favourite haunt of the major investigations team, a good place to go when a change of scenery and a fresh perspective was needed. The proprietor Yolande showed little respect for rank, and possessed a seemingly exhaustive knowledge of her customers' preferences.

'Soya milk cappuccino,' she said with disdain before plonking a mug in front of Paulsen. Finn's mild amusement vanished as he received his Americano in similar fashion, but there was a pleasant smile reserved for Ojo as she was served a cup of camomile tea. The DS shrugged, and they proceeded to business.

'Let's start with the Sulemans,' said Finn. 'Claire's gone to stay with her family until the funerals. Sami's with them at the moment, but I take it you're happy to resume as joint FLO now you're back, Mattie?'

'Of course. I'll catch up with Sami when he gets back.'

'Be aware she'll now be the story as far as the media are concerned. They'll all want a piece of her and I want to protect her from that.'

'I think it's more than just the media you need to worry about,' said Ojo. 'She's lost her daughter and her husband in

152

the space of a week. Christ alone knows what state her head's in.'

Paulsen looked at her as if sensing an implied criticism.

'I'm not implying anything, Mattie. I'm sure you were carrying out the VAF properly. If the signs weren't there, then you can't prevent something like this from happening – that's always the risk. And the signs weren't there, were they?' she said evenly.

Suddenly the cafe, usually murmuring with chatter and chinking spoons, seemed like the quietest place on the planet.

'I *was* watching them closely. They were struggling, but I didn't see enough to warrant a Merlin report. And I stand by that,' said Paulsen, but her voice sounded hollow.

'Jackie's right,' said Finn. 'It's easy after something like this to say we should have prevented it, and maybe some people will say that. But Karl was a strong-willed man who refused all offers of counselling and support. And he wasn't a prisoner – it's not as if we could have put him on suicide watch.'

The irony of his words bounced straight back at him as he said them: 'a strong-willed man who refused all offers of counselling and support'. He fleetingly checked Paulsen and Ojo's faces and was grateful they hadn't appeared to have made the same connection; seen the hypocrisy of it.

'He was crucified by the media though, and we – I – left him exposed,' said Paulsen.

'We advised him not to give an interview and he did anyway,' said Finn.

'Because he wasn't thinking straight. We should have prevented it.'

Ojo looked up sharply.

'The person who's to blame is the man who murdered Karl's daughter, don't you think, Mattie?' she said.

There was a silence and Paulsen nodded. But Finn could see enough in her eyes to know what was going on in there. She was lost in a place they'd all been at some stage in their careers – in the corridor between responsibility and account-ability. Only she knew if she'd applied the right judgement regarding Karl's mental health. But these were questions they'd have to return to later.

'There'll be plenty of time for navel-gazing after we've got the killer under lock and key,' he said. 'But we've got another murder to deal with now. Which brings me to Jamie Baker. Jo Corcoran spent the night in hospital under sedation. When she's feeling up to it we need to take her statement. The door-to-doors have given us absolutely nothing. It was a quiet Monday night and aside from the family who let Jo in, no one else seems to have seen or heard a thing.'

'What about forensics?' said Ojo.

'Still at the scene, but so far there's nothing to work with. Once the post-mortem's been completed there'll hopefully be some DNA we can try and match with what was found on Leah's body. It's also a back road adjacent to the railway line – there's no CCTV, so the only witness we've got is Jo,' said Finn.

'When can we talk to her?' said Ojo.

He frowned and took a sip of his coffee.

'The hospital wanted to check her over this morning. Physically I think she's fine. It's her mother who they're more concerned with – she's elderly and was pretty shaken up. I'll give them another call, but the doctors were talking about midday.'

'This has got to be linked to what happened in the park,' said Paulsen. 'It can't be random. It's a specific address, these three were targeted. And that means Leah and Karl were too.'

'That's still circumstantial at this point,' said Finn.

154

'Of course it is. But if these were random attacks, the second one would have been somewhere a lot less specific. He *sought* these two out. We have to start looking at this in a different way.'

'What are you trying to say?' said Ojo. Paulsen slumped back into her seat, not even bothering to try and hide her frustration.

'Since you asked, that I think we're making a bit of a dog's breakfast out of this. We've got two almost identical murders and one suicide. Nobody in the frame, and no idea what connects any of it. You want to tell me what our next move is? Because right now I'm struggling to see it.'

Finn closed his eyes as he listened, and tried to centre his thoughts. He couldn't blame Paulsen for feeling emotional – she blamed herself for Karl's death. And she was right – as they sat there drinking coffee, there was far too little to work with. But she lacked his and Ojo's experience. The breakthrough would come, but through patience and investigation, not on its own. He opened his eyes and looked directly at her.

'You're right. There is some sort of connection between these murders, so let's start thinking out of the box and try and find out what it is. What do we know about Jamie Baker?'

'People in the street said they were a very friendly couple. He'd helped a few of them over the years, doing some jobs for free, that kind of thing. Nobody really had a bad word to say about him,' said Ojo.

Just like Leah Suleman, Finn thought. He was satisfied there weren't any skeletons in Leah's closet. She'd been textbook ordinary, in the nicest possible way.

'So let's look at Jo. We know Karl wasn't the most popular guy, so if this is about the person left behind, let's dig into her.'

'She's a nurse . . .' said Paulsen.

'Her job doesn't mean a thing – it's the human being I'm interested in.' He took a sip of his drink, allowing his own train of thought to run. Think out of the box, he'd told them.

'We know Karl had a taste for coke. Now we've got these two – a nurse and an electrician living in a comfortable terraced house,' he said.

'Perhaps it's about middle-class drug crime then?' said Ojo, nodding.

'Potentially – maybe a particularly violent dealer. The proximity, the profile of the victims, the level of sadism . . . it all lends itself. First things first, we need to know a lot more about Jo and Jamie.'

'So what do you want to do?'

'Mattie, you talk to Claire, then have a look in the system for some of the dealers who work the area close to where the Sulemans live. They're only a couple of miles from Jo's house. That might be the common denominator. Dig some of them out and pull them in if you need to. See if anyone knows who Karl might have been buying his gear from.'

'I'll look into Jamie,' said Ojo. 'We're going through his phone and his laptop. I'll see if there's anything drug-related. We're still in the process of looking at who his friends are, and who his clients were.'

Finn nodded and drained his coffee as Ojo started reaching for her bag. Paulsen remained still.

'What are the press going to do when they get hold of this?' she said.

Finn shook his head firmly.

'No, I'm not having it. Not again. I won't let anyone get vilified the same way as Karl was. I've already briefed everyone on the team, and made sure uniform and CID have been given the same message. I don't want anyone who isn't a police officer knowing Jo left her partner to die.'

'And what if this isn't about the people left behind?' said Paulsen.

'How do you mean?'

'You said think out of the box – what if the only reason the killer has targeted these people is the actual choice itself? Let's say it all begins when he chances on Karl and Leah in the park and realises they're father and daughter. And then he gets a taste for it – so he finds another set of victims to target. Maybe he met Jo in hospital and found out she lived with her mother, or overheard Jamie talking about Jo and her mum in the pub.'

'Go on,' said Finn.

'In other words, the killer has no link to the victims themselves – but he's finding people who fit his MO and targeting them. And if that's why he's doing this, he might only just be getting started . . .'

21

'I was hungry. Isn't that weird? Absolutely ravenous this morning. I bought a full fry-up, then felt ashamed for eating it. Jamie was murdered last night. How can I even be thinking about food?'

Jo Corcoran shook her head, genuinely mystified. The words were chatty but her tone was flat. She and Finn were sat in a small room full of medical supplies at St George's Hospital in Tooting. It was close to the ward where Jo's mother was still sleeping, the only place that offered some privacy. Even though the door was shut, the bustle outside was still intrusively loud, Jo occasionally wincing as a gurney came trundling past or a porter shouted down the corridor. Finn was balancing a pad on his lap in order to take her statement. It was still blank – he'd wanted to make sure she was comfortable about reliving the horror of the previous night first.

'You're in shock and you hadn't eaten since yesterday lunchtime. It's no wonder you were hungry. There's no reason to feel guilty about it,' he said.

She nodded like a woman who knew this already, who offered similar words of comfort all the time in her day job. Who knew words of reassurance meant precious little right now.

As Finn watched her it was hard not to feel the shadow of Karl Suleman over the conversation. News of his suicide was on the front page of the *London Evening Standard*. They'd illustrated the story with a screenshot from his television interview, and that haggard face with its beseeching eyes seemed to be staring out from everywhere. Free copies were available in the hospital reception and he hoped Jo hadn't seen them. Everything about her demeanour was all too familiar, with Karl's fate a sober reminder of where things could go.

'You must think I'm a terrible person,' she said. Outside, a nurse was barking orders at someone. Finn waited for them to quieten down before continuing.

'Of course I don't.'

'I just didn't have time to think.'

'That's what this person wanted – to put you on the spot like that.'

'Why, in God's name?'

'I wish I knew.'

She met his gaze head-on. It felt like she was building to something important. She swallowed then took a deep breath.

'Please . . . as a police officer, tell me – what was the right thing to do last night? What *should* I have done?'

Finn considered the question. *Really* thought about it, not wanting to add to this woman's guilt, but also wanting to be truthful with her.

'You only had the illusion of choice. If you'd tried to raise the alarm you might be dead now. If you'd disobeyed the instructions you were given, your mother might be dead too. It was a no-win scenario. I'd say you did the only thing you could do.'

She listened, but the answer brought no comfort. She put her head in her hands, kneaded her fingers through her hair and looked up again with reddening eyes.

'You *think* you'd do anything for the person you love. If it comes to it, you'd lay down your life for them. I always thought so anyway. And I did love Jamie, I want that clear. But when the moment came and I saw that knife . . . the size of it. The fear was too much.' The tears were coming now. There was a pause while she blew her nose. The handkerchief she pulled from her pocket was patched with Jamie Baker's dried blood. 'I just didn't want him to use it on me. And the idea of that thing being used on my mother . . .'

'I hate to ask this, but is there any reason why someone would have wanted to do this to you and your partner?' asked Finn.

She shook her head instantly.

'No, of course not. Jamie wouldn't have hurt a fly. And as for me . . .' She broke off for a moment. 'I suppose there is one thing. I worked in a care home before I joined the NHS. Some patients died, and the relatives claimed they'd been neglected. And they were right, frankly. It's a long story but I was nothing to do with it – I ended up leaving. There was a lot of anger at the time and things got ugly.'

'How ugly?' said Finn.

'There were death threats. I got one in the post. The police were told; I'm sure there must be a record of it somewhere.'

'Which care home was this?'

'Rectory Park in Caterham. I left in March 2017.'

Finn frowned, trying to place it, but shook his head.

'You think someone might still be holding a grudge?'

'I've no idea.'

Finn nodded. He was missing something; he could feel it. Jo had told Ojo at the house last night that she didn't know the Sulemans. It could be a lie, but he doubted it. This was about Jo though, he was certain of it. In that crucible moment she could have chosen her mother, allowed Jamie to live – and how would that change the dynamic? The truth was it wouldn't. She'd still be sitting in front of him now and someone she cared about would still be dead. And that was the point. This was about her just as Leah's death was about Karl. Something connected them, even if Jo didn't know it herself. The words instantly recycled in his mind: *even if Jo didn't know it herself.*

'This is going to sound a bit odd, but do you mind if I ask you a few questions about your life with Jamie?'

She shrugged.

'If it helps.'

He ran through where they shopped, where they drank, where they exercised. He asked about their routine, how often they ate out, where they ate, when they saw their friends, who their friends were – but nothing presented itself. And the nagging feeling persisted that something important was hidden in plain sight. He thought about her address and its proximity to the Sulemans.

'How do you get to work?'

'I get the train, from Penge East to Victoria.'

A fragment of another conversation suddenly came back to him. Something Phil Wadham had said.

'That stops at Brixton, doesn't it?'

'Yes – but what's that got to do with anything?'

'Were you on a train that derailed back in January, by any chance?'

She looked at him, nonplussed.

'Yes. They made us walk along the trackside afterwards. It was in the papers the next day.'

He noticed he had stopped writing as he listened, and quickly started jotting on his pad again.

'I think Karl Suleman might also have been on that train.'

Jo looked bemused.

'I don't understand.'

Nor did Finn frankly, but he could feel his adrenaline coursing now. A sense this might be a piece of the puzzle somehow.

161

He wasn't too bothered that he didn't understand its significance yet. Like an archaeologist unearthing a scrap of pottery, the context of the find would come later. The first priority was simply to get it out of the ground.

'Can you tell me what actually happened that morning?'

'It was just an ordinary journey to work. We were between Herne Hill and Brixton. The train suddenly began to brake sharply and everybody went flying. It felt like the carriage was going to overturn.'

'But it didn't?'

'No, the emergency services and the rail officials – when they finally got there – escorted us all away. The worst that happened was I got to work late. What on earth has that got to do with what happened to Jamie?'

Good question, thought Finn, and he didn't have an answer – or even a theory – yet.

'Maybe nothing at all, but any link needs properly investigating, however small it might seem.'

She nodded, but the dullness was back in her eyes, and he wasn't sure how much his words were even registering.

'There's something I need to warn you about, Jo,' he said, moving the conversation on. 'There's a possibility the killer might try and contact you. It happened with Karl, and he may do the same with you.'

She looked at him in alarm.

'Why? What on earth for?'

'He sent Karl some upsetting pictures from the crime scene.'

Jo looked appalled. 'But I'm going to need my phone. It's hardly the moment to be telling people I'm on a different number.' She looked torn. 'I don't see how this person could even get my number anyway.'

'It's entirely up to you. But we obviously want to try and shield you from any further distress.'

'I'll risk it if that's okay.'

'Sure – but let us know straight away if you receive anything out of the ordinary.'

She nodded.

'Counselling is available for you, if you want it,' he continued. 'And there'll also be family liaison officers working with you. The uniform PC who's outside your mother's room will stay there until she's discharged too.'

Jo nodded, but looked as though the words were just bouncing off her now. The idea that the killer might try and make contact was clearly disturbing her. Finn was also aware he still needed to take her statement.

'I keep playing that conversation in the hallway out in my head. I should have called out to Jamie. I thought about it but didn't. I'll never forgive myself for that – the two of us might have been able to overcome him, scare him off or something.'

'Or you both could have died. You can't torment yourself like that.'

'Can't I? The only thing that's certain is I left him to die. I keep thinking of him dying alone on that floor, wondering why I wasn't there. He must have been so scared.'

This time Finn had no answer for her.

'Two murders and a suicide and you're telling me you've got nothing,' snapped John Skegman as Finn brought him up to speed in his office. So much seemed to have happened in the four days since Karl Suleman had met his daughter for their abortive curry. And yet Finn's summary of the double investigation had been indecently brief.

'I wouldn't say *nothing*. The care home Jo mentioned is a decent lead.'

'How does that link with the Sulemans?'

Finn bit his tongue. Skegman knew the answer – that there was a team of detectives down the corridor already digging into it. The DCI was getting twitchy because of the ever-increasing press interest. A lot of the media requests were being directed towards him, and he didn't fancy standing in front of the cameras without having something concrete.

Skegman's criticism was harsh, thought Finn. His team were working flat out, and after Paulsen's outburst in YoYo's earlier, another dissenting voice – even if it belonged to the DCI – was more than he needed this late in the evening.

'What do you want me to do, bullshit you that we're close to an arrest?' he said. When it was just the two of them, there seemed to be an unwritten rule that the gloves could come off a little.

Skegman gave an exaggerated eye-roll. Finn continued, trying to keep his point on the right side of reasonable.

'We've got a few more pieces to work with tonight. In addition to what Jo told us about the care home, we know Karl upset some people too – he'd just laid off some employees. He kept secrets from his wife, including a coke habit, so it's possible there were other skeletons in his cupboard.'

'So what are you saying – this is vigilantism of some kind?'

'Why not? Someone punishing people they think deserve it.'

Skegman mulled it. For all the occasional moments of friction between the pair, they usually weren't far apart in their analysis of an investigation.

Finn continued. 'I think Paulsen must be at least partly right. That choice he gives them is bang at the heart of this. It matters to him, putting them into that vice. Identify *why*, and you'll get closer to identifying *who*.'

Skegman was still concentrating, tapping his foot ever more quickly under his desk.

'And where else are you looking on that front?'

'There's another angle that's come up today – a derailed train both Karl and Jo were on.'

Finn had now skimmed through the Rail Accident Investigation Branch's report on the derailment and gave Skegman a precis of what he'd read. The accident had been a low-speed collision between a passenger train and an engineering wagon, which had caused the front carriage of the train to come off the tracks. In the grand scheme of things, it was hardly a major incident.

'Surely that's coincidental?' said Skegman. 'Karl lived in Dulwich, Jo's in Penge and they both work in central London. There are hundreds, if not thousands, of people that could apply to. How in God's name does that connect to these deaths?'

'I honestly don't know, but it's the single thing we've got that draws a line between the two families.'

'I vaguely remember it – was anyone hurt?'

'Just some minor injuries which were treated by the LAS at the scene. Nothing serious, although I think some woman had a stroke afterwards.'

'And that was it?'

'The RAIB said human error was the cause, to cut a long story short.'

'Does the report specifically mention either Karl or Jo?'

'No.'

Skegman shook his head.

'Talk to the RAIB. These reports can be dry. They might be able to colour in some of the details for you. It could be coincidental, or there might be more than is in the official version.'

Finn nodded. There was a pause, as Skegman seemed to be weighing something up.

'We haven't talked about Paulsen.'

'What about her?'

Skegman looked him directly in the eye.

'Did she screw up with Karl Suleman?'

Finn looked out of the window at the deserted car park below. He saw his own car sitting alone in the darkness and wished he was in it.

'In my judgement she was applying the vulnerability assessment framework diligently. These are fine margins – she thought he was holding up.'

'He hung himself.'

'Yes, after giving a car crash of an interview on national television. Which he went ahead with against our advice. She couldn't have prevented that.'

'No, but maybe *you* could have.'

The words hung for a moment.

'With respect, sir—'

'You wanted to give Paulsen the FLO role, and you said you'd take responsibility, remember?'

'And I do. But I didn't realise just how tied up Sami would be. In the circumstances she did damn well and her log book will reflect that. I don't think *anyone* could have prevented Karl's death. She was updating me regularly throughout, and I agreed with her judgement of his mental state. There was no indication he was going to do what he did.'

'And yet . . .'

Skegman held out his hands as if the point was childishly obvious.

'He was a stubborn man who wasn't interested in receiving support.'

'Who does that remind me of?'

'Piss off, John,' said Finn, giving up the ghost of keeping it formal. 'If you think either me or one of my team has fucked up, then make it formal. Otherwise . . .'

166

Skegman shook his head in semi-surrender.

'Alright. I'll accept what you're saying for the moment. But there's a lot going on right now that I don't like. The choices you're making, some of the lines of enquiry you're prioritising, the general lack of progress across the board.'

Finn said nothing, but didn't bother keeping the contempt off his face.

'You've got a problem, Alex, and you're in denial about it. But at some point it *is* going to affect the job.' He pointed a finger at Finn. 'And I know you – I know what you're thinking.'

'What's that, then?'

'That you won't allow that to happen. But nobody's a machine. If the thin ice you're skating on finally cracks . . .'

Skegman didn't finish the sentence, because he didn't need to. There was a silence, an understanding of sorts between them. Finn nodded very slowly, then turned and walked out.

22

The following day came a breakthrough. Jackie Ojo was in a newsagent close to Cedar House when the call came; she'd been assessing two equally soggy-looking sandwiches in the vain hope of grabbing a quick lunch break. She listened to what DS Vincent had to say, paid for what looked like a cheese and tomato sponge, and hurried to her car.

When she arrived at the Hope Estate, a uniform PC manning the cordon at the crime scene pointed to a cul-de-sac on the other side of the road where two blue-gowned forensic officers were huddled over a drain grill with a detective constable from CID. One of the SOCOs was kneeling, working carefully at the edge of the drain. But it was the other one, stood next to him, who caught her eye. He was holding a long transparent evidence container, the type specifically used for the recovery of knives. As Ojo got closer she could clearly see what was inside: a zombie knife with dark, rust-coloured stains on its teeth.

At Cedar House, Finn was at his desk, struggling to get much done. He was barking orders, giving the impression of a man in charge, but he wasn't deceiving himself. He could feel a growing skittishness at his own lack of productivity. Skegman's warning from the previous night had lodged. The pair often went back and forth on things, sniping at each other with no little pettiness. But it was rare there was a genuine needle between them, and this time he'd seen anger in the DCI's face and heard it in his voice. And if Finn was honest, it was hard to dispute Skegman's analysis of his behaviour. Where once he'd been able to compartmentalise – keep his pain from impinging on his work life – now the edges were blurring. The small voices of discontent around him were starting to become a cacophony. He knew if he didn't do something to arrest this, it was going to become a problem.

His thoughts were interrupted by his phone. It was Ojo, who brought him up to speed with what she'd found.

'So is that the knife that was used on Mark Connors?' he said.

'It's very close to where he was stabbed. But it's a zombie knife, guv . . .'

If his attention had been wayward a few minutes earlier, now there was genuine focus. The Hope Estate was barely a five-minute journey from the house Jo Corcoran shared with Jamie Baker. Close enough – it was just possible they might have found their murder weapon. The same knife, too, that was used to kill Leah Suleman.

'Where is it now?'

'On its way to the lab. It shouldn't take long to test it and then we'll know.'

'What about fingerprints?' said Finn.

'SOCO say it was submerged underwater, but it was stuck on a ledge with a fair amount of mud on top – so some bits of it are still bloodstained. It's possible we can pull some DNA off it.'

'And were Connors' injuries consistent with a zombie knife?'

'No, not according to what the doctors told me. Sounds like his wounds came from a smaller blade.'

Finn contained his excitement. He knew better than to jump to conclusions before the science supported them.

'At the risk of being overcautious, this could be coincidental. God knows how long that knife might have been down there.'

'Maybe. But we've got CCTV of the killer heading in this direction, and now a zombie knife bang in the centre of the estate. It'd be a hell of a coincidence. What do you make of the timeline?'

He thought it through logically. Jamie Baker was murdered around half an hour or so before Mark Connors was stabbed. Just enough of a window for the killer to have gone to the estate and disposed of the weapon. Just a little later and he'd have found the place crawling with police.

'It works potentially. Where are CID now with the Connors stabbing?'

'They've got a partial number plate from a guy who saw the attackers leave. We also know what colour the vehicle was and what make it is. They're checking it out – there should be enough to get a name. I'll call in when I've heard something.'

He finished the call and sat staring absently at a coffee ring on his desk while he tried to order his thoughts. If this was the murder weapon, it was possible the killer could have dropped it on his way somewhere else. But there was also a decent chance it tied the killer to the Hope Estate – and that was a big step forward.

Yet his earlier edginess lingered on. Where usually there was a clarity to his thinking, right now there was just fog. And in that haze, the potential for a mistake. He felt slightly sick, light-headed. Normally a breakthrough like this had the opposite effect: cleared out all the distractions, and centred his mind. It was precisely what Skegman had warned of. He looked around the room and saw his team working quietly and efficiently, oblivious to his difficulties. He needed to get his head straight and as quickly as possible. He stood and grabbed his coat.

'Guv, I've just spoken to this care home where Jo Corcoran worked,' said Dattani, intercepting him.

'You got something, Sami?'

'I'm not sure.'

'Then it'll have to wait,' said Finn and headed for the exit, to Dattani's undisguised frustration. He pushed through the double doors and skipped down the stairs to the main entrance with the urgency of a man who knew where he was going. Except he didn't – all he knew was that he needed to get out.

'What's going on, Alex?' said Karin.

'Not now,' he said under his breath.

'Where are you going?' This time he ignored her. *'You know this isn't normal, don't you?'*

He carried on striding, maintaining an impressive pace. It was helping – he could feel the blood pumping through his system now. He was fairly sure he wasn't having a panic attack. There'd been one or two of those over the past year; terrifying, suffocating experiences which left him short of breath, paralysed and soaked in sweat. This was something else – from the same family, but not quite the same thing. It would pass, he told himself. He'd walk it off, grab a coffee, return to his desk and get on top of things again. No one would be any the wiser. He walked through the trading estate where Cedar House was situated and out into the adjacent street of nearby shops. He took some deep breaths, trying and failing to suppress the sense of rising hysteria.

As he walked, he passed a large red-brick building of office space. There was a sign taped to the door which caught his eye. Written in black marker ink were the words: 'Do you need help? All welcome!' Below was a blue triangle with the letters

'AA' in the centre. Each side of the triangle was lined with a single word: 'unity', 'service' and 'recovery'. He stopped and looked at it as if hypnotised. His casual description of Karl in YoYo's came back to him: 'a strong-willed man who refused all offers of counselling and support'. He'd felt like a hypocrite when he'd said it; doubly so now. *'Read those words again,'* whispered Karin. And he did.

He stood on the threshold, not entirely sure what he was doing, and pushed the door open.

He walked down a small corridor until he reached a door with the same sign as he'd seen outside taped to it. He pushed it open and found a middle-aged man with light brown hair racking some plastic chairs. The man turned and smiled at him.

'I'm so sorry, I'm afraid you're too late. We wrapped up about ten minutes ago. But if it's something urgent ...' He held out his hands, palms up. 'Is it something urgent?' He spoke with a gentle Glaswegian burr.

'I don't know,' said Finn truthfully.

'Sounds like it might be,' said the man carefully.

'I'm sorry. I think I'm here under false pretences. I shouldn't have come in.'

'How so?'

There was still a friendly smile on the man's face but there was now a look of professional appraisal in his eyes too.

'I don't really know what brought me in here, to be honest. It was curiosity, I suppose.'

'I think maybe I can guess. When did you last have a drink?'

'It's not that.'

'Do you want a drink?'

Finn exhaled; the slight insanity of what he was doing was starting to hit him. There was also the matter of his team at

Cedar House who needed him right now. A flash of guilt struck him at the way he'd brushed Dattani aside. He really should just go.

'My problem isn't alcohol. My wife died about a year ago.'

The words just came out – a sense he wasn't quite in control of what he was saying or doing. He felt unravelled.

'It's alright. Go on . . .' said the man.

'I don't really . . . I mean . . . I guess I don't really have anyone I'm able to talk to about it.'

As he said it, he realised it was perhaps the single most honest thing he'd said to anyone about his bereavement since Karin's death.

'Out of choice?'

Finn thought about it.

'No. I'm just not brilliant at letting people in.'

'If you don't mind me saying, that does sound like a choice.'

'I suppose. It doesn't really feel like it though.'

'There are a lot of bereavement counsellors out there. I could recommend one. You'd be surprised how much it goes hand in glove with what happens here.'

Finn wasn't surprised at all.

'Not my thing, I'm afraid. Which is stupid, I know. I spend half my life telling people where they can get counselling.'

'Are you a doctor?'

'No.'

'A policeman?'

'Yes.'

The man nodded, as if something had slotted into place.

'First and foremost, don't apologise for coming here. Looks like you needed some help, and there's no crime in that. But I can't solve your problem with a quick pep chat and I think you know that.'

'You're right, I'm sorry.'

'Don't say sorry. Go and get yourself some proper counselling. Find the time, don't listen to your own excuses – just do it. It'll be the best move you could possibly make. That kind of pain runs deep. You need to talk it out, properly. Not like this.'

Finn knew it was more than just good advice – it was the right advice. But was he *really* going to take it? If he was honest, deep down he thought he probably wouldn't. He'd go home and decide tonight he could solve his own problems – as he always did. And it would all get just that bit worse. The man seemed to be reading his thoughts.

'I know what happens when people bottle things up. It won't get better and eventually it'll reach a crisis point. I don't know you, so I don't know how it'll manifest in your case. But it will, trust me . . . it always does.'

Finn tried to find an answer but couldn't.

'We're here tomorrow if you want to chat again. Maybe best before or after the meeting though – I don't want to confuse the others. But you'd really be better off finding a specialist. That's the best advice I can give you.'

Finn nodded.

'Thank you. I don't even know your name.'

'It's Murray, Murray Saunders.'

He smiled and the two men shook hands. And much later, lying face down in the dirt with his blood pooling around him, it was a conversation that would come back to Finn.

23

'Is this urgent, Jonas?' said Paulsen. She was standing in a backstreet of Peckham, increasingly convinced she'd been stood up by the drug dealer she was there to meet. She was hoping to find out more about Karl's coke habit. But as ever – as it had always been – when Jonas wanted her attention he expected the world to stop for him.

'When is a good time, Mat? There's never a good time.'

'How about tonight? When I'm off shift – just a wild thought.'

'I can't tonight, I'm out.'

Paulsen checked her watch. This was time she didn't have to waste.

'Alright, two minutes. What's the matter?'

'What do you think it is? I'm angry – really angry. Why didn't they tell us Dad had already been diagnosed?'

'Because they wanted some privacy? A chance to get their heads around it?'

'I get that, but it's like being a child again – them making big decisions without telling us. I've been worried sick and they knew all along.'

'Don't you think you're missing the point? The fact it's confirmed now is the important detail. Never mind when they told us, we've got bigger shit to deal with now.'

There was a silence. He already knew that. And she knew he knew. He'd just wanted to talk, to rationalise it, and she understood that impulse too – she was still trying to do the same herself.

'What are we going to do then?'

She was about to try and answer when she saw a nervous-looking man in a denim jacket walking towards her. He was looking over his shoulder, checking they were alone.

'I'm going to have to call you back.'

'Mat!'

'I'm sorry, Jonas – I'll call you later.'

'This guy told you what?' said Finn at his desk, scrolling through his emails. Paulsen was standing next to him, glaring because she only seemed to have about thirty-three per cent of his attention.

'He reckoned he knew a dealer who was selling to Karl. A guy called Danny Howells. He operates around Tulse Hill,' said Paulsen, trying again.

Finn nodded, still focused on finding the email that was apparently eluding him.

'That's close enough to both crime scenes – and the Hope Estate for that matter. How solid do you think it is?'

'Fifty-fifty – might be bollocks, might be something.'

Finn didn't reply.

'Are you listening to me, guv?'

He swivelled his chair round and Paulsen saw for the first time just how tired he was looking. He was a man who usually took pride in his appearance but his normally moisturised skin seemed dry, his eyes were an unhealthy shade of pink and his complexion was vampire white. He looked like he should be just about anywhere but in this room.

'Of course,' he said. 'Who was this guy you got it from, again?'

She fought the Herculean desire to slap him.

'One of Dave McElligott's snouts. He said this Howells character was mouthing off about the "bloke in the news" – claimed he knew him.'

'And how much do we know about Howells?'

'Not much, he's not in the system. This dealer I spoke to says he doesn't like police and can get a bit lively. He's also been known to carry a knife apparently.'

Finally, she seemed to have his undivided attention.

'Lively enough to stab two people to death?'

Paulsen shrugged.

'I can't even confirm he knows Karl yet – it's just hearsay.'

'When were you going to pick him up?'

'I was just about to leave.'

'Who with?'

'Dave's coming with me.'

'Stand him down. I'll go instead. And let's take a couple of TSGs too. If there's any chance this actually *is* our guy, I don't want to take any unnecessary risks.'

Finn briefed the territorial support group commander before they set off. The link to Karl was spurious at best – just a dealer gobbing off in a pub by the sounds of it. There was also nothing yet to suggest either Jo Corcoran or Jamie Baker were drug users. But he preferred to be safe than sorry, and half an hour later the two TSG officers joined Finn and Paulsen close to the address she'd found for Howells. They were waiting by a small strip of shops in West Norwood. Howells' front door was tucked between a bookies and a Thai massage parlour. A pile of litter was gathered by the step, and unintelligible graffiti tags were sprayed across the door and on to the adjacent brickwork.

'You guys hold back unless we need you,' said Finn to the TSGs. 'If he's got a problem with police I'd rather not wind him up unnecessarily.'

He and Paulsen walked up to the door and Finn rang the bell. After a moment, a thin wiry man with close-cropped hair answered. He was wearing a parka and seemed almost surprised to see Finn, as if he was just on his way out anyway.

'Danny Howells? I'm DI Finn, this is DC Paulsen. We—'

Before he could continue, the door slammed in his face. Finn exchanged a glance with Paulsen and then called out Howells' name again. They waited, but there was no reply. Finn signalled to the TSGs for assistance and one of them ran back to their van to retrieve an Enforcer – the large battering ram used for situations like this.

As was standard practice, Paulsen ran immediately round the side of the massage parlour and down the adjacent side street to head off any potential escape via the back of the building. At the end of the road she could see the perimeter of West Norwood cemetery, the huge forty-acre site that dominated this corner of south London. She looked across and saw the fur trim of a parka as Howells emerged into the street from a back door. She ran towards him and he sprinted towards the fence ahead of him. He jumped, grabbed the top and hauled himself over into the cemetery.

Finn was now running to join her. She was guessing the two TSG officers were now inside Howells' flat. She pointed at the cemetery fence.

'He's in there. I'll go after him, you head him off in the car.'

Finn turned and ran back up to the main road. She looked at the fence, took a running jump and levered herself over and in.

It was like jumping into another world. The place was vast and overgrown, century-old gravestones standing next to shiny new ones. She'd almost landed in a fresh bunch of pink peonies, and despite the urgency instinctively stepped to one side. She weaved down through the graves on to a concrete pathway where she could now see Howells running into the middle distance. He was glancing over his shoulder but didn't seem to have seen her, and was slowing down to a jog. Paulsen increased her own pace as stealthily as she could. As she got closer Howells turned his head.

'Police, stop!' she shouted, and he began to sprint again. There was a gate ahead and he ran up a shallow incline of graves towards it. As she caught up, she could see it was chained. He'd cornered himself, and he span around to face her.

'Stand still, you're under arrest,' she shouted.

He pulled something from his pocket, but it wasn't a knife. Instead it was a metal canister of some sort.

'*Acid*. Back off!' he snarled, removing the lid and holding it forwards.

Paulsen stopped and they stood eyeing each other like modern-day gunslingers, the advantage suddenly all his.

'Put that down and let's talk,' she said calmly. He took a step closer and jerked his hand. She saw the liquid in flight, felt it splash on her face and screamed.

24

She could feel it in her eyes, dripping down her face to her throat. There was a split second of grace as she waited for the searing pain to hit. But it didn't come. Realisation dawned – it was water, just water. She whimpered, unable to contain her relief. And then there *was* pain, sudden and sharp as the 'acid' bottle smashed into the side of her skull. It knocked her sideways, and then Howells brought his arm around again, crashing it into the other side of her head. She could taste blood now, mingling with the water. Everything was a scarlet blur. Wiping the liquid from her eyes, she staggered back to her feet. When the murk finally cleared, he was gone.

Finn had radioed the TSG officers while running back to his car. He followed the road around to the cemetery entrance, and sped through a large stone Gothic archway. Slowing down to get his bearings, a fresh bunch of flowers close by caught his eye.

Jason Schofield
2011-2012

A split second of his attention, but almost a decade of pain for someone – it was as if bereavement was stalking him. He looked up and saw a figure in a parka running towards him. There was no sign of Paulsen. He put his foot down again and drove straight at Howells, before swinging the car round to block his path. Behind him he could hear the roar of the TSG officers' van. He let them skid to a halt and watched the briefest of mismatches as the two men in body armour jumped out and intercepted their man. Finn was more concerned about Paulsen. By all rights she should have been just seconds behind. On foot now, he followed the path past a large domed mausoleum until he saw her. She was walking along quite calmly, blood streaming from an ugly gash on the side of her head.

'Jesus! Are you okay?' he said.

She didn't reply, just spat out a gobbet of blood and nodded. She looked past him, visibly grateful to see Howells now being bundled into the back of the TSG van. She took several deep breaths and slowly sat down on a nearby bench.

An hour later Finn was back at Cedar House, while Paulsen was being stitched up in hospital. The good news was she hadn't been concussed, but he told her to take the afternoon off anyway.

'At least we know why Howells ran,' Finn told Ojo as they reconvened in the incident room. 'We found a fair quantity of coke and cannabis on him – he must have been on his way out to work when we turned up.'

'So what do you think – is this our guy?'

Finn blew through his teeth.

'We've got a sample of his DNA now, so we'll know soon enough if it matches what was found on Leah's body. But he's taller and older than the description both Karl and Jo gave us, and we've found nothing useful in his flat. All of which makes me sceptical.'

'So what do you want to do?'

'Interview him, see if he really did know Karl. Then I want to hold a briefing . . .' he looked at his watch, 'at 5 p.m.' He was about to say more when in walked Paulsen, sporting an ugly purple bruise on one side of her face and a newly sutured scar around her temple on the other side.

'I thought I told you to go home,' he said.

'Why would I want to do that, when I'm having such fun?'

She was, Finn thought, the only person he knew who could effectively combine a glare with a smile.

'I haven't killed anyone.'

Danny Howells was loud and belligerent. His solicitor seemed to be in no rush to settle him down either. Finn was guessing she'd handled men like this before and was timing her intervention carefully. Karin had been a solicitor and he'd learnt a few tricks of the trade from her.

'Where were you last Friday night at around seven o'clock?' asked Paulsen.

'In a pub in Camberwell. And I've got a lot of mates who can back that up.'

'Which pub?'

'The Ship and Anchor.'

'What time did you arrive?'

'About half past six?'

'And what about Monday evening? At around nine o'clock?'

Paulsen was virtually spitting the questions out now, doing little to hide her contempt.

'With my ex-girlfriend, visiting my kid. You're welcome to check with her.'

'We will. And we'll also check with the Ship and Anchor,' said Paulsen.

'We've been told you know Karl Suleman. Have been bragging about it . . .' said Finn.

'Didn't even know his name until I saw it in the paper. But yeah, I knew him.'

'How?'

'He used to buy coke off me.'

'How do we know you're not lying?' said Paulsen.

'Why would I do that?'

'To make yourself look important. The whole country knows who Karl is right now,' she countered. He shook his head dismissively, not bothered by her hostility. 'So when did he start buying from you then?'

Howells thought about it for a moment.

'Back when it was snowing – must have been around the end of January.'

'How did he find you in the first place?' said Finn.

'I sell to a mate of his. I'm guessing he must have told him about me.'

'And who supplies you?' said Finn suddenly. Howells pulled a face.

'I'm not telling you that.'

'I suppose it depends how long . . .' replied Finn. Howells looked confused. So did his solicitor. '. . . you want to go without seeing your kid?' he continued. 'You assaulted a police officer, and then there's the stash of drugs we found in your coat. So, do you want to do yourself a favour and cooperate?'

Howells looked across at the solicitor. She didn't need to say anything, her stony expression answering his silent question. He rolled his eyes and sat up straight.

'A couple of guys on the Hope Estate.'

'Do these guys have names?'

Howells shifted around uncomfortably on his seat.

'Andy Forbes and Hayden Simms.'

Finn contained his reaction.

'Did Karl give you any idea why he suddenly wanted this stuff?' asked Finn, returning to the previous line of questioning.

Howells frowned, remembering.

'Yeah . . . it was weird. He said something had happened which had freaked him out. Told me he needed to take the edge off it. I told him to take a puff of weed, but he insisted on coke.' Howells flashed a smile, revealing a set of yellowing teeth. 'And you know what they say – the customer is always right. Doubt it took the edge off though.'

Finn leant in.

'Did he tell you what this something was?'

Howells shook his head.

'I didn't ask, I'm not a fucking counsellor. It had shook him up though, that much was obvious.'

'I think we can rule Danny Howells out as a suspect – if he was ever in,' said Finn. 'We'll run his DNA against the sample from Leah Suleman's body, but I think his alibis will stand up.'

The whole team had gathered in the briefing room, and Finn was addressing them all. Images of Leah and Karl Suleman, Jamie Baker and Jo Corcoran were pinned to the boards behind him. There was a separate one with an image of Mark Connors, and a photograph of the knife they'd recovered from the drain. There was also a map of south-east London with flags pinned at the key sites of the investigation.

'Howells didn't know Jamie or Jo, and if his alibis do check out, I think it's unlikely this is connected to drugs.'

'So we're back to square one,' said Paulsen.

'Not at all. Sami – do you want to tell us what you've found?'

Dattani nodded quickly.

'So Jo Corcoran was employed by Rectory Park Care Home initially in October 2016. Hold on.' He broke off and started leafing through the paperwork balancing on his lap. 'Here we go. Sorry, she wasn't employed by the care home, she was contracted by the private healthcare provider who ran it: Shawcross. Five people died between 2013 and 2017. The coroner said the place was riddled with institutionalised abuse.'

'And was Jo implicated in that?' said Ojo.

Dattani shook his head.

'No, the official report exonerated her of any involvement with the fatalities. However, there were several statements given at the time accusing her of turning a blind eye.'

'If someone really believes that, it's a strong enough motive for murder. You could see why someone might want to make her suffer,' said Paulsen.

'How much do we know about the death threats?' asked Finn. Dattani scanned his paperwork again.

'A complaint was made to Surrey Police in March 2017. She received one through the post, handwritten. But Jo was never blamed directly for anyone's death – it was guilt by association.'

There was a lot folded into that, thought Finn as he watched the room filter the information. And enough unknowns in it to make him uncomfortable as well. Paulsen's point was well made; there'd been plenty of time since 2017 for a grudge to fester with someone.

'Who sent her the death threat – do we know?' said Finn. Dattani shook his head. 'Then talk to Surrey again – find out who they were looking at.'

'I don't understand,' came a voice from the back. It was DC Dave McElligott. He wasn't the smartest cookie in the jar, but occasionally surprised everyone with a flash of genuine inspiration. 'Why would the same person who killed Leah Suleman go after this woman because of what happened at a care home a few years back?'

'Very good question, Dave. And since you've raised it, perhaps you'd like to look into whether Karl or Leah had any links to that care home too? Some family or friends we don't know about, maybe? Sami – can you help Dave with that?'

Finn didn't wait for a response, pointing immediately instead at another board where a collection of photocopied newspaper articles was pinned up.

'I'm also still keen on this.'

The headlines were all variations on the same theme: 'Passengers face delays after Brixton derailment', 'Second day of travel chaos following train derailment'.

'We know both Karl and Jo were on this train. We have the Rail Accident Investigation Branch report, but all that tells me is the technical details of what took place. I want to know what actually *happened* on that train. Mattie, can you see if we can find some more of the passengers who were on board?'

'What am I looking for in particular?'

'Anything out of the ordinary that's not in the RAIB report or the press coverage. Phil Wadham told us Karl had been spooked by the accident, and what Howells has told us all but confirms that. I'll get in touch with the RAIB and see if there's any more to it from their side.'

The room was quiet now, and Finn knew that was never a good sign. They were all experienced officers, who could tell the difference between an investigation gathering momentum and one that was stalling. There were too many strands, and all of them loose; Karl's drug use and general ability to piss people off, the care home, the train. And the biggest question remained unanswered – why these two? Why Leah Suleman and Jamie Baker – or, indeed, why Karl and Jo? He couldn't see the pattern, and underneath it all Finn could still feel a beating drum of self-doubt.

'How can you help anyone, when you won't help yourself?' whispered Karin.

He turned momentarily, pretending to cough as he gathered himself. 'Jacks, have forensics come back on the knife we found?' he said, affecting an authority he wasn't feeling.

'No, but it shouldn't be long now,' Ojo replied.

'Did any of the people you've spoken to about the Connors stabbing see anything?'

'Nothing's come up – but it may be worth double-checking.'

Finn nodded.

'If it is the murder weapon, judging by the state of the crime scene, the killer would have been covered in blood. If he was wandering around the estate on Monday night, he'd have been pretty conspicuous. Same as the night Leah died.'

Finn's eye settled on the map again.

'And that's the point, isn't it? The Hope Estate is bang in the middle of this – Howells just gave us a couple of names as well. It's the second time Hayden Simms has cropped up in the course of this. So, let's bring him in – I think it's time we had a chat.'

25

'When was the last time you did something silly?'

Jade laughed at Hayden's frown. They were in a Nando's in Streatham – her idea – an evening off, away from the estate. His shaking hand was evidence, she said, that he needed to give himself a break. His appetite was another clue. They were sharing a plate of wings, but he'd barely touched them.

'What do you mean?'

'When you just did something for fun. Like go to the cinema or have a dance? You don't seem to have mates you can do that with.'

He was about to reply when she held up a finger.

'And don't talk to me about Andy . . .'

He sighed.

'Someone tried to stab me on Sunday. Someone I know *did* get stabbed on Monday night. Andy thinks I should be out there right now doing something about it. Instead I'm here with you, eating wings. How chilled do you need me to be?'

The words came out harder than he meant. He picked at one of the fries in front of him and bit the end off.

'You don't ever really talk about yourself – it's something I've noticed. You've never told me what happened to your mum, for instance,' said Jade.

He washed down the chip with a sip of beer, watched a couple at the neighbouring table laughing at something on their phones. He was an introvert by nature, didn't really like opening up, either about himself or his family history. Her expression suggested she wasn't going to be put off easily though. He took himself back into the memory and felt a wave of melancholy.

'She died when I was fifteen. Before then I was nothing, really. I was invisible. Didn't upset anyone, didn't do anything to stand out. But everything at home was okay. Dad worked and Mum brought us up.'

'So what happened?'

'Cancer. Took her in a few weeks. Everything changed after that.'

'And that's why you joined a gang? Because your mum died?'

Hayden scowled.

'I was never in a gang. Hung around with a few people who were ... but I wasn't stupid. Andy was the same, we just looked out for each other. It was more about getting away from home.'

'Why? Was that when you fell out with your dad?'

The questions were sharp, felt punchy.

'I don't want to talk about that.'

He was trying not to snap at her. The truth was, whatever was going on with his hand was unnerving him. He didn't understand it, and what he didn't understand scared him. He didn't know if he was simply tired, or whether there was actually something properly wrong. It was nagging at him, making him irritable. Jade was just about the only person he could turn to, and he'd much rather spend time with her just chilling. The incessant questions were wearing.

'I want to know everything about you,' she said, coming at him again. 'All you've ever said is you and him don't talk, and you've never told me why. What did he do that was so bad?'

There was clearly no avoiding it. And so he didn't. He told her how it all went wrong in the days and weeks that followed his mother's death. How his father had grown distant, even as the two boys cried in bed at night. How few words of comfort there'd actually been.

'He probably didn't know how to help you. You've got to remember he was dealing with his own grief,' said Jade.

Hayden snorted with derision.

'He had a responsibility.'

'So what happened?'

He forced himself to remember. The niggly little arguments that began when they should have been mourning. Small things that became big things. And finally the explosion it'd all been leading up to. Words were screamed which couldn't be simply forgotten. Corrosive like acid, they burnt deep. The only common ground in the aftermath was the shared desire to no longer be related. The scar it left inside was as significant to Hayden as the one on his face.

'How did it start?' said Jade carefully.

'He caught me carrying a knife.'

Jade nodded, said nothing.

'I was young, didn't understand the impact of it. Despite everything . . .'

'Did you actually come to blows?'

'Almost. He threw me out. Or I walked out – I can't even remember which it was. We've hardly spoken since.'

Jade shook her head.

'That's nuts. Just one row. Surely it's fixable?'

'No chance.'

'You were both grieving. It affects how you think.'

Now he was watching her carefully.

'Sounds like you know how that feels?' he said.

Jade's eyes narrowed at the memory. Her turn to look uncomfortable.

'Yeah – I lost my mum too.'

'What happened?'

Pain flickered across her face.

'You don't have to . . .' he said.

'It was sudden. She was more like my best friend. We used to talk for hours – any old rubbish really. About boyfriends, food, reality TV. I miss her.'

'What about your dad?' There was a silence, and Hayden felt he'd crossed some sort of line. 'I'm sorry. I didn't mean to dig anything up.'

'You didn't. He's dead too. And before you say you're sorry again – I'm not.'

He nodded gently, understanding enough without needing to probe further.

'I can relate to that.'

'No. It's different. My dad wasn't a good man – yours is. And he's still alive. You've still got time to fix things.'

He thought about what she was saying, imagined himself trying, then slowly shook his head.

Finn was working late again. He'd spent the remainder of his day trying to avoid going home. After his conversation with Murray in the AA meeting room, he felt slightly nervous of finding himself alone in the flat. Ojo had been dispatched to the Hope Estate to bring in Hayden Simms but there'd been no sign of him. The incident room was still busy though. In a few hours the night shift would take over, and Finn's major hope was that a double murder investigation wouldn't turn overnight into a triple one.

He'd devoted his energies to tracking down the author of the RAIB report into the Brixton derailment. After some initial prickliness at being rung at home in the evening, the man in question – an investigator called David Edwards – was now opening up.

'Of course we only look into the actual cause of incidents, it's not our place to apportion blame,' said Edwards, in a slightly-too-chummy tone.

He was someone who clearly liked the sound of his own voice. Try as he did, Finn couldn't shake the image of an old-fashioned geography teacher – all diagrams and chaotic hair.

'I mean, off the record . . . it's a completely different story. Some of the stuff I come across would make your eyes water. I mean, take this one – absolute shitshow, really. They didn't properly vet the guy who tested the equipment, so you have some idiot passing a set of points as safe, then three weeks later – bang! They were lucky it wasn't a damned sight worse. I think I picked my words quite carefully in the report, all things considered.' He chuckled smugly at his own smugness. Finn contained his irritation.

'Did you personally interview any of the passengers who were on board?'

'Of course, and we also had that backed up by statements BTP took on the day. I was happy I had a pretty rounded picture of what had happened. To be honest, the real detective work was in establishing how those points failed in the first place. There was quite a trail of incompetence . . .'

There was a brief pause, Edwards clearly waiting to be asked to elaborate. But Finn was far more interested in the people who'd been on board.

'What I could really use is transcripts of everything you've got and a full list of passengers. We've managed to track down quite a few of them, but our list is by no means exhaustive.'

'Neither was ours, but it's probably a bit more than you've got. The two you've asked about, by the way . . .' Finn heard the tapping of a keyboard, 'Karl Suleman and Jo Corcoran – they were both in the carriage that actually derailed. Fortunately, we've got the names of nearly everyone else who was on that one.' A few clicks of a mouse. 'There, you should get that in a moment.'

'Was there nothing else that struck you as odd?'

'No, it was exactly what you'd imagine it to be. People panicking, then half an hour later standing by a track grumbling they were going to be late for work. My main priority was finding out what caused the collision in the first place. The passengers were only relevant in terms of the train's safety protocols. And that all checked out, I might add. What were you expecting?'

Finn watched a couple of tired detectives bantering in the corner of the room beneath the sunny smile of Leah Suleman, her photograph pinned to the incident room wall. Jamie Baker was next to her, raising a pint.

'I wish I knew.'

Finn finished the conversation and put the phone down, and turned to his screen where Edwards' emails were sitting in his inbox. He opened the first and scrolled through the list of passengers. One name suddenly caught his eye as it flashed past and disappeared. He swore under his breath and quickly scrolled back. There it was again – in black and white: *Hayden Simms*.

Hayden and Jade had finished their meal and were now walking down Streatham High Road together. They reached her bus stop and sat down on the red plastic bar which passed for a bench. A man was walking past reading the back page of the *Evening Standard*. Karl Suleman's anguished face stared out at them from the front page.

'Have you seen? That guy ended up killing himself,' said Jade.

Hayden nodded. 'That's the thing – people think they're heroes, but when shit happens for real . . . they're not, trust me.'

His hand went up automatically to the scar on his face.

'Do you want to tell me how you got that?' she said, though her eyes had already telegraphed the question.

'Not really.'

She gave him the same look she'd given him in the restaurant; the one that suggested their whole relationship might crumble if he didn't give her some straight answers to these questions.

'You want all my secrets tonight, don't you?' he said, then pointed at the scar. 'This happened not long after Mum died. I was doing a bit of dealing.'

'I thought you said you didn't used to do that kind of thing?'

'I've done a little bit over the years – just for money. Thing is I was doing it somewhere I shouldn't, only I didn't know it. I was with a couple of others; it wasn't as if I was alone. Suddenly there was a group of them. They came on bikes . . .' He broke off as he saw Jade's bus approaching the stop.

'Never mind that,' she said. The bus came to a halt, and its doors swished open. Hayden looked at her quizzically.

'You sure?'

'I wanna know . . .'

He shrugged, and they got up and began walking again.

'I wasn't going to run. There were three of us, five of them. That worked for me. But suddenly I'm on my own.'

'Your mates ran away?'

'Yeah. Then it's five against one. I was lucky, they could have killed me. Instead they gave me a beating. I think it was about sending a message. To the people who ran things back then.'

He ran his finger slowly across the criss-cross pattern of the scar.

'They marked me. Sometimes it comes back when I'm asleep. What it felt like – being held down, the blade cutting into my cheek . . . the fear.'

He broke off and looked at his fingers as if he was expecting to find blood there now. There was something though. They were wet. He stopped and looked at them almost in disbelief. He put his hand back up to his cheek and double-checked. Tears. He'd been crying, completely oblivious.

'Hayden, it's okay. You're allowed.'

He looked nervously around.

'You don't tell anyone you saw this, yeah?'

He looked scared, angry.

'I mean it – I don't live in the same world as these people.' He gestured randomly. 'The streets I walk down, people would see this as weakness.'

'Baby . . .'

She leant in close, until the anger softened.

'Of course I won't. But this is what worries me about you – you've got no one.'

He looked confused.

'What do you mean? I've got you. I've got Mikey.'

'Everyone needs family.'

He realised what she meant and shook his head.

'If you're talking about my dad, forget it.'

'It just seems sad.'

'Well, then it's sad. That's how it is.'

'Maybe if you tried talking to each other . . .'

'No.'

'What would you do,' persisted Jade, 'if you were like that guy in the park, and you had to choose . . .'

'What – between you and my dad? You, every time.'

He laughed.

'*Every* time, baby.'

26

The joint funeral for Karl and Leah Suleman was held the following morning at a church in a small village just outside Guildford. It was where Karl grew up, a bland collection of post-war houses interspersed with soulless new builds and a small strip of shops at its centre. Grey skies hung threateningly overhead, the clouds swirling together as if debating options. Paulsen felt uncomfortable. It wasn't just that she was in another graveyard so soon after her experience in West Norwood, or that she was an outsider at such an intensely private occasion. It was more the look on the other mourners' faces that was so unsettling. This wasn't a beloved grandparent finally coming to rest. It was a young woman butchered for reasons that still weren't clear, by a killer who remained free. In the adjacent coffin was the body of her father, a man who'd run in the opposite direction while she died.

As the service began, Paulsen was struck by the lack of tears or even noise around her. The lack of anything. There was little emotion on display, people simply reduced by the horror of it to mute stillness. Claire was bearing up remarkably well despite the appalling circumstances. Her face was a determinedly cool mask, save for the occasional flash of warmth as old family friends stopped to pay their condolences. Whatever she was feeling, there was clearly an effort to keep it contained. But the façade crumbled away when she stood at the lectern to make a speech, choking on her words as a hall of horrified people watched, wrestling to keep their own composure. A middle-aged woman – it was hard to tell whether she was a friend or part of the extended family – stepped forwards, put a consoling arm around her and led her gently away.

Afterwards the coffins were taken outside for burial. Paulsen noticed they were close to two relatively fresh gravestones, which appeared to be those of Karl's parents. His father had died in 2015, his mother two years later. He didn't have any brothers or sisters, so an entire family unit was now gone. Another by-product of those two minutes of madness in Crystal Palace Park.

As the mourners tossed soil and flowers into the grave, Paulsen found it impossible not to think of the day when she'd be doing this for her father. Would they just be feeling relieved by then? Glad for all concerned he was finally out of his misery? Or would they make it a celebration of his life, something upbeat? And then there was her mother – it was difficult to imagine her in a world where Christer wasn't there. She was still relatively young – what would she do afterwards? Would she reinvent herself, or lock herself away, lost in grief? Paulsen felt her eyes beginning to tear up and discreetly lowered her head, embarrassed not by the emotion itself but because it wasn't for the two people in front of her.

'Thank you for coming,' said Claire later. She seemed to have recovered some measure of composure after her moment at the lectern. They were still in the graveyard. A few photographers were there too, keeping their distance – though if they were bothering Claire, she wasn't showing it. People were beginning to drift away now, heading off to the wake. It felt like an intrusion too far for Paulsen.

'I'm so sorry again,' she said.

'How's the investigation progressing?'

'We're pursuing a number of leads, but haven't made any arrests yet. As soon as there's something to tell you, I'll be straight in touch.'

'I really appreciate everything you've done since Leah died. I know Karl didn't treat you very well, but—'

'Please,' said Paulsen, unable to contain herself. 'I'm sorry I wasn't there. I should have been. I feel like I'm partly to blame for what happened.'

It was starting to rain now, spitting slightly as if chivvying them along.

'Don't be ridiculous. The last thing I told him was that it should be him dead, not Leah. How do you think that makes me feel?'

She said the words softly so as not to be overheard.

'For what it's worth, I judged him harshly when I first met him too,' said Paulsen. 'None of us can really know what we'd have done in the same position.'

Claire's face hardened.

'I may wish he hadn't killed himself, but it doesn't change how I feel about what he did. I know *I* wouldn't have run away. Leah was my child and I'd have died for her. Karl always put himself first – the biggest surprise about what he did was that it *wasn't* a surprise.'

'Claire—'

'There's stuff you don't know about him. And you should know it now.' She lowered her voice some more. 'Karl was involved in a hit and run years ago, just after we got married. It left a young kid in a wheelchair. I've kept that secret for literally decades.'

Claire looked away guiltily as Paulsen took it in. There had always been the sense of some secrets between the pair, she realised in hindsight. It had underscored the tension in the house. Now she knew why. Claire turned back with a renewed defiance.

'I'm just saying he always put himself first. Back then. In the park with Leah. And even at the end when he took his own life. I spent a marriage being second best, so don't you dare blame yourself for anything.'

But even as Paulsen took in the words of absolution, her mind was working furiously to process the significance of what she'd just been told.

27

Jo Corcoran was staying at the local Travelodge close to the hospital where her mother was still recovering. Maeve seemed to have developed a small temperature, so the hotel stay had been longer than she'd expected. The sudden jump from the cosy routine of her life with Jamie to this soulless non-existence had been jarring. She'd been visited frequently by DC Nishat Adams, one of the FLOs Finn had assigned her. She'd also been referred to Victim Support and had spoken to a team from the charity. And that was the problem: people were rushing to help, when underneath it all she didn't feel like she deserved it. That she was as responsible for this as the grotesque creature who'd actually pushed the knife into Jamie's body.

Jamie's family had also been desperately trying to get hold of her. She'd spoken briefly to his mother on the phone but deliberately steered the conversation towards the emotions, and away from the hard details of what had taken place. Her shock and grief were useful in providing some cloud cover, but she was aware the truth would come out eventually – what exactly had happened to Jamie and where she'd been while it was happening.

She kept replaying the conversation with the intruder in her mind, as if trying to identify a plot hole in a film. She was convinced there was a moment she'd missed, an instant where she could have prevented this. She'd always think that, always believe that if she hadn't panicked, Jamie would still be alive. The guilt felt like ever-tightening hands around her throat. Overshadowing it all was the choice she'd made – *why* had she chosen her mother? Even now she didn't know what criteria she'd applied, what it said about her or Jamie. She hadn't let herself think too hard about that. She feared whatever tenuous grip she had on her sanity might just loosen for good if she went there.

It was hard not to be aware of Karl Suleman's fate too. She'd read the headlines, seen what people were saying about him online – that he was a coward who deserved to burn in hell for deserting his daughter. Now she was perhaps the only person on the planet who knew what he'd gone through. She was acutely aware that he must have spent his last few nights going through the same set of emotions she was feeling now. Somewhere around three that morning she'd convinced herself she was on the same inevitable trajectory – that this would end with her deciding she couldn't live with the guilt either. But by six o'clock, as she showered in the room's cramped bathroom, she'd found a new resolve to fight that fate. Whether it was just bluster or genuine intent, even she didn't know.

As she sat eating tepid porridge in the Travelodge's restaurant she tried to focus on the more pressing problems in front of her now. She expected her mother to be finally discharged later that day. They'd need somewhere to go. For a moment she could see Jamie looking across the breakfast table at her, grabbing his cutlery with relish as he always did before attacking a fry-up. She'd never be able to explain it to him, she thought – why she'd done what she'd done. She tried to imagine the conversation, pictured him nodding understandingly.

'*Whatever you do, you know I'm always on your side.*'

That's what he'd always said when she'd found herself in tight spots over the years. Would he say it now, about this? She'd never know for certain. She hadn't even said goodbye to him. In the space of three minutes she'd decided his fate and coldly left him to it. Slowly she put down her spoon, rose and calmly walked down the corridor until she found the toilets. She looked at her reflection in the mirror and began to retch into the sink.

'What I don't understand is where you were?' said Maeve Corcoran about an hour or so later. Jo was at her bedside, pouring her some water from a jug.

'Are you sure you don't want a hot drink, Ma? A cup of tea or something?'

'When I came down the stairs . . .' Maeve stopped, her eyes widening as she remembered.

Jo hadn't thought about that when she'd made her choice – that her mother might be the one to find Jamie's body. She was seventy-six years old and now deeply traumatised for whatever remained of her life.

'You still haven't said where you were?'

'I did tell you. I went out. To the shop.'

Maeve looked at her, almost as if she was too scared to challenge the answer. In return, Jo could barely meet her eye. Her phone pinged with a text. She looked at the handset, which she'd carefully placed face down on the bedside table. She lifted it to read the incoming message.

Next time it'll be your mum ☺

Finn had gathered his core team of Ojo, Paulsen and Dattani for a mini briefing – a lot seemed to have happened. Jo had rung the incident room as soon as she'd received the anonymous text message. She'd been calm as she explained it to the DC who took the call, and Finn was grateful he'd been able to forewarn her. He wasn't fooled though – they'd all thought Karl was coping and look how that turned out. He'd decided on the spot to move Jo and her mother to a safe house. The two DCs he'd assigned as family liaison officers, Nishat Adams and Amy Hunt, would alternate their time with them. After what had happened to Karl, he was determined to protect Jo, from both the media and the killer. Nishat and Amy were both experienced and he knew he could trust them not just to handle a delicate situation sensitively, but also to probe for any useful scraps of information that might help the investigation. The sense Jo, like Karl before her, held the critical, missing piece of information wouldn't leave him.

'It's personal. Has to be,' said Finn. 'We just still don't have any idea why he's targeted these two. Mattie, have you looked into this hit and run Claire told you about?'

Paulsen sighed. There was little to go on. The incident occurred in Crouch End close to Christmas 1998, and would take some digging into. She knew from experience how tricky tracking down historical paperwork could be.

'Still – it's a decent line all the same,' said Ojo. 'We know someone had a grudge against Jo, sent her death threats over that care home business. What if the same person knew about the hit and run too? Backs up the idea it's some kind of vigilante?'

Finn had been considering the same possibility, but like everything else with this investigation, there was nothing substantial to support it. Just another theory to throw in with all the rest.

'I think we need a lot more concrete information before we can say that for certain. Claire told Mattie she'd kept this a secret for decades. I doubt Karl was shouting his mouth off about it either. If *we're* struggling to find out about it, how does the killer know it happened?'

He looked at his team and saw no one was rushing to answer.

'We'll deal with that one as and when more information comes to hand. Meanwhile . . .'

He walked over to the board where the details of the train derailment were pinned. 'I was on the phone last night to a guy from the RAIB. It turns out there was someone else we've come across who was on that train with Karl and Jo, and in the same carriage too: Hayden Simms.'

It took a moment to sink in.

'My head's hurting,' said Ojo.

'So's mine,' said Dattani. 'What are you saying – that this kid's potentially the killer?'

Finn held out his hands as if balancing a pair of weights.

'From the description we've been given he's the wrong height and build, and the wrong age. Hayden's in his early twenties – and both Karl and Jo described a teenager.'

'Given the circumstances they could have been confused,' said Ojo.

'True. Which is why it would certainly help if we could talk to him, Jacks.'

Both Dattani and Paulsen automatically looked across at Ojo. She'd been the one tasked with finding Simms. If Finn meant the question as an implied criticism, he wasn't letting it show. If Ojo was *taking* the question as an implied criticism, she wasn't letting it show either. Nevertheless, there was suddenly an undercurrent in the room.

'It's not been for the want of trying. We did a sweep last night and there was no sign of him. Unless you can magic up some extra bodies from your non-existent budget, that's how it is,' said Ojo. 'We'll get him when we get him.'

Paulsen and Dattani now exchanged an awkward glance between themselves. Only Jackie O could get away with talking to Finn like that and it was hard to escape the sense of Mum and Dad having a row. 'If Simms was on the train with Karl and Jo, what do we think happened then?' said Paulsen, quickly filling the awkward gap.

'I think we should be careful of jumping to any quick conclusions,' said Ojo. 'They all live in the same corner of south-east London. They might have all been in the same pub that week, or the same Tesco's. If we're not careful, we could . . .' She groped for the right word.

'Derail ourselves?' said Dattani. Ojo glowered at him.

'You're a fucking comedian, Sami. You know what I'm saying. Maybe we shouldn't read too much into it.'

Finn was nodding but before he could respond, his computer chimed with an email. Instinctively he glanced across at it, then reached over to open it.

'It's the lab. They've finished analysing the bloodstains on that knife. The DNA's a confirmed match for Jamie Baker. Looks like we've found our murder weapon.'

The news helped dissipate the slight tension that had been building in the room. It was a genuine development and they all knew it.

'So it all comes back to the Hope Estate. Again,' said Ojo, who at that moment received a call on her mobile and walked away to take it.

It did come back to the Hope Estate, thought Finn – but he was far from displeased by that. Finally there was a focus to the lens of this investigation.

He instantly issued a series of rapid-fire instructions. He was particularly keen to start building a timeline of the night Jamie Baker died. Now that they could pretty much confirm the likely route the killer took after leaving Jo's house, a few things opened up. He gave instructions to widen the door-to-door enquiries, as well as expanding the search for CCTV footage. Another thought suddenly struck him.

'Sami, why don't you organise a reconstruction in Crystal Palace Park of Leah Suleman's murder. The media will be all over it – they've already been given the stills from the CCTV footage of the guy in the dark jacket. Release some of the footage itself – let's use their interest to our advantage and make a new appeal for information. I want to start building some pressure on whoever this is.'

'What do you need me to do, guv?' asked Paulsen. 'I've got calls in on this hit and run, but I'm not expecting anything back imminently.'

Finn's phone buzzed on his desk. He looked down and found himself thrown as Cally Hunter's name stared up at him.

When are we meeting again?

He grimaced with irritation, and turned the handset face down, aware Paulsen was watching him with interest.

'We still don't know half as much as I'd like to about the derailment. It might, as Jacks says, be coincidental – but it might not. I want a more first-hand picture of what actually happened – both on board that first carriage and by the tracks afterwards.'

'Picture of what, though?' said Paulsen. 'You've got the RAIB report, read the witness statements, spoken to the man who wrote it . . . what's left?'

He thought for a moment.

'The woman who suffered that stroke trackside. It might be worth chatting to her family – see if they can add anything. I'm willing to bet the events of that day must be burnt into

206

their minds. If anyone's going to remember the small details it'll be them.'

Paulsen nodded, a little unconvinced, as Ojo re-joined them.

'CID have got positive IDs of the two men who stabbed Connors. One's in South Norwood, the other's in Thornton Heath.'

Finn nodded.

'Stick with that for the moment – sit in on the interview when they're brought in.'

'Are you sure? It'll take me away from Simms.'

Finn nodded, remembering Skegman's warning to him about delegating work and deciding to ignore it.

'Don't worry, leave Simms with me.'

He was already reaching for his coat before she could reply.

28

Paulsen walked down the narrow corridor and grimaced at the smell, a combination of detergent and mashed potato. It seemed to be a fundamental rule of the universe that primary schools the world over smelt like this. She was there to meet Hannah Knolls, the daughter of Joyce Knolls, the woman who'd suffered the stroke in the snow by the derailed train carriage. Hannah worked at Tenby Primary School in Sydenham as a teaching assistant and hadn't seemed too perturbed when Paulsen called, asking if they could meet.

But as she walked through the empty playground, Paulsen felt a rare sense of uncertainty. She now increasingly felt there was something specific both Karl and Jo had done that had led the killer to target them. The train seemed too tenuous a connection and it was hard to understand what could possibly have happened that morning. An argument or a fist fight was probably the best bet. Karl's temperament certainly lent weight to that theory and it was easy enough to imagine him losing his temper in the heat of the moment. But what about Jo? And surely no impromptu row between strangers could have been so bad as to provoke the kind of retribution they'd received.

The tragedy that befell Hannah Knolls' family looked incidental, and asking her to relive that day felt unnecessary. She couldn't shake the feeling that Finn hadn't really thought it through. The more she watched him at the moment, the more ragged he seemed to be. Ojo had already expressed her concerns and now a few more were openly expressing similar views. She'd kept her own counsel on that front, but with each passing day it felt like someone really needed to sort this out. Skegman, for example.

An attractive woman in her early twenties, Hannah flashed a wide, engaging smile as she greeted the detective.

'Let's find an empty space where we can talk. It's almost chucking-out time and you don't want to be standing here when that happens,' she said.

She led Paulsen to the school hall, peered through the door to check it was empty and let her in. It was freezing and smelt of floor polish – another universal law, thought Paulsen. Hannah grabbed a couple of chairs from the side of the room and they both sat.

'I don't really know what more I can tell you, to be honest. I thought I'd pretty much said it all on the phone earlier.'

'I'm so sorry for your loss again,' said Paulsen. Although Joyce Knolls had suffered the stroke in January, she'd survived another couple of months before dying in hospital.

'Thank you, but in a funny sort of way it's a relief. Mum wasn't living much of a life at the end. Why are you so interested in what happened on the train anyway – I thought that'd already been looked into?'

Paulsen shifted uncomfortably on her seat.

'It's something that's come up in the course of a separate investigation. I'm sorry for asking, but would you be able to talk me through what happened from your perspective?'

Hannah gave a resigned look and took a deep intake of breath.

'Sure. Mum was taking us – me and my little brother – up to see a show in the West End.'

Paulsen consulted her notes.

'Your brother . . . Anthony, is that right?'

'Tony, yes. We started doing this for him when he was a kid. It sort of became a family tradition.'

'So when you say your little brother . . . ?'

Hannah smiled.

'He's not so little. Nineteen now, in fact. But Mum used to enjoy it – we all did – and that's why we kept it going.'

Paulsen nodded, made a note and motioned to Hannah to continue.

'We were going to do some shopping in the morning, grab some lunch then head to the theatre.' Her voice held the same breezy tone, but her eyes were betraying the deep well of pain underneath. 'Everything was normal, we were chatting, and then the train suddenly started braking really hard. I mean, *really* hard. It felt like the whole carriage was . . . bouncing, until it came to a halt.'

'What did you think had happened?'

'It was obviously quite serious. But pretty quickly you could tell nobody had been seriously hurt. There was a lot of panic – I think one or two people thought it was a terror attack or something. I was just concerned about my mum and Tony.' Again, there was that slight wince of pain, the one Paulsen had seen so many times in Finn's face. 'And it was while we were waiting by the tracks afterwards she had the stroke.'

'And do you think that incident directly caused it?' said Paulsen.

'Who knows? The doctors weren't sure. She had high blood pressure anyway. Her cholesterol wasn't great, so it could have happened at any time. It can't have helped though.'

'And there's nothing else that you remember that stands out?'

Hannah shrugged. 'Such as?'

'Anything involving the other passengers? An argument or a fight maybe?'

Just for a brief instant Paulsen got the sense Hannah was holding something back. A quick narrowing of the eyes as she remembered.

'I honestly wasn't really focusing on them. Like I say, I was just worried about my own family.'

The conversation dried into an awkward silence. Out in the corridor there was excited screaming as the school emptied out for the afternoon.

'If you must know, it was all a bit like that,' said Hannah, nodding at the door. Paulsen smiled, but the other woman's face remained sombre. 'When people are scared, that's what happens – they turn into screaming children.'

And briefly, Paulsen could very easily picture the scene. Scared commuters bundling for the doors, only concerned for themselves. Suddenly she saw Christer, that confused look on his face, standing in the middle of it, and she shivered.

Finn pulled his coat around him, feeling the wind as it blew through the Hope Estate. He'd kept it from the team, but his private worry now was of a third murder. There was absolutely nothing to suggest the killer was finished. And it could come in any form – a mother being forced to choose between two children, an elderly parent sacrificed for a baby's life. The permutations were appalling, and he knew that if he could conjure them, so could the person they were chasing.

While it wasn't a full-on manhunt for Hayden Simms, every officer in the area had been given his description and was aware that he was a person of interest. They'd tried his flat again without success, and Finn knew better than to ask Isiah where he might be. Ahead, he saw a uniform PC talking to a local resident and he hurried over to join them.

Isiah Simms walked into the small reception of the MOT service centre where he worked and was surprised to find a young woman waiting for him. He'd been summoned off the shop floor, told there was a visitor, but assumed it was an impatient customer keen for an update on their vehicle. He wiped his oil-streaked palms on his blue overalls.

'I probably shouldn't shake your hand,' he said with an affable smile. 'What's your reg number?'

'I'm not here about a car. I'm actually a friend of your son's.'

'Michael? Has something happened to him?' His eyes widened with sudden alarm, but the young woman smiled.

'No, not Mikey. Hayden. I'm his girlfriend.'

It took a moment for the words to penetrate, as he processed the oddness of someone he didn't know using the nickname 'Mikey'.

'Have you got a minute?' she asked him. 'It's really important. Well, I think it is, anyway.'

He looked at her with suspicion. 'Very briefly.'

He led her through to an empty waiting room next to the main workshop, and pulled out a couple of plastic orange chairs. The faint sounds of a radio, men shouting and laughing, and the intermittent whine of a drill all collided in the background. The woman seemed friendly enough, but the mention of his boy had thrown him. She must have sensed it, because her smile broadened again.

'I know this must seem odd, and I'm very sorry for bothering you at work, but I'm worried about him.'

'You haven't even told me your name yet.'

'Jade. And I know what the situation is between the two of you . . .'

He digested this, wondering exactly what Hayden had told this young woman.

'If you know what the situation is, then you already know you wasted your time coming here.'

'Please – just a few minutes of your time, that's all I'm asking.'

She patiently explained what she'd seen over the last few days. Hayden's shaking hand, the nightmares, the spontaneous tears in the street in Streatham. Isiah listened to it all impassively.

'What are you saying – is he ill?'

'In a way. I think a lot of things are coming to a head and I don't know how to help him if I'm honest.'

She didn't have to say it. He knew why she was there and what she wanted from him. He shook his head.

'The door's always been open for him. But he's never shown any desire to come home. He's never reached out. Never shown any contrition. So I'm sorry, I can't help you.'

The woman didn't move, kept her eyes on his. A sense that there was some steel behind that pleasant smile, he thought.

'He's changed. He's not how you remember him, I'm sure of it.'

He pursed his lips. It was possible, he supposed. Hayden had been no more than a boy when they'd fallen out. He felt on the brink of asking this woman to leave.

'Go on . . .'

'I know he cares deeply about his brother and I honestly think he's ready to build some bridges with you.'

'And you've had this conversation with him?'

'Yes. He says it's too late to fix anything. But I know him, and I think he'd like to change things deep down.'

Isiah smiled wryly. 'You seem very sure of yourself.'

'Please. One conversation is all I'm asking. What have you got to lose? Something good might actually come out of it. If not for me, then for Mikey. And I know you both care about him,' she said.

Isiah thought about it as the sound of hissing and grinding echoed in the background. He felt tired and worn down. Not by this conversation, but by the years that had gone by. He sighed.

'If you get him to agree, and he's serious about it, I'll listen to what he has to say. But I'm making no promises.'

The reason Hayden hadn't been at home was because he'd been with Andy. Given the quantity of police on the estate it seemed prudent to keep their business well away for the time being. They'd spent the afternoon strategising – or at least Andy had. Hayden's appetite for their business was decreasing by the day. He'd listened and nodded along, keener to try and establish when he'd actually see some of this money he'd been promised. They were travelling in opposite directions, he realised. He'd listened to Andy's ambitions of expansion and none of it sounded like a world he wanted to be a part of. Instead, he'd thought about what he could do with the cash. A course somewhere maybe, a chance to improve himself, an existence less hand to mouth. Something safer and more honest.

As he made his way home, he became aware that there were now even more police on the estate. He was conscious too of the knife he was carrying. It was for his own protection, but it made him feel uncomfortable – he knew what his dad would think as well, and that nagged at him. Despite everything he'd told Jade the previous night, his father's approval still mattered on some level. He was becoming precisely the kind of man he'd always insisted he wasn't.

As he turned a corner he saw a policeman in a high-vis uniform, who immediately started to size him up. Hayden knew the drill – look calm, walk calm, don't do anything to suggest you've got something to hide. But as he got closer, this felt different; the officer was looking hard at his face.

'Hayden Simms?'

Hayden stopped.

'Are you Hayden Simms?'

If he searched him, he'd find the knife. It was a simple choice – run and risk the consequences, or stay and risk being searched. He turned on his heels and accelerated. To his surprise, the policeman didn't follow; instead he heard him shouting into his radio. It didn't matter why they wanted him, what was important was what he was carrying. He turned a corner, saw a skip and tossed the knife into it. As he ran on, a police van skidded to a halt in the street ahead. Three uniform officers bundled out and sprinted straight at him. He veered off in a diagonal away from them. They were big men, weighed down by stab vests, belts loaded with batons, handcuffs and pepper spray cans. Very briefly he thought he might just outpace them. As he looked for an out, he became aware of someone else now running towards him. A tall man with glasses making up surprisingly quick ground with powerful long strides. He recognised him instantly as the man who'd been talking to his dad earlier that week. Hayden felt a streak of fear – whatever it was they wanted with him, all this seemed excessive. He slowed to a halt. The man with the glasses motioned at the pursuing officers to hold back.

'Hayden Simms?'

This time Hayden nodded in acknowledgement.

'What have I done?'

The man smiled unexpectedly.

'Nothing, as far as I know. Fancy a cup of tea?'

29

An hour later they were sitting in one of Cedar House's interview rooms. Hayden was reluctantly there of his own volition, having been assured he wasn't going to be arrested.

'So why were there so many of you chasing after me then?' he said.

'Because you ran from an officer who just wanted to confirm your identity,' said Finn.

Paulsen was with them, having returned from her visit to Hannah Knolls. 'What is it you want, then?' asked Hayden.

'Just to talk. Your name's come up a few times in the last few days.'

Hayden shifted warily in his seat, as if suspecting a trick.

'Let's start with Mark Connors,' said Finn.

'What about him?'

'Do you know who he is?'

'I know he's a dealer and I know what happened to him – but that was nothing to do with me.'

'Maybe not directly,' said Finn. 'But it's been suggested to us you've been stepping up recently. That you know quite a bit about the drug supply in and around the Hope Estate these days.'

Hayden slumped back into his seat and didn't reply.

Finn had done enough of these interviews over the years. They went one of two ways usually – cocky youths sat wisecracking, or angry young men sullen and uncooperative. But that wasn't what he was seeing here. At the mention of Connors, Hayden's hand had gone straight to his face, gently touching the prominent scar on his cheek. There was a glisten of sweat on his forehead too, and his breathing was getting heavier. On the surface they all looked like visible indicators of guilt, but Finn wasn't getting that from him either. There was another layer to this – he looked more like a man carrying the weight of the world on his shoulders.

'Shouldn't I have a lawyer here if you're going to say stuff like that?' said Hayden.

'We've been told what happened to Connors might have been a reprisal for another incident the day before,' said Paulsen.

'News to me.'

'I hope so, because we're currently interviewing the men we arrested for stabbing Mark. If your name comes up again, then we might need to make this conversation formal,' countered Paulsen.

'Knock yourselves out.'

He wiped the moisture gathering on his forehead with his sleeve, sniffed and swallowed uncomfortably. There was a jug of water on the table and he poured himself a cup, draining it in one. Finn was watching him closely. There was neither anger or resistance there, just more of the same weariness. Simms looked like someone with little appetite for playing games. Something didn't smell quite right about any of his reactions.

'It isn't just Connors we want to talk to you about,' he said. 'We're also investigating two murders: a woman in Crystal Palace Park last Friday night, and a man in Penge on Monday evening.'

Hayden sighed and shook his head.

'I don't know shit about any of that.'

'We found the murder weapon in a drain on the Hope Estate.'

Hayden looked genuinely surprised.

'And what – you think I put it there? Seriously?'

He swallowed, as if finding it slightly difficult to breathe. He poured out another cup of water and gulped it down noisily. Finn gave him a moment before continuing. Another bead of sweat was already forming on his forehead.

'No, but you live there and have your ear to the ground. Is there anything you've heard that can help us?'

Hayden seemed almost overwhelmed by the question. If he was part of the new regime, a man potentially running a county lines operation, he didn't look like it right now. He looked instead like a young man, with an old face, in desperate need of some rest.

'No, nothing at all. Why would I?'

'Come on, Hayden, it's been all over the TV news, in every newspaper. Don't tell me you haven't seen it?' said Finn.

'What do you want me to say? I can only tell you the truth – I've heard nothing about it.' A hand fell heavily on the table, his irritation turning now to anger. 'I don't under-stand why you've singled me out.'

Finn had been waiting carefully for this moment, trying to lead the conversation here in stages.

'Because we think there may be a connection between those deaths and a train derailment which took place earlier this year. A train you were on,' he said.

Hayden looked genuinely thrown. Finn picked up a brown envelope from his lap and took out four photographs. He laid them out slowly one after the other, giving Hayden a chance to take in each image in turn.

'Do you recognise any of these people?'

Hayden looked, shook his head.

'Karl Suleman was the father of Leah, the girl who died in the park. Jo Corcoran was Jamie Baker's partner.' He pointed at each of the quartet as he named them. 'Are you sure you don't know any of them?'

'No. Why would I?'

'Karl and Jo were on the same train that morning. In the same carriage as you.'

In fairness, thought Finn, Hayden's response to that wasn't a million miles from his own team's. He seemed genuinely at a loss to know how to respond. He was still slumped back in his seat, and with an effort propped himself back up again.

'Just tell us what happened, from your perspective,' said Paulsen.

There was a pause while Hayden remembered.

'It was mad that morning, the train was rammed. I was with my little brother. We were going up to Oxford Street to buy some clothes.'

'How old's your brother?' said Finn.

'Thirteen.'

Finn and Paulsen exchanged a glance and Hayden caught it, his eyes narrowing.

'Just so we've got a clear picture,' said Finn quickly and motioned at him to continue.

Hayden's breathing seemed laboured as he picked up.

'The train suddenly braked. All the people standing by the doors went flying. And there's this sound, like metal on metal, and the carriage swerved. Finally, it stops and we're at this weird angle – you could tell it'd come off the tracks. Someone shouted it was a bomb, and then it all kind of kicked off after that.'

'What do you mean "kicked off"?' said Finn.

'People being stupid, screaming at each other. It obviously wasn't a bomb. I mean, there hadn't been an explosion – all I was thinking about was Mikey.'

'Your brother?'

'Yeah. I had a seat, beat him to it when we got on. I couldn't really see him from where I was. There were too many people in the way.'

Finn leant in, sensing something important.

'And what happened next?'

'This schoolgirl's shouting it's an attack, pointing at these two guys with beards. They were yelling back at her.' He took another gulp from the paper cup. Finn could see his hand was trembling now, spilling water on to the table. Hayden stopped, looking almost accusingly at his errant fingers.

'Take your time,' said Finn. But his concern was growing by the second – what the hell was happening to this guy?

'I just wanted to find Mikey. People started trying to force the doors to get off. I got up, tried to push my way through, but . . .'

He stopped mid-sentence. His hand flapped towards the cup again but didn't make it this time. His eyes, pupils dilated, swivelled back and his head slowly dropped forwards. He began to twitch, whooping for air, a streak of something wet dribbling from his mouth. He slipped off his chair and fell to the ground almost in slow motion. Finn jumped to his feet and raced round, as Paulsen ran immediately to the door to get help. Hayden was convulsing as Finn reached him. He threw the chair he'd been sitting on out of the way and rolled him over on to his side. Outside he could hear frantic shouting as he pulled off his jacket, rolled it up and used it as a makeshift pillow. There was a strange strangulated noise coming from his throat and Finn quickly unbuttoned the top of his shirt. For one horrible moment he thought Hayden might actually be dying in front of him. Behind him, the door to the interview room crashed open and help mercifully arrived.

'The paramedics have checked him out and say he's fine. They can't find anything wrong. There's no history of epilepsy either,' said Finn a short while later. He and Paulsen were back in the incident room, still shocked themselves by what they'd seen. Hayden was resting in the station's medical examination room. He'd recovered extraordinarily quickly all things considered. He seemed more embarrassed by what had happened than worried, and was keen to leave, but there was no chance of that until they were certain he was okay. For his sake and theirs.

'What the hell was that then?' said Paulsen.

Finn was at his desk, Hayden's record open on the screen in front of him.

'He deteriorated when we started talking about the derailment. Mind you, he looked like he was struggling from the start – but it was the train that seemed to provoke the reaction.'

He looked at Paulsen for confirmation and she nodded slowly in agreement.

'This is a guy who's potentially running a county lines operation? Why would a minor train shunt affect him like that?' she said.

Finn was starting to build a picture now of the level of panic that morning. That much at least the RAIB report hadn't conveyed accurately. He already knew how much it'd affected Karl, to the extent that he'd started taking drugs in the aftermath. Jo, too, had spoken of her initial fear, while Hannah Knolls had given a similar account to Paulsen. Now he'd seen potentially the most dramatic reaction of all. But none of it explained why Leah Suleman and Jamie Baker were both dead and why the killer was going after their loved ones.

'Maybe he's just got a dicky stomach? Shouldn't think his diet's kombucha and kefir somehow,' said Paulsen.

'Maybe, but it looked to me like something more deep-rooted.'

'Could be about his brother rather than the derailment. Did we know he was on the train?' said Paulsen.

Before Finn could answer they were joined by a uniform PC.

'Sorry to interrupt, but there's someone at the front desk – a Jade Clarke – says she's Simms's girlfriend and wants to know what's happening.'

'Tell her to wait, he won't be long now,' said Paulsen.

'I can do that,' said Finn suddenly. He stood. 'Maybe she can help shed some light on this.'

He entered the waiting area and saw a young woman in a denim jacket and grey tracksuit bottoms sitting on her own. She glanced up pensively and he smiled reassuringly, introducing himself as he sat down next to her.

'They said Hayden had been taken ill, but that's all I was told. I've been worried sick.'

'It's alright – he's okay,' said Finn. 'He had some sort of seizure while we were talking, but the paramedics have checked him out and can't find anything wrong. We're just making sure he's definitely okay before we let him go.' Far from calming her, this seemed to make Jade more worried, her face creasing with concern. 'Do you know if anything like this has happened before?' Finn continued.

'What – a seizure? No. But . . .'

She stopped as if unsure of what to say next.

'Go on . . .' he said.

'There have been a few things recently . . .'

She told him about the shaking hand, the night terrors, the tears he hadn't noticed as he'd explained the scar on his cheek. Finn nodded as he listened. The truth was dawning on him and he kicked himself for not putting it together earlier. It'd literally been staring him in the face.

'I think what you're describing is post-traumatic stress disorder. I've seen it before in gang members.'

She glared at him sharply.

'Hayden isn't in a gang. Unless you think all young working-class black men are automatically gangsters,' she said.

Finn winced; he'd been thinking aloud and it'd been a stupid thing to say. Nevertheless, however well-made her point was, Hayden's precise status on the estate still remained far from clear. He held up a palm by way of apology.

'Maybe he's not in a gang, but that scar on his cheek tells me he's been through a few things. I think there may be another issue to it as well.'

'What do you mean?'

He told her about the train and Hayden's reaction to his questions. Jade remained passive at first, as if there was a delay between her hearing his words and her brain processing them. 'I know it doesn't seem too serious. No one was hurt, nobody died ... but it sounds like a pretty scary thing to have been caught up in. It might well have upset him more than he realised.'

'I don't think so.'

She said it quickly and it seemed an odd choice of words to Finn.

'How do you mean?'

'I don't think Hayden's the sort of guy who'd be affected by something like that.' She said it with an absolute conviction. 'That's just not who he is.'

★　　★　　★

223

As he returned to the incident room, Finn tried to make sense of what he'd seen and heard. If what Jade had just told him was true, and Hayden wasn't involved with a gang, then he wondered what had caused his PTSD. It might well be connected to the scar on his face; the way his hand constantly moved there suggested what had happened had deeply affected him. But he was sure, too, that the conversation about the derailment had been the trigger for the fit. Jade's dismissal had been unequivocal, but he wasn't convinced by that. His suspicion was now turning into a much more concrete belief that something *else* happened that day. Something that might just have led to the deaths of two people, and the suicide of a third.

30

'What's the matter with you? You've hardly said a word all night,' said Nancy as Mattie stood at the open door of their fridge, assessing its contents.

'I don't know if I want a yoghurt or a beer,' she replied.

'Have both. And mix them with some cheese and nails,' muttered Nancy. This had been the general level of conversation since she'd arrived home and her patience was now clearly wearing thin.

Mattie grabbed a bottle of beer, shut the door and turned with an absent frown.

'You what?'

Nancy shook her head.

'Nothing. What is it, Mat? Your dad? Your job? Me?'

'Not you. Why would it be you?' She walked across the room and slumped into the sofa. Nancy came over and joined her.

'There's clearly something bothering you. What is it?'

Mattie frowned and took a swig of beer. In truth there were multiple causes for her mood. Her father was one of the reasons. His diagnosis was hanging over her like a cloud. Some problems couldn't be easily solved. There was no simple solution to be ordered off eBay or Amazon. It would have to be endured for its duration. And in that respect she felt some empathy with Finn. The key difference was that she wasn't letting it affect her work. But in the months and years to come, who knew what would happen. She felt a sudden stab of guilt at some of the opinions she'd formed about him recently. Don't knock it till you've tried it, she thought.

But her father was only part of it – Karl Suleman's fate wouldn't leave her either, despite Claire's words at the funeral. She'd been given the FLO role on trust and it had ended with a suicide. Finn had made it clear he didn't hold her responsible, though she wasn't so sure about Skegman. She stood by her judgement. She hadn't seen a reason to escalate Karl into the vulnerable category. But it felt like his subsequent actions had made a nonsense of that. A Merlin report would have triggered a multi-agency response and might just have saved his life. What she couldn't stop asking herself was where her attention had been – on Karl, professionally assessing his mental well-being, or on her father? Had his plight distracted at her right at the critical moment?

She explained to Nancy how she was feeling, but it felt easy telling a sympathetic ear. And she didn't want sympathy – she wanted to be told that she'd fucked up. That her selfishness had cost a man his life. But it didn't come.

'It's a big moment in your family's life – you were *right* to go home,' said Nancy, resting a hand on Mattie's knee.

'So why do I feel so bad then?'

'Because beating yourself up is written in your DNA. And I know what you're like when you find a good reason to do it.'

Paulsen felt a burst of irritation, largely because Nancy had, quite accurately, put her finger on it.

'What's that supposed to mean?' she said anyway.

'For a start, do you want to tell me more about those stitches on your face? All you've told me is that it was a difficult arrest.'

Mattie looked away. It was a conversation she'd thought she'd avoided.

226

'The man who did this – he chucked water at me, but for a moment I thought it was acid.'

Nancy looked appalled.

'Where was Detective Inspector Goldenballs when this was happening?'

'Trying to catch up – I went after this guy alone.'

It was the answer Nancy expected and dreaded in equal measure.

'You could have died. Or it *could* have been acid, and you—'

'I know what *could* have happened,' said Mattie, interrupting. 'I lost control.'

'Again,' said Nancy.

Finn sat down on the bench and looked out at the Thames, glittering under the moonlight. He opened up the small box of noodles he'd just overpaid a street vendor for. The London Eye was lit up to his left, the Oxo Tower to his right, and he cut an anonymous figure among the teeming throngs around him. It wasn't the first time he'd headed to the South Bank on his own after work. He liked coming here, noise-cancelling headphones on with an audiobook playing in his ears. Especially when it felt like there was too much rattling around his head.

He was going through a phase of biographies, particularly of his beloved American sport stars. The current was Bill Belichick, the record-breaking coach of the New England Patriots. It allowed his brain to relax, roll the day's events around in the background. It was like sifting for gold in the murk of his mind. He often returned home with at least one useful insight gleaned. Forking some spicy carbs into his mouth, he paused to let the heat rush warm him.

A couple caught his eye as they walked past. Their body language was awkward. He may be out of practice, but good money said they were on a first date. He saw a lot of that on the South Bank. The place seemed to attract them like honey to a bee. The guy was trying to fill the silence; the woman with him didn't seem that bothered. Finn wasn't sure which one he sympathised with the most. Irritatingly it made him think about his conversation with Cally Hunter. He still hadn't responded to her latest text. There'd be another one tomorrow morning if he didn't get back to her. He shook his head – there were other matters which were more important. The investigation, for a start.

Skegman was right about one thing: the clock was ticking, and Finn's brain wasn't functioning the way it usually did under pressure. He still didn't know *why* two people were dead and the longer he was in the dark, the more the possibility of another attack grew. He was also angry with himself for missing Hayden's PTSD. It was a bad mistake and out of character. Proof once more that Skegman's criticisms weren't unfounded. He felt himself on the brink of a critical mistake. He'd been skirting it, but at some stage his luck would run out.

He'd come to the South Bank to try and find a little bit of the old Finn. He wanted to kick-start things after spending the remainder of his day looking at the list of passengers who were in that carriage with Hayden, Jo and Karl. There was also now Michael Simms to add to the mix. He fitted the age bracket of the person they were looking for, but there was nothing in the witness statements and the RAIB documentation that even mentioned him. And why would a thirteen-year-old boy have hunted down two families like this? It didn't make sense, but then none of it did.

'*Look too hard at the other side of the road, and you'll walk into a lorry,*' said Karin.

'Hello you,' he said softly under his breath.

228

And suddenly there it was – the clarity he'd been looking for hitting him with a rush of adrenalin. He stood instinctively and began to walk. It was drizzling now but he didn't mind; the cogs were finally turning. Karin was right – he'd been looking too hard at it, missing the blindingly obvious.

He'd been working on the assumption that there was a connection between Karl, Jo and Hayden. But if you were connecting those three, then in parallel shouldn't you also connect Leah and Jamie . . . with someone close to Hayden? The through-line of his own logic stopped him in his tracks: *Isiah or Mikey?*

'Stress? Fuck off,' said Hayden. He was sat on his sofa attacking the contents of a plastic pot of rice, alternating with heavy swigs of beer from a can. Jade was wrapped in a towel having just emerged from the shower. He'd been too exhausted to fight her when she'd insisted on staying over for the night.

'I'd have cooked if you'd waited,' she said. He waved a dismissive hand. 'And you still haven't told me what happened to you.'

'It was just really hot in there – I got a bit light-headed, that's all.'

'That's not what they said. I was told you had a seizure.'

'That's bollocks.'

He reached for the TV remote.

'Hayden, wait – can we talk about it?' she persisted. 'The man I spoke to said something about a train crash. You've never mentioned anything about that before.'

He tossed the remote across the sofa in irritation.

'Because it was nothing.'

'Doesn't sound like nothing,' she snapped sharply. 'Are you sure that's all it was to you?'

He turned, surprised by the reaction.

'I can barely remember it. I wasn't hurt, and neither was Mikey – that's all that happened. It was just a ball-ache – it took us hours to get into London.'

Jade visibly checked herself, as if she didn't believe him. He reached out to stroke her back but she shrugged him off.

'Don't be angry with me, baby – not tonight.'

'It must be something or they wouldn't have asked you about it.'

'They said it's to do with the bloke whose daughter died in the park. That's nothing to do with me.' She still didn't look convinced. 'Honestly, they were taking a punt.'

'So you don't think you've got PTSD then?'

'They were just trying to get in your head.'

'How do you mean?'

'That if they make out it's something medical, I'll trip up – tell some doctor something they can use against me. They know what me and Andy are doing. This guy was playing you.' He tapped the side of his head. 'You've got to use this.'

He put the empty pot of rice to one side and put his arms around her, giving her a beery kiss on the neck. This time she didn't resist. 'You're the only person I need to tell stuff to.'

'Do you remember what I said to you in Streatham? This is what I meant.'

He sighed, dropping his head with exaggerated weariness. 'If you're talking about my old man again, what good would he have been today?'

'Hayden, don't be angry with me . . .'

He softened, moved his face in close and smiled.

'Why would I be angry with you?'

'Because I went to see him earlier.'

He let go of her, straightened up.

'You did *what*?'

230

'Just to talk, that's all. I wanted to see if he'd meet with you.'

'Why?'

'Because I think you should.'

'Fuck's sake, Jade.'

'He said he would, if you would.'

Hayden looked genuinely shocked.

'For real?'

'Yes – he's prepared to hear what you have to say.'

'There you go – he wants *me* to do it. *He's* the one who needs to apologise.'

'Why don't you think about Mikey? Where would he be if anything happened to either of you? Have you ever thought about that? Or is it always about you?'

Invoking his little brother's name produced a reaction, as it always did, and Jade didn't give him the chance to regroup.

'Who do you want to be, Hayden? A gangster? Or a brother? Or a father, maybe?'

'A father?'

She looked him in the eye, nodded.

'One day. Why not?'

His hand went automatically up to his face, absently rubbing at the scar again.

'What would I even say to him?'

'We can figure that out.'

Hayden necked what was left of his beer. He felt exhausted in every sense.

'Alright then. For whatever good it'll do.'

The rest of the evening was uneventful and they went to bed early. There were no night terrors this time and Hayden fell into a deep sleep. Jade watched him for a while, listening to the gentle bellow of his lungs. She rolled on to her back and stared at the ceiling for a while, thinking about the chain of events that had led them to this point. Quietly she swung her legs and climbed out of bed, careful not to wake him. She reached down to the side table, picked up her phone and tiptoed to the door. She slowly held the handle down and pushed, a shard of light instantly illuminating the room. Satisfied Hayden was still sleeping, she stepped out and slipped into the living room. In the distance she could hear the dim wail of sirens somewhere. She could also see now what was causing the bright white light – a full moon, framed in the sky high above the Hope Estate. She went over and sat on the sofa, bathing in the glow for a moment, then flipped her phone round and tapped out a text message.

It's on. They've both agreed.

31

'I don't understand what you're trying to say to me.'

Isiah Simms was looking at Finn with confusion as much as concern. They were standing in the same small waiting area of the MOT centre where he'd met with Jade the previous day. On the shop floor a small karaoke was taking place as his colleagues sang in sync with the radio, interspersed by short bursts of an ear-piercing drill.

'I know how this sounds, but I wouldn't be here if I didn't think it was important,' said Finn.

'Why would anyone want to hurt me?'

'I think it's more about trying to hurt Hayden *through* you.'

Isiah shook his head in bemusement.

'Then they've picked the wrong family. I'm not sure my son could care less about me.' A thought seemed to strike him. 'Mikey's not in any danger, is he?'

Finn had thought hard about this conversation on the way over. He wanted to establish exactly where the youngest Simms boy had been on the night of the two murders without alarming Isiah. It was a delicate tightrope – he wasn't sure if the teenager was in genuine danger, or a potential suspect.

'All I'm saying is you might want to be a bit more vigilant than normal for the next few days. And that includes Mikey—'

'That's easier said than done,' said Isiah, interrupting.

'Forgive me for asking, but do you have any particular worries about him at the moment? Any small changes in his behaviour, for example,' said Finn carefully.

'Why do you want to know?' said Isiah suspiciously.

Finn spread his hands.

'I'm just trying to build as complete a picture as I can. The more I know, the more I can tell you how much of a threat there might actually be.'

It was woolly and he knew it, but it was also essentially true. There was a pause before Isiah answered. Yes, Mikey's behaviour had been erratic recently, his school reporting some unexpected absences. On the night Leah was killed the boy had been out, and his father clearly didn't know where. The following Monday evening, while Jamie Baker was being murdered in his own living room, Mikey was at home watching TV. Finn digested the information without comment.

He was well aware there was no proof the Simms family were even in danger. He didn't have the authority or even the manpower to provide them with any kind of formal protection. The best he could do was try and warn Isiah.

'Just be careful who you answer the door to, that kind of thing. Hopefully I'm wrong.' He pulled a card from his pocket. 'If there's anything at all that seems unusual, you can call me directly on this. Day or night.'

Isiah took the card but looked troubled.

'Why would someone go after Hayden?'

'We're still investigating that.' Finn waited for another burst of drilling to finish before resuming. 'But there's something else you should know too.'

He explained Hayden's fit in the interview room, the conversation with Jade afterwards, and what he suspected was the underlying reason for it.

'PTSD . . . are you sure?'

234

'No. I can't say for certain. But I've seen a lot of it in different contexts over the years. What Jade was describing to me, what I saw yesterday – I'd say it's a very strong possibility.'

There was a loud peal of jarring laughter from the workshop.

'I've let him down, haven't I?' said Isiah with genuine distress. 'Let my wife down too – this isn't what she would have wanted.'

'Ring any bells, sunshine?' said Karin.

'It can't have been easy,' said Finn, ignoring her. He was desperately trying to find the right words but couldn't. Bereavement was like a vampire, he thought. It drained its victims, left them lifeless, their emotional faculties damaged and diminished by it. Whoever came up with the phrase 'time heals everything' probably wasn't worth getting a second opinion from.

'What do you think I should do?' said Isiah.

'I'm trying to get hold of Hayden, to warn him too. But if the pair of you were able to reach some sort of understanding . . . I think it might help in all sorts of ways.'

It was becoming a familiar feeling, Finn thought as he drove away afterwards – that *cheapness*. The sense of cajoling people into showing precisely the kind of emotional courage he couldn't – or wouldn't – find in himself.

'I'm sorry, I'm not buying this connection to the train. Not when you've got stronger lines of enquiry to work with,' said John Skegman as Finn and Paulsen brought him up to speed later. Finn was trying to explain his chain of logic, why he thought Isiah and Mikey might potentially be in danger.

'I'm not neglecting those other leads,' he said with a patience that verged on patronising. 'I just think this is potentially the most pressing one right now.'

Skegman glared at him, not caring for the tone.

'We've got a hit and run no one else knew about, and a nurse connected to a dodgy care home where people died. They both look like solid motives to me. Your killer could just be the hired muscle for someone who thought these two deserved it.'

'I agree, and we've been looking on the dark web for signs these might have been professional hits, but we haven't found anything to suggest it,' said Finn.

'Nobody you've spoken to has given even the slightest hint that something else happened on that train. You've got the RAIB report, not to mention all the statements BTP took – and there's *nothing*.' Skegman banged his desk with his palm like a card player throwing down a winning hand.

'I'm aware of that,' said Finn, in that same tone again. 'But I'm still not convinced we have a complete picture yet.'

Skegman's ratty little eyes darted down, then across, the frustration intensifying.

'They all live in the same part of south London. They could all use the same gym, or belong to the same doctor's surgery. You could probably find them on that train most days of the year.'

Finn smiled, largely because he knew it would probably wind Skegman up a little bit more.

'Karl, Jo and Hayden weren't just on the same train – they were in the same *carriage*, the only one which actually came off the tracks.'

'And I accept it needs looking into. I'm just keen it doesn't become a distraction. I've got the media knocking incessantly on my door and it feels to me like you've become bogged down with this.'

'I haven't,' said Finn, through gritted teeth. 'The killer's DNA isn't on the database. He's new, whoever he is, and you

236

know how difficult that makes things. The only *direct* connection we've established between the two murders so far *is* the train.'

Skegman visibly controlled himself.

'Mattie, tell me more about this hit and run involving Karl – what have you found?' he said, turning his head away from Finn.

'I've been trying to establish if an accident report book was submitted at the time, but Claire's been pretty vague on the details. It's all second-hand information from what Karl told her back in the day. For all I know it never even happened.'

Skegman pursed his lips and turned his attention back to Finn.

'And this care home scandal Jo was involved in?'

Finn updated him with Dattani and McElligott's progress, insofar as there was any. Both had made the good point to him earlier that there were others involved whose hands were far dirtier than Jo's, if this was indeed about revenge.

Sensing Skegman was reaching the limit of his patience, Finn explained his plan to hold a reconstruction of Leah Suleman's murder in Crystal Palace Park later that evening. It was exactly seven days on now and was a good opportunity to make a fresh appeal for witnesses and information. They were sure now the killer would have tracked Karl and Leah before he attacked them. It was possible someone might have seen something – maybe even the killer without his mask on. The idea seemed to placate Skegman, largely because it involved Finn taking the burden of the press off his shoulders.

'Have the media made any connection between Leah Suleman's murder and Jamie Baker's yet?'

Finn stifled a scowl. He'd been called by a journalist he knew and trusted on his way back to the station earlier. While they talked he'd been careful not to link the two investigations formally, but when pushed on whether they were being stretched had inadvertently mentioned a 'pooling' of resources. It was a brief slip but a slip nonetheless, and it was nibbling at him. He was usually meticulous in his conversations with the media. The mistake had been clumsy and he could only hope he'd got away with it.

'Not as far as I'm aware, but with Amy and Nishat keeping a close eye on Jo at the safe house we shouldn't get a repeat of what happened with Karl,' he said, hoping he was right.

'Has she received any more messages from the killer?'

'No, but that's hardly a surprise – he'd be pretty stupid to think we're not monitoring her phone now. Or that we wouldn't have warned her. That one message was probably enough to make his point though.'

'Okay, fine. Investigate the train link by all means, but please – *please* – don't get bogged down in it. I just don't think it's worth it.'

'As you've already made perfectly clear, sir,' said Finn, smiling briskly as he turned on his heels, the smile quickly evaporating.

'Well that was a productive fifteen minutes,' said Paulsen as they walked back to the incident room. Finn muttered something under his breath – she didn't quite catch it, but she got the drift. He barged the door open and walked over to his desk. Paulsen watched as he recalibrated himself. Petulance giving way to concentration. He leant forwards, tapped out his password, and his PC screen unlocked.

'You better get stuck into that hit and run.'

'Sure – what are you going to do?'

He glanced at his inbox, smiled with satisfaction. 'I'm going to have a look at this: CCTV from the trackside cameras at Brixton, courtesy of the RAIB.' He plucked a sheet of A4 from a packet of printer paper, rummaged around his desk until he found a pen. 'Because sometimes to draw a picture, you really *do* have to draw a picture . . .'

As she stared at him with bemusement, a rare grin began to spread across his face.

Isiah Simms walked across the Hope Estate, catching a whiff in the wind of his own sweat mixed with motor oil. As was his habit, he'd have a shower when he got home, a fresh change of clothes before settling down for the evening.

His conversation with Finn earlier was still troubling him. He stopped and looked up at Ashbank Tower. He could remember arriving back here after his wedding, carrying his new wife over the threshold. He'd loved living here then. Strange how the same surroundings now felt so ominous, when once they'd been so welcoming. Bricks and mortar don't change though, it's the people who live inside, he thought. Or maybe it was just him; he really couldn't tell any more.

'Mr Simms?'

He turned and saw Jade walking towards him.

'I was just on my way to your flat to see you, I was hoping you'd be in.' He didn't reply, slightly thrown as she caught up with him. 'Are you okay?' she said, smiling that same big smile she'd given him when they'd first met. It was infectious and he couldn't help but return it.

'I've spoken to Hayden. He's open to talking with you. Tonight, if you're free?'

Isiah nodded. He'd been thinking about nothing else all day, the desire to reach out to his son still tempered by his pride. He wanted to do this, he just didn't know *how* yet.

239

'You're both as bad as each other,' said Jade, misunderstanding his muted response. 'You can both stand looking at one another in silence if you like, or you can actually try talking.'

Isiah's smile returned. A gentle warmth to it this time.

'Like father, like son, I suppose?'

'Totally. He'll be here at 9 p.m.' She pointed to a cluster of benches in the centre of the forecourt. 'By those benches – if you want to go ahead.'

Isiah nodded.

'Okay,' he said. 'Okay.' He repeated the word quietly almost for his own benefit. And then he continued on his way.

Jade watched as Isiah walked away, waiting until he was out of sight before pulling out her phone and sending a text. The reply came back almost instantly.

Meet me at my place. 15 mins.

A quarter of an hour later Jade was sitting in a small flat in one of the backstreets on the western side of the Hope Estate. Superficially its layout mirrored the one Hayden lived in. There the similarity ended. This wasn't someone's home; more a place its occupant used to eat, sleep and defecate in. It smelt of body odour and the stale fruity perfume of a vape pen. Used pizza boxes lay discarded on the floor, together with shoes, shopping bags and random dumbbells. A short, stocky white man was sitting with her on a battered leather sofa.

'What time tonight?' said Andy.

'Nine.'

'Good – you've done the right thing.'

She looked uncertain.

'Have I though?'

'Hayden's not well – you know it and I know it. So it's good you told me about it. He's better off out of it. Let him make peace with his dad. I'll do what needs to be done.'

He opened his jacket a little and Jade saw the black metallic handle of a gun. His mouth widened into a crooked smile.

32

'Shit,' said Finn, staring down a large green iguanodon. It felt like months had passed since he was last in Crystal Palace, but it'd only been a week. He was walking up through the dinosaur park to the railway station at the top of the small hill which overlooked it. Passing a park bench, his eye had been drawn to a discarded copy of the *Evening Standard*. Its front-page splash read:

LEAH COPS INVESTIGATE SECOND KILLING

The small slip he'd made on the phone had indeed been picked up on. Finn knew if queried he could bluff it out – another uniform PC somewhere who must have said too much again. But he also knew by his own standards it was a bad error. Instead of leading the wolves away from Jo, he'd clumsily pointed them towards her.

As he turned the corner he saw the small gaggle of journalists and cameramen who'd gathered for the reconstruction of Leah Suleman's last moments. At least he'd have the chance now to apply some damage control, he thought.

Standing by the station entrance was Sami Dattani, together with a woman Finn just about recognised as Lauren Oxley, one of the uniform PCs. She was dressed in the same clothes Leah had been wearing on the night of her death and was also sporting an ill-fitting wig. A similar height and build, from a distance Oxley presented a reasonable silhouette of the woman whose steps she was about to retrace. With Lauren and Sami was a man Finn recognised as one of the Cedar House cleaners. He was wearing Karl's signature designer suit, and Finn briefly felt the hairs on the back of his neck rise as father and daughter stood reunited before him. Just seven days ago, Karl and Leah had simply been meeting for a meal – now the whole country knew their names.

'Everything under control, Sami?'

'This bit is – but you're going to have your hands full.' Dattani nodded at the journalists. 'I don't think they're that interested in these two any more. You've seen the *Standard*, I take it?' Finn nodded and watched as a short, pink-faced man laughed raucously with one of the cameramen. 'How the fuck did they get hold of that?' asked Sami.

'Usual way, I expect – someone somewhere hasn't engaged their brain,' muttered Finn. He was grateful when the pink-faced man pointed at something and the cameraman suddenly started scrambling into action. Finn turned to see what had caught their attention. Walking towards them was a hooded figure in a dark metallic blue coat. There was no face, just an oval mirror where the features should be. The overall impression was of something not entirely human.

'Jesus,' said Finn involuntarily. Even though he was well aware of the killer's appearance, actually seeing it in front of him now was another thing altogether. Reflected in the mask were the watching press corps, and it struck him that's how Karl and Jo would have seen themselves. Leah and Jamie too – the last faces they saw as they died their own, screaming back at them.

'This isn't just about concealing his identity, it's a costume,' he said, as much to himself as to Dattani. 'He's thought about how he wants to look. The blank face – it's about dispensing justice without emotion.'

'It's also fucking horrible,' said Dattani under his breath.

The light was fading fast and Finn checked his watch – it was just gone seven. The conditions were now exactly as they'd been one week before.

'What have you got planned?' he said to Dattani.

'Our own photographer's here now, so I think we can start.' He pointed at the ersatz Karl and Leah. 'We're just going to get these two to walk down from the station to the crime scene. We'll also retrace the distance we think Karl covered before he turned back.'

'And him?' Finn motioned at the masked figure.

'They can grab some pictures and then we'll take him to the street outside where the CCTV cameras picked him up.'

Finn nodded. There'd been a steady stream of people exiting the station while they'd been talking. Some, tired after a long day, kept their heads down as they passed, while others stopped to see what was going on. A large percentage of them would probably be regular commuters at this time. There was a high chance some would have seen Karl arriving, been on the same train even.

'Detective Inspector Finn?'

He turned and found himself facing a stern young woman with short dark hair.

'I'm Nicky Paige, I'm—'

'I know who you are,' said Finn. 'You're the reporter who interviewed Karl Suleman the day he died.'

He said the words without emotion. She'd just been doing her job, he understood that. He didn't blame her for Karl's death either – if anything he blamed himself for not preventing the interview in the first place. But it didn't hurt to repeat the fact of it; he liked to think it would give her pause for thought at least. But if that was the case, she wasn't showing it.

244

'Can you confirm you're linking this investigation with the murder of Jamie Baker in Penge last Monday?'

The other reporters were now flocking around, thrusting iPhones and microphones under his nose while cameras were being hoisted on to shoulders. He'd intended to hold a brief Q&A after the reconstruction, but it looked like that was happening now whether he liked it or not. He wasn't too displeased – it was a chance to regain some control after his earlier slip and there wasn't much point in hiding the connection any more.

'Yes, we're formally linking the murder in Penge with the tragic death of Leah Suleman here last Friday night. Their families are currently being supported by specialist officers. Our investigation's still in its early stages and at this time we're pursuing a number of leads to try to establish exactly what chain of events led to these two people losing their lives.'

'Can you confirm too that the partner of the second victim also left the scene?' shouted the pink-faced reporter he'd seen earlier.

'At this point I'd rather not comment on specifics.'

'But is it true he made the second victim choose – like Karl Suleman?' said Paige.

'Like I say, I'd prefer not to comment.'

'That's not a denial then?'

'We're here today to see if anyone can remember anything which can help us with our investigation. The smallest thing could prove crucial, even if it may seem insignificant.'

'But it's a second random attack,' said another reporter. 'How concerned should Londoners be?'

'And what would your advice be to people living in the area?' said another before Finn could answer. The DI paused, deliberately trying to take the heat out of the questions.

'My advice would be to stay vigilant, if you're out and about. Be mindful of your surroundings and—'

'Do you think this might be the work of a serial killer, Detective Inspector?' said a tall blond man, cutting him off. He was young and Finn didn't recognise him, but at least some of the more experienced reporters were rolling their eyes.

Finn controlled himself. He'd handled situations like this many times before. But it was a sign of how much the Sulemans' fate still remained part of the national conversation. He'd heard his own officers discussing what they'd have done in the same position as Karl or Jo and he imagined that conversation had been replicated in homes and workplaces around the country. It was something he didn't want to feed, aware it might well be part of the killer's agenda.

'We're completing a detailed review of all the facts available so far, and it would be wrong to speculate about the killer's motives until an arrest is made.' He fashioned a pleasant smile and turned to Dattani. 'Which of course brings us to the reason why we're here.'

The reconstruction itself was a straightforward affair. Finn didn't hang around once it was over – they'd got their pound of flesh from him. Back at Cedar House, he was working late again when Skegman caught up with him.

'There's been another one, Alex.'

'Another what?' said Finn without turning.

'My counterpart at Greater Manchester Police has just been on the phone. A young couple with a pram in Salford were stopped by a man in a mask.'

Finn wheeled round in astonishment. It felt like everything he thought he understood about this investigation had just instantly been reduced to rubble.

'The attacker told the mother to go or he'd stab her child. Strung it out apparently, put the blade to the baby's forehead while he made her think about it.'

'Jesus,' said Finn.

'She refused, and her partner tried to take the knife off him. He's now in hospital in a critical condition.' Skegman held up a hand. 'It's not our man – they've made an arrest. Someone well known to them up there, apparently.'

'A copycat?'

Skegman nodded.

'The guy they've got in custody claims his mate put him up to it – filmed the whole thing to stick up on YouTube. They're investigating.'

'If we're not careful, this might catch on,' said Finn.

'I agree – we could use an arrest to nip it in the bud. God forbid there's another attack. Did the reconstruction prompt anything?'

'Yes, we've had a few calls, Sami's sifting through them now.'

'And the hit and run?'

'Paulsen's got a name she thinks might be a fit from Crouch End – she's trying to track them down.'

'Then go home, Alex.'

Finn stopped, stymied in his tracks.

'It's not a request,' continued Skegman. 'You look absolutely shattered. Let's really not have this conversation again – for both our sakes. I don't think I could face it.'

Skegman's expression was more sympathetic than the words sounded, and Finn got the message. One thing was certainly true: he was simply too tired to argue.

It was just before nine when he collapsed into his favourite chair at home. He'd thrown some pasta into a pot, overcooked it and washed the congealed mess down with a glass of two-day-old wine. His stomach felt full, and beyond that he didn't care.

He couldn't shake the conversation in the AA meeting room from his head. It'd been sitting in the back of his mind for a couple of days now. Needless to say he hadn't taken the advice Murray had given him. A man he'd only met for a few minutes seemed to have got the measure of him in a way that others hadn't, and Finn felt a strange guilt at letting him down. He looked across at his sofa, saw for a moment his late wife lounging on it, in a flat she'd never set foot in.

The problem always seemed so simple, that was the absurdity of it – a truth tattooed on the inside of his head.

'For as long as I walk this earth, I will never see her again.'

Over and over it kept coming back to that, like an anchor pulling him back, and no therapist or counsellor could change it. But he'd solve it his way, he thought. Make the time later, think it out – find a solution. That was how he solved most things in life – bigger puzzle boxes than bereavement, too. And it was a question of priorities – he needed to catch this killer before he could grant himself the luxury of fixing himself.

The sudden clarity of the thought gave him a boost. He grabbed his phone and rang Cally Hunter before he could change his mind.

'Finally . . .' came the familiar gravelly voice. He could hear cutlery clinking in the background. 'I was wondering if you were ever going to call. Or whether you were hoping I'd leave you alone.'

'It's not a bad time, is it?'

'Evening service. It's been a decent night though, I'm not complaining. What can I do for you?'

'This is a bit awkward, but I've been thinking a lot about what we talked about the other day. My situation. Your situation too. Why Karin left you those instructions. I understand, I really do. I promise you, no one knew me better than her.'

'But?'

'I do have a problem with my loss and how I'm dealing with it – that much is clear to me.'

'Good,' said Cally cautiously. 'That you recognise it is a healthy thing.'

'And I *will* sort it out. But I need to do it properly – and right now I'm up to my eyes. There's a killer, and I don't think he's finished yet. It's nothing personal, but I just don't have the time for this with you right now.'

There was a long silence.

'It's your life and I can't make you do anything. You're a grown man, after all. But for what it's worth – I think Karin was right about you, Alex. You're making excuses, retreating into yourself, and it won't do you any good in the long run.'

'You're actually the second person to say that to me this week. I won't let it fester, I promise. For Karin's sake,' he said unconvincingly.

'Sure.'

The phone went dead.

33

Mikey was late home for the second time that week. When Isiah questioned him about it, he was evasive and vague. The cheeky boy was becoming an insolent young man and it gave his father a heavy heart. Finn's warning to Isiah earlier was also weighing on his mind. A look of bemusement had spread across his son's face as he tried to explain the need to be careful.

'I don't understand. Who'd want to hurt us?' he'd said.

And that was half the problem – Isiah didn't really know himself. It was probably just a policeman being overcautious. All the same, he shared Finn's concern.

'Humour me. Just for a few days.'

He'd bought a huge bag of fish and chips for dinner, and smiled despite himself at the glee with which his youngest was attacking the feast.

'We should do this more . . .' said Mikey, wiping grease off his chin with the back of his hand. He was rotating at speed between throwing chips into his mouth, checking his phone, and grinning with sheer delight.

Isiah couldn't help but compare the scene with his own childhood dinners around the table. It was all rather different back then, austere occasions which took place at six o'clock every evening on the dot. White lace placemats on a wooden table so polished you could see your reflection. And then there was his mother's cooking. In the bleak landscape of the 1970s, her menu was a spectacular assortment of salt-fish fritters, curried goat, and patties which melted in your mouth. He'd give his right arm for one more taste of her food.

His father wouldn't have tolerated what was going on now though – he'd have probably slapped the boy in front of him by this point. The phone – or indeed any distraction at the table – would have been tossed out of the nearest open window. But times change, and Isiah found his son's obvious pleasure rather endearing. He'd noticed this recently, the slight softening of some long-held attitudes. He wasn't quite sure what he made of it. He'd always been a man of clearly defined principles and ethics. He'd never questioned himself. But now Jade, this young woman who'd chosen to involve herself in his family's business, was making him look at things anew.

Isiah could remember his noble intentions when Hayden was born. The son he'd hoped to raise in his own image. Even after all these years, he didn't quite know how it'd come to this. He was quite sure, deep down, that Hayden possessed a good heart, but Isiah also believed a man was the master of his own house and challenging that was inviolate – a red line. He'd been disrespected by his eldest son and backing down was simply not an option. But straight lines had a tendency to blur. The day Hayden's face was cut open, for example. It'd happened about a year after his son had walked out. Despite this, Isiah had gone straight to the hospital to talk to the doctors as soon as he'd learnt what had happened. He left before his son even knew he was there. To this day he didn't know if Hayden knew that.

As the years went by, it had become clear neither party was interested in a thaw. He'd see Hayden around the estate occasionally, and it hurt like an open wound. It'd taken Jade to truly make him confront his feelings again, and he honestly didn't know how this was going to play out tonight. In truth, he expected the conversation to be short. He expected a row, and he expected things to stay the same.

A single question had been sitting at the back of Hayden's mind for years. If Isiah keeled over one day, would he even go to the funeral? Would he really abandon Mikey in his hour of need, just as Isiah abandoned him once? He simply didn't know, but the thought occasionally pulled at him. He poured himself a glass of chalky tap water, watched it slowly turn transparent while his own expression clouded over with doubt. The flat was silent for a change. He'd got used to his brother's uninvited visits and Jade making herself at home there.

He held out his hand – it was rock solid and he nodded approvingly. So much for stress or trauma or whatever shit it was that cop was trying to sell. He'd just been tired, that's all. There'd been multiple messages from the same guy on his phone warning him of some unspecified danger – just more bullshit. Whatever game the police were playing with him, he wasn't interested.

He looked at the clock on the wall. It was almost time. There were butterflies in his belly, which was unlike him. He'd dealt with scarier situations than this, and instinctively felt for the scar on his cheek. Downing the rest of the water, he tried calling Jade. It went straight to answerphone and he didn't bother leaving a message. She knew where he was going and he was surprised she hadn't been in touch given how important it was to her. He sent a text.

About to go. I'll call u when I'm back. Love u

He grabbed his jacket, checked himself in the mirror and opened the front door. As was his habit now, he carefully glanced to the left and right before leaving. He stepped out on to the walkway and looked down on to the forecourt.

Isiah was already there, sat on one of the benches, illuminated by the full moon above. As if sensing his son's presence, his head jerked up. He was too far away and even in the moonlight it was too dark to make direct eye contact, but it felt as if the world was standing still as they became aware of each other. Hayden felt his hand start to tremble again.

His footsteps echoed as he walked across the concrete to join his father. Isiah was staring ahead impassively. Typical, thought Hayden; he's not going to give a single inch of ground. He sat down on the bench next to him, clutching his phone. There'd been no reply from Jade. The other hand, the errant hand, he kept tucked in his jacket pocket.

'Alright,' he said casually. The word cut through the air like a blade. Slowly the older man turned his head, nodded, said nothing. Like it or not, Hayden knew he'd have to go first.

'So does Mikey know where you are?'

'He always knows where I am.'

'Does he know what you're doing?'

'No.'

The wind blew around them, tossing litter and leaves in the air. Hayden decided to stop dancing.

'What do you want from this, Dad? Why are you even here?'

There was a long pause, but this time when Isiah turned, he looked him straight in the eye.

'Because your friend got through to me.'

'Yeah, well, she has that effect.'

Isiah didn't smile.

'What have you got yourself caught up in, boy?'

'What do you mean?'

'The police say your brother and I are in danger, because of you.'

Hayden rolled his eyes.

'It's nothing – it's bullshit. They're just playing games.'

'Doesn't sound like games. They told me about this fit you had. PTSD, is what they said . . .'

'Which is more bullshit. And it wasn't a fit.'

The older man gave a dismissive wave of his hand. Nothing seemed to have changed, Hayden thought. It would be easy to get up and go, never have to bother with him again. And then he looked at his father's features – close enough to touch for the first time in years – and he found he didn't want to. The feeling surprised him.

'If it's bullshit, show me your hand. Why are you keeping it in your pocket like that,' said Isiah.

Before Hayden could answer, his phone vibrated, the glare of the display distracting them both. Automatically he glanced down and the image on the screen stopped him cold. It was Jade, tearstained and clearly in distress. Blood was dripping from a nasty-looking cut above her eye. The handset buzzed again, a second picture replacing the first. Closer in, this one showed her anguished expression more clearly. There was an ugly smudge of blood on her cheek. Some words flashed up across the screen: 'DO AS YOU'RE TOLD, OR SHE DIES'.

Hayden couldn't quite take it in. Isiah had seen the pictures too, and was wearing the same horrified expression.

'Hayden!'

The shout came from a dark hooded figure striding towards them. Hayden stood and peered, trying to make out a face. As the intruder got closer he could see a mirror-like mask. Just some kid in a Halloween outfit trying to mess with him. But they'd picked the wrong man. He took a step forwards then stopped, the fury dissolving as quickly as it'd formed, a sick feeling in his stomach replacing it instead. There was just enough light to see the figure was holding a gun. With his other hand he seemed to be pulling something out from the folds of his jacket. He threw the object towards Hayden, and

254

there was a clatter on the ground by his feet. In the moonlight he could see the blade of a machete.

'Kill the old man and Jade can go. Or you can both walk away – and she dies. It's your choice.'

The threat was hissed, and Hayden struggled to place it – something almost familiar in its tone. He forced himself to think. This was the guy who'd killed the girl in the park, made that bloke run away. The description from the papers was exactly the same. But why was he here? Why now? And what did he want with them?

'Decide!' yelled the figure.

Slowly Hayden bent down, curling his fingers around the grip of the machete, feeling the heft of the weapon in his hand. There was no way he could or would use this thing on the man behind him – he knew that instantly. He turned and looked at Isiah. They locked eyes and finally there was a genuine understanding between them.

'I'm sorry . . . for all of it,' whispered Hayden.

Isiah nodded, the smallest of movements, and later that would matter.

'*I will cut her fucking throat!*' the figure screamed.

Hayden swivelled back round.

'Don't make me do this. Whatever this is, it's not worth it.'

'Last chance . . .'

And suddenly everything was quite clear to Hayden. There weren't two choices, he reasoned. There really was only one.

With a roar, he charged forwards. The figure wasn't expecting it and took an instinctive step backwards. There was a sound like a thunder crack, deafening in the enclosed space of the forecourt. It stopped Hayden in his tracks, and it took him an instant to realise the gun had actually been fired. He checked, and almost to his own astonishment realised there was no wound, no blood, and that he was okay. The gunman

255

was reeling in front of him now, apparently in shock as well. Just a kid, thought Hayden again, and realised this was his chance. He was about to launch at him with the machete, when he heard a groan from behind. He turned and saw Isiah lying prone on his back. Something dark was pooling beneath him. Instantly Hayden broke off his attack and sprinted back.

'No, no, no,' he said under his breath. He knelt and heard a thick gurgling coming from his father's throat. Helpless, he looked up and waited for the inevitable second shot – but it didn't come. The gunman had gone. He snatched up his phone and quickly dialled 999. As he waited for it to connect, a message flashed up:

What happens next is on you.

34

Paulsen had woken early. She'd come into the living room so as to not wake Nancy. There was a message on her phone from Finn informing her of the shooting on the Hope Estate the previous night. She was struggling to make sense of it – her initial thought was that the use of a gun surely meant it was a different assailant to the one they were hunting. But she was mindful too that Finn had warned them Hayden Simms might be targeted, remembering as well that Skegman hadn't been convinced. Now Isiah Simms was in hospital fighting for his life. Another major incident, not just in the same corner of south-east London, but on that estate too – the eye of the storm. Her concentration wasn't helped by another poor night's sleep. She'd been jumpy since the fake acid attack in the cemetery and was becoming aware it had affected her more than she'd initially realised. There were enough distracting thoughts crashing around her head as it was.

On a whim she texted her father.

Are you up?

It wasn't a complete stab in the dark. He'd always been an early riser, either walking the dogs back when they'd had them, or using the time to get some work done. It wasn't uncommon either to come downstairs in the morning and find him reading a book with a large mug of coffee by his side. A reply came back pleasingly swiftly.

Yes, it's late. Why are you up? x

She smiled, hearing exactly the tone of voice, seeing precisely the gentle smile that accompanied it. Encouraged too by the gentle wit of the words. She rang him, drawing her knees up to her chin on the sofa while she waited for the call to connect.

'This can't be good – is everything okay?' he said.

'I couldn't sleep.'

'And why was that?'

She pondered whether to lie and just chat lightly, simply grateful to hear his voice, or tell the truth and get some much-needed advice.

'I fucked up, Dad.'

The words tumbled out. There was a sigh, a slurp of coffee, the sound telling her exactly where he was and what he was doing.

'Bet you haven't. Bet you just think you did, and you're beating yourself up unnecessarily.'

She told him about Danny Howells. How she'd pursued him on her own. What might have happened. She realised there was also something new as she spoke – a sense of being on a clock, an edge to the conversation because she couldn't be sure how long he'd be present and correct for it. It was a horrible feeling. The new reality.

'Maybe I'm a foolish old man, but let me ask you a question. Have you ever got yourself into a situation where you were out of your depth? I mean, this is the girl the school bullies swerved for their own safety, as I recall.'

Mattie smiled; he wasn't wrong.

'No one's ever laid a hand on me, really. Not until this week.'

'Well, there you are. That tells me you know what you're doing. Have *always* known what you're doing.'

A sudden memory of it again: the metal canister smashing into her temple, blood running down the side of her face.

'Maybe I've just been lucky.'

'Or maybe you should have more faith in your instincts, stop doubting yourself so much. You don't tend to misjudge these moments from what I can see. You think you keep getting yourself into trouble, when actually you have a knack for avoiding it.'

'I lost my temper. I was so angry with this man that I didn't think.'

And that was the heart of it – her temper again. There was a silence. Another slurp of coffee. She could hear him breathing heavily now.

'Dad?'

'I'm sorry, Mathilde. Which man? You'll have to remind me.' The question felt like a physical jolt.

'The man I just told you about – the one in the cemetery.'

Another long silence.

'A cemetery? Why were we talking about graveyards? I'm not dead yet.'

She felt a tear starting to form and tried in vain to quash it.

'Have I told you about this book I'm reading, by the way?' he said with a sudden joviality. 'Jonas recommended it. I usually hate historical fiction, always feels like homework, but this one's a cracker.'

Hayden stood in the hospital corridor like a drunk caught in the middle of a busy dual carriageway. He was looking for somewhere that sold hot food. Not for him, he wasn't even close to hungry, but he'd heard Mikey's stomach rumbling and it'd given him something to do. The clock on the wall was

259

nudging towards 6 a.m., but it felt like he'd been there for half a lifetime.

Croydon's Mayday Hospital was rather cruelly nicknamed the 'May die' by locals. As he watched the harassed staff rushing back and forth, the joke didn't seem very funny. The ambulance he'd called for Isiah only just arrived ahead of the vans containing armed police. There'd been multiple reports of shots fired, and just for once he was happy to see the place flooded with law enforcement. The paramedics had worked furiously on Isiah, stabilising his condition before transferring him to hospital. Hayden had accompanied him before belatedly remembering his little brother, alone at home waiting for his father. He'd told the police officer at the hospital who'd come to take his statement, and a highly distressed Mikey was collected and brought in.

After that, they'd simply sat and waited. Each moment twice as torturous for Hayden, because Jade's fate remained unclear. He hadn't received any new messages, and could only hope the worst hadn't happened. He'd rung Andy and told him about it all. Once his friend got over the shock, he'd started promising hard and swift retribution.

'Just find Jade' was all Hayden could manage in response. Without a clue who was behind this or where she might be, there was little he could do. Leaving Mikey alone was simply not an option either. He felt powerless and beaten. If this was hell, then he'd dragged them all there and now didn't have a clue what to do about it.

Finally, in the last hour had come some relief – Isiah was stable. But that was all they knew. Any immediate threat to his life was over, but the tired-looking doctor who'd informed them stressed he wasn't out of danger yet. So the waiting went on.

'What does stable mean?' Mikey had asked. 'Does that mean he's going to be okay?'

Hayden didn't know, but for now it would have to do.

There was an armed officer guarding Isiah, and a plain-clothed detective with them in the waiting room. He'd given the latter a statement, or *a* version of events anyway – he hadn't mentioned anything about Jade to him. Beyond an ingrained distrust, he didn't have the time to waste. The police would move in slow motion while Andy would already be all over it. Blood had been spilt and now blood needed to be spilt.

Finn had been informed about the shooting shortly after the first 999 call had been received. He was now driving to the Mayday with mounting questions. He'd wanted to go straight to the Hope Estate the previous night, but had been told in no uncertain terms by Skegman to stay away and get some sleep. There hadn't been much chance of that. He'd spent most of the night striding the length of his flat, trying to follow events on his phone. His worst fears over Isiah had come to pass and he'd been furious. Angry with himself for failing to prevent it, livid with Skegman for not listening.

Logic dictated this was the same person who'd murdered Leah in the park and butchered Jamie Baker in his own front room. So why a gun this time? He was certain Hayden had been given a choice and was desperate to speak to him. He felt a step closer to the truth, but was aware it had come at a price. When he thought about Hayden, it was hard not to see the hollowed-out faces of Karl Suleman and Jo Corcoran too.

Jackie Ojo's call as he was parking up at the hospital provided some answers. This time there hadn't been a shortage of witnesses. Residents saw Isiah and Hayden talking together from their windows. They'd also seen the arrival of a dark figure wearing a bizarre mask. The CCTV on the estate was in good working order as well. One of the uniform officers going through the footage had found something and told Ojo, who'd immediately rung Finn.

'The pictures speak for themselves, guv,' said Ojo. 'He was offering them a choice; I'd stake my life on it.'

Finn was now sure of one thing: it was about the train. Everything else – the hit and run, the care home deaths, the potential drug links – had all been false trails. The only consolation was that this time they weren't opening a new murder investigation. Dave McElligott had taken the statement from Hayden at the hospital overnight, but Finn was certain it only told a fraction of the story. Now with Isiah out of danger that was going to have to change.

He was surprised to find Paulsen already waiting for him in the hospital's main reception. She looked absolutely shattered and was sitting with a face like thunder, nursing a cup of coffee. She took a sip from it, winced as if it were neat scotch and glared up at him by way of welcome. There was something about her relentless attitude he almost found endearing.

'Couldn't sleep, so I came straight here,' she said by way of explanation.

He brought her up to speed with what Ojo had told him.

'Another choice then,' said Paulsen, before shaking her head. 'Probably told Hayden to take a hike while he threatened to cut his father's eyeballs out . . . or something.'

'I haven't seen the pictures myself, but Jackie's convinced by them and that's good enough for me. We're trying to establish where the shooter went. I'm hoping there'll be some more witness statements later – sounds like a lot of people saw something this time. Ballistics are down there and the knife we recovered is with forensics.'

'What about the estate? Isiah getting shot – that's going to have some impact,' said Paulsen.

'There's a Section 60 in place for twenty-four hours, which hopefully will give us some breathing space.'

A Section 60 order was routinely used in situations like this. It gave police the power to stop and search anyone within a certain area without requiring reasonable grounds to do so. It was usually used after an act of serious violence, or when there was a genuine fear that something significant was about to happen.

A heavy police presence was one way to try and calm tensions, but it carried its own risks too. The longer the person who shot Isiah Simms was at liberty, the more feelings would be running high and the greater the chance that tinderbox could catch alight. Finn didn't want to think of the consequences if Isiah died.

He turned, and flashed his warrant card at the reception desk. After establishing where Isiah was, the pair started walking down one of the long corridors.

'What I'd like to know is what Hayden and Isiah were even doing,' he said. 'I got the impression there was more chance of Liam and Noel Gallagher having a quiet cup of tea.'

'Their timing was unlucky to say the least,' said Paulsen. 'They decide to have a family reunion for the first time in years, and this happens.'

'You're right. How did the gunman know they'd be meeting? And how did he know where and when? And why the gun this time – it's an escalation from the knife.'

'You haven't mentioned the train yet,' said Paulsen. 'Doesn't this pretty much seal the connection? A third person from the same carriage?'

'You'd think . . .' said Finn.

'So what *is* the connection?'

He shook his head.

'I only wish I knew.'

They turned the corner and found themselves in a secluded waiting area, the rows of moulded green plastic chairs making it look like a rather sparse school assembly. They were greeted immediately by Dave McElligott. There was none of his usual laddish nonsense though. He looked paler than the polished white floors after spending most of the night there. Sitting at the back was Hayden Simms, staring hard into space while his brother dozed on his shoulder.

'How's it been, Dave?' said Finn.

'Isiah came out of surgery around 5 a.m.' McElligott tried and failed to stifle a yawn. 'Sorry. He's still stable but the doctors reckon the next few hours will be key.'

'And those two?'

Hayden had now clocked Finn and Paulsen, recognising them from their previous encounter, and was tracking them across the room with his eyes.

'Good as gold, but I think you're right – I think he's only given up half the story. Given the circumstances I haven't pushed it, though.'

'You did the right thing. Now go and get yourself some sleep. We can pick this up.'

McElligott nodded gratefully and wasted no time in leaving. Finn and Paulsen walked over to the Simms brothers.

'I'm so sorry this happened, Hayden.'

Mikey's eyes opened and he looked up suspiciously at the two detectives. Finn smiled at the boy, but it wasn't returned.

'Mind if we have a chat?' said Finn to Hayden.

'I've already given a statement.'

'All you've done is given us a description of the attacker – and not much more. We've seen the CCTV. We know you spoke to the gunman.'

'H . . . ?' said Mikey uncertainly. Hayden remained impassive.

'We've got a theory,' said Paulsen. 'We think he gave you a

choice to make. Does that ring a bell?' From his reaction, it clearly did. 'What did he ask you to do? To kill Isiah?'

They waited but there was no response. Mikey was looking at his brother intently now too.

'You're not the first person he's done this to, as I'm sure you're aware,' said Finn. 'We just want to find out who he is and why he's doing this. Will you help us?'

There was a buzzing sound and Hayden pulled his phone from his pocket. He read the text on the display, his face still giving nothing away, before slipping the handset back into the folds of his jacket.

'I need to go,' he said slowly. 'Can you look after my brother?'

He rose to his feet and the boy reacted instantly.

'Where are you going, H? You can't leave.'

'He's right. I think you should stay, Hayden. Tell us what this is all about,' said Finn.

Hayden turned to Mikey.

'I'll be back, I promise. But there's something I've got to do.'

'No, no, no . . . you can't go now.'

Mikey looked exactly like what he was: a frightened little boy.

'*You stay here,*' said Hayden. His tone made it clear the instruction wasn't to be argued with.

'Don't go looking for retribution, Hayden. That would be a very bad idea. You could jeopardise the investigation into your father's shooting and put yourself at risk. Help us instead,' said Finn.

Hayden ignored him again, strode instead towards the corridor they'd just walked up.

'If not for us, for your brother . . .' Finn shouted after him.

He took no notice and carried on walking. Finn shook his head.

'Do you want me to go after him?' said Paulsen.

'Why? We can't force him.'

Finn turned his attention to Michael. The boy looked on the brink of tears and it was hard to blame him. He was picking absently now at the peeling plastic on the chair. Finn got a sudden sense that Hayden's presence was the only thing that'd been holding Mikey together.

'It's okay, nobody's going to leave you alone, Michael. Why don't you tell me what's been happening?'

Finn sat down next to him as the boy looked up uncertainly. Paulsen watched Hayden disappearing down the corridor and turned back round in exasperation.

'Give Jackie a call and see if anything else has come up, while me and this young man have a little chat,' said Finn. He smiled pleasantly at her and she rolled her eyes.

Hayden walked out of the hospital doors and into the car park. Finn's parting jibe had hurt. The last thing he'd wanted to do was abandon Mikey while their father was in this state. He'd stayed with his brother through the night because he owed him that, but he'd run out of choices. He pulled out his phone again and re-read the text he'd just received.

You were warned what would happen.

Paulsen had taken the hint and left Finn alone with Mikey. She guessed he was somehow going to try and question him about the train derailment. He'd been in that carriage too, after all. She still couldn't see how it connected or where the anger behind these crimes was coming from. But she understood rage, recognised the smell of it when it was in the air. Whoever was doing this saw themselves not as a villain, but as the hero of their own story. Karl, Jo and Hayden crossed boundaries of gender, race and class, but all had found themselves on the wrong end of the same righteous fury. This was someone whose anger far outweighed their fear. Her phone rang and she saw it was Ojo, the person she guiltily realised she was supposed to be calling.

'Where's the DI – I thought he was with you? I need to talk to him.'

'I think he's illegally interviewing a minor – don't ask.'

'This is important.'

A few moments later Paulsen ran back into the waiting room. Some more people were now dotted around the seats. Finn was sitting, quietly listening as Michael Simms spoke.

'Guv, sorry to interrupt . . .'

He glared up in irritation.

'Can't it wait?'

'Not really – forensics have just pulled a print off that machete. It belongs to an Andy Forbes – lives on the Hope Estate. He's got previous: two convictions for possession of class A drugs with intent to supply.'

Finn seemed to take a second to properly register the information, almost irritated at his lack of recognition.

'*Who?*'

35

They found Andy easily enough, inside a flat on the western side of Ashbank Tower. With enough police already in the area to form a small militia, marshalling a team at short notice wasn't difficult. A gun, a dark blue jacket and the distinctive mirror-like mask were all quickly recovered from the same property. They'd been stuffed into a bag at the back of a cupboard and were now being pored over by the relevant forensic experts. Despite furious denials, Andy was arrested on suspicion of murder and taken straight to Cedar House to be processed and interviewed.

Despite the apparent breakthrough, the mood in the incident room was strangely muted. Finn was making little effort to hide his scepticism.

'None of this makes sense. If it's this guy, I don't get why. What's his motive? I mean, I can see why he might go after Hayden – that's a power grab. But Karl and Jo? Why?'

'Because he's a psycho?' said Sami Dattani. 'Maybe it's as simple as that. Sometimes I think we look too hard.'

'What's that supposed to mean?' said Paulsen.

'That just once in a while it's *exactly* what it looks like.' He tapped the side of his head. 'A nutjob. We don't know his history – what he's seen, what's been done to him. Perhaps the end product of all that is someone who does crazy shit like this, which we then spend half our lives trying to figure out.'

'Sorry, Sami, I think that's bollocks,' said Finn. Whatever theories he'd been privately working up about the train derailment, this arrest drove a tractor straight through them, and he wasn't happy. The fact they might have caught their man was almost secondary to his irritation at the fact he hadn't put the pieces of the puzzle together first.

'Forbes doesn't even match the description of the killer. He's too old, too stocky and I doubt that jacket even fits him.' He was almost spitting the words out.

'Do we know if he was on the train?' asked Paulsen tentatively.

'No. Not as far as I can tell, though the passenger list isn't exhaustive, so who knows.'

'Is there any connection between Andy and the two victims, Leah and Jamie?' said Ojo.

'None. Or at least none that we've found. What do we know about him anyway?' said Finn.

'Neighbours are telling us he and Hayden were joined at the hip. They often saw them around together,' Ojo replied.

'So maybe Andy ordered it then?' said Paulsen. 'If they were using kids to move drugs and money around, maybe he got one of them to do it for him?'

'No,' said Finn, shaking his head. 'What happened was too personal. Whoever did this was a cold-blooded killer, not a child press-ganged into it. None of this makes *any* sense.'

He looked around the room balefully, and right there and then no one had an answer for him.

In the interview room Andy was aggressive and jumpy, frequently ignoring the duty solicitor's attempts to calm him. He denied shooting Isiah the previous night, was vague about his whereabouts and dismissed any suggestion that he'd put someone up to do it.

'For the benefit of the recording, I'm showing the suspect four photographs,' said Finn.

He carefully spread the A4-sized images out in front of him.

'Do you recognise any of these people?'

Andy took a cursory look at the pictures and shook his head with genuine bewilderment. Finn asked him where he was at the time of each murder.

'Last Friday week I was out. On the Monday night, I was at home, chilling.'

'Out where on the Friday? Just after seven o'clock?'

'I don't know. Seeing people.'

'Do you understand the seriousness of this? Two of these people were murdered,' said Finn. He pointed at the pictures of Leah and Jamie. 'Stabbed to death by someone wearing a jacket and mask matching the ones we found in your flat. We also found a gun in your flat, the morning after a shooting smack in the middle of the estate. We've got ballistics and forensic officers working on these items right now, trying to identify fibres, DNA and fingerprints. We've already found your fingerprints on the machete. If you committed or ordered these murders we'll find out, we'll make the case in court. Your life – as you know it to be – will be over.'

'I didn't kill anyone. That stuff isn't mine and I don't know how it got into my flat.' He looked at them both with a depth that hadn't been there before. 'You *know* it.'

He slammed his fist down on the table, and the uniform officer standing by the door took a step forwards. Finn waved him back.

'You've never seen that jacket before? Or the mask?' said Paulsen.

The solicitor whispered forcefully in Andy's ear.

'No comment.'

270

'What about the gun – is that yours?'

'No comment.'

'How did your fingerprints come to be on the machete we found?'

'No comment.'

'Did you intend to shoot Isiah last night, or was that an accident? Was it Hayden you were after?'

'Neither, because I wasn't there.' He held up a hand before his solicitor could interrupt. 'You don't know me and Hayden, how far we go back. He's my brother – I'd never hurt him. Or his old man.'

'So where were you then?' said Paulsen.

'Out. With mates – I don't take notice what time it is.' He stopped to think. Really think about it this time. 'I was eating about nine. The McDonald's in Forest Hill. On the high street.' A look of dawning realisation spread across his features. 'They've got cameras in there – I've seen them.' He laughed, the dark clouds suddenly dispersing. 'Go and look for yourselves. I'll be there, eating a Big Mac. Fuck you. Fuck you both.'

He sat back, crossed his arms and smirked.

'Doesn't mean you weren't behind any of this. That you didn't order it,' said Finn. Andy's face hardened again and he pointed at the photographs. 'I don't know these people. I don't *care* about them – I didn't kill any of them.'

'I believe him,' said Finn afterwards. They were in Skegman's office trying to bring the strands together. The mood was one of frustration, the problem like a barrel with three holes and two corks. Whenever they found a potential answer to one part of it, more questions seemed to leak from elsewhere.

'Why?' said Skegman.

'I don't think he's our killer. He simply doesn't match the description or possess a motive. And probably has an alibi.'

Paulsen nodded in agreement.

'So is he protecting someone?' said Skegman.

Finn sucked his teeth.

'That's more difficult to determine. I can't tell you defini-tively that he isn't, but I'd need a lot of convincing . . .'

'Is this about that bloody train again?'

Finn smiled politely.

'No. Andy swears he wasn't on it and reckons he can prove it. I did ask, in case you're wondering.'

Skegman opened out his hands.

'So?'

'Here's my problem. These crimes are vindictive. This is someone wanting to make their victims suffer, taunting them in order to pour salt into their wounds. What they did to the Sulemans – that wasn't just a murder, it was a *project*. The killer relished it. The choices these people were offered – if Andy was driving it he'd want to be there, to see it for himself.'

'Are we saying someone's set him up then?' said Skegman.

'Logically, yes,' replied Finn. 'My guess is we'll find Andy's DNA and fingerprints all over the jacket and mask. How's Isiah, by the way?'

'I just rang the hospital – no change,' said Ojo. 'Someone's going to have to talk to Michael Simms at some point. He lives alone with his dad. We'll need emergency foster care for him.' Another DC from the team was currently with Mikey at the hospital, but Ojo was thinking further down the line.

'He does have a brother,' said Finn.

'And where is Hayden right now?' said Skegman.

'He ran off. I'm not too worried though. It's not like he's going to go very far, he'll have to come back for his brother. I'd rather talk to him when he's cooled down.'

'What about your other lines of enquiry – the hit and run involving Karl?'

Paulsen reached for some notes in a sheaf on her lap.

'There's one unsolved collision that broadly fits the dates, time and location which Claire gave me. It took place close to midnight on Salisbury Avenue, Crouch End on the seventeenth of June 1998. The victim's name was Keith Redmond – he was left with life-changing injuries, and they never traced the driver. Thing is, Keith died seven years ago. His mother died two years later, and there's no surviving family. If this is revenge for that, I don't know who'd be behind it.'

Skegman sighed.

'And Jo Corcoran and the care home?'

'Sami hasn't found anything else. She wasn't directly linked to any of the deaths. There's a suggestion she turned a blind eye to a few things, but there were others who were accused of much more – far more obvious targets if that was your motive,' said Finn.

Skegman wrung his hands.

'So tell me, Alex, where is this investigation going?'

'Back to where it was always going to go.'

'Let me guess – the fucking train.'

Finn smiled and produced a sheet of A4 from his inside pocket on which he'd sketched something out with a Sharpie. It looked from a distance like a child's picture you'd see pinned on a fridge door.

'Thanks to the RAIB, statements taken on the day by transport police, and some phoning around, I've managed to build a picture not just of who was on the carriage that derailed, but very specifically where they were sitting.' He held up the picture, which showed two banks of seats divided by an aisle. 'Karl Suleman, Jo Corcoran and Hayden Simms weren't all just in the same carriage, they were all sitting in the same group of seats. I think something very specific happened in the few minutes between the derailment and the evacuation of that train. Something that has cost three people their lives.'

He looked around the room. Skegman was frowning hard, his beady eyes concentrating fiercely. Nobody was treating the theory as just a coincidence now.

'I'm not pretending I've got the answer,' said Finn. 'But in my opinion, there is a direct link between that carriage and the Hope Estate. When we find out what it is, we're halfway there.' He continued. 'There's more. Joyce Knolls was sitting in the same group of seats too, along with Hannah Knolls and her brother Anthony.'

Skegman turned to Paulsen. 'What did Hannah say to you?' he asked with a new urgency.

Paulsen shrugged.

'Same as everyone else – that it was chaotic, but it quickly settled down.'

'And Joyce was the woman who had the stroke?' said Ojo.

'Yes,' said Finn. 'They were one side of the aisle with Karl. Jo was by the window on the other side. There was a schoolgirl called Stella Galloway, but she'd moved to the doors by the time the accident happened. Opposite Jo were two students from SOAS: Amir Ansari and Haroon Siddiqui. In the imme-diate aftermath people thought it was a terror attack, started panicking and pointing the finger at them. It sounds like things got a bit stupid for a while. In fact, they helped to calm it down. I've got eyewitnesses who saw them helping Joyce off the train just before she suffered her stroke.'

'Have you spoken to either of them?' said Skegman.

'Briefly on the phone. They corroborated what everyone else has described. But they saw Joyce on the floor of the carriage after everyone had got off. Nobody else has mentioned that – it's a small discrepancy but I'd like to follow up on it. Everything that happened at that point I think might be important.'

'When I spoke to Hannah, I also left a message with her brother – I'll chase him up,' said Paulsen.

'Do it – I want to talk to as many people who were on that carriage as possible,' said Finn.

'And Andy Forbes?' said Skegman.

'Let's see what the CCTV at the McDonald's in Forest Hill shows. We've still got plenty of time before we have to kick him loose. You're all focusing on who the killer is, but I'll say it one more time: it's about the *why*.'

36

In the end they tracked Tony Knolls down at the gym in Bromley where he worked as a part-time fitness instructor. Finn and Paulsen waited for him in a small cafe area close to the front desk. It was like watching a strange game of before and after, Paulsen thought. Smiling, happy people bouncing in – sweaty, exhausted ones passing them on the way out. When Hannah Knolls' little brother finally emerged, freshly showered from the changing rooms, she immediately noticed the family resemblance. He was a clean-cut young man in his late teens with closely cropped black hair. As they made their introductions, she noticed Finn was also studying him intently.

'So what's this all about? I thought they'd investigated the thing with the train?' said Tony.

'It's nothing to be suspicious of,' said Finn. 'It's just come up as part of something else. It would really help if you could tell us what happened though, in your words.'

Tony looked at him warily.

'You want me to relive the morning my mum had a stroke?'

'Actually, it's the bit before then I'm interested in. But you don't have to talk about anything that makes you feel uncomfortable.'

Tony considered it.

'Okay. My sister's probably told you this already, but we always used to take Mum up to London for a show after

Christmas. She loved musicals, especially at that time of year. Anyway, we were sitting on the train—'

'Sorry to interrupt,' said Finn, cutting in abruptly. 'But to be specific – your sister *wasn't* sitting, was she? Not at the moment it derailed.' He consulted his notes. 'She was actually by the doors at that point, as I understand it?'

Paulsen raised an eyebrow. Even she hadn't realised how much research Finn had done on this. At least she now knew what he'd been doing with those early starts. He was projecting a warm and reassuring front for Tony, but she knew him well enough to know something was up. There'd been an intensity to him from the moment he'd laid eyes on the young man – she could hear it in his voice too.

'Yeah, that's right, she was by the doors,' said Tony. 'How could you know that?'

Finn checked his notes again.

'That's what Hannah told the British Transport Police in her statement . . .' he shuffled his papers, 'and the two students from SOAS corroborated it when I spoke to them on the phone.'

Tony looked slightly taken aback at the level of detail.

'Yeah, she got up to chuck a water bottle in one of the bins. Everything happened really fast. It was scary, like a giant hand reached down and shook the whole carriage.'

Finn smiled but his jaw tightened briefly too, and that's when Paulsen realised that he didn't just have a vague suspicion any more – there was something much more solid going through his mind. She felt her own pulse quicken in tandem.

'There was this screech, like a million fingers coming down a blackboard,' Tony continued, 'and then a huge bang. I was thrown to the ground. Mum got tipped forwards on to her feet. Then there was a lot of shouting and screaming. These guys in robes, the two students, I think?' Finn nodded quickly in confirmation. 'People were blaming them. They were shouting back as well, holding their hands out to show they weren't carrying anything. Then everyone bundled for the doors.'

'And where was your mother at that point?' said Finn. Paulsen could hear the increasing urgency in his voice.

'I couldn't really see her. This man next to me got in the way . . .'

Finn didn't need to glance at his notes this time.

'Karl Suleman.'

Tony looked at Finn vaguely, not apparently recognising the name.

'That's when I noticed I'd cut my head. It was only small but it was bleeding. One of the two guys with beards came over and asked if I was alright. Then I saw Mum on the ground. The other man, the first guy's friend, helped her up. Hannah was there by that point.'

Finn was scribbling all this down at speed in his pocketbook. Paulsen was listening, still not quite understanding what Finn was seeing.

'Where was everybody else at that moment?'

'Trying to get out. Like I say, there'd been this huge scrum for the doors. They were all trying to get off.'

'But to be clear, at that point, you're still by your seat. Your mother's on the ground in the aisle. The two students are helping the pair of you – and Hannah has come down the carriage from the doors to re-join you?'

Finn spoke slowly, making sure to emphasise each statement carefully, like bullet points.

'Yes . . . that's it exactly. But what is it you want me to say? I told the police all this in January.'

Finn was nodding furiously.

'I'm trying to build a picture of exactly what was happening as close to real time as I can. You said your mother was thrown from her seat on to her feet, then shortly afterwards you saw her on the ground. Did you get a sense of *how* that happened? Did she fall? Or might she have been pushed?'

Tony looked bemused.

'I didn't see. She was quite frail, so I assumed she must have fell in the confusion. The train wasn't exactly stable.'

'If you don't mind me saying, why would you assume that – if you didn't see?' said Finn, leaning in now.

Paulsen was still trying to second-guess him. Was Tony a suspect? Was that where this was going? Physically it was credible – he was about the right height and age.

'Do you mind me asking why all this is so important?' said Tony.

'Because I think I'm starting to understand what might have happened,' Finn said.

'I don't suppose you feel like sharing?' said Paulsen.

'Apart from the stroke, did your mother sustain any other injuries that morning?' said Finn, ignoring her.

'Yeah, some bad bruising.'

'Where exactly?'

'All over – her chest, legs, side of her face. We assumed it was from the tumble she took.'

Tony's phone lit up for a moment as a text arrived. He glanced down automatically.

'Sorry, I should have turned this off.'

Finn was also staring at the device now.

'Do you mind?' he said, holding out his hand. Tony looked confused.

'It's just my boss. She wants to know when you're going to be finished with me.'

'That's fine, I'm not interested in the message,' Finn said. Tony shrugged and passed him the phone. Finn looked closely at the screen. The wallpaper was a picture of Tony with his mother and sister, all of them laughing in happier times.

279

'How close would you say your sister and your mother were?' he said.

'Very. Didn't you talk to Hannah already though?'

Paulsen nodded.

'I thought you seemed familiar,' said Finn quietly, looking at the screen.

'I don't understand,' said Tony.

Finn finally looked up.

'I think I've already met your sister. Except she wasn't calling herself Hannah. She told me her name was Jade.'

37

Four Months Ago

He used to love the snow when he was a kid, thought Karl Suleman. Tobogganing in the park, building snowmen in the backyard. Now the stuff was just a pain. His train was already late, the wrong kind of snow, doubtless – too white and cold for them, they'd probably say. As he looked down the tracks there was no sign of the damned thing. The electronic board above his head, still lying about its impending arrival. He retreated into his phone along with the rest of the waiting commuters. There was a WhatsApp message he'd missed from Leah.

> Katie spent Xmas in Tromso – says it's amazing!!! We have to go one year!! ☺

The hint of a smile crossed his face. He didn't even know who Katie was.

A good nine minutes after its scheduled arrival the train finally crawled into view like an apologetic slug. As it came to a halt, he found he was standing on the wrong part of the platform, caught between two carriages. He swore under his breath, adrift as the scrum converged on the doors. When he did finally board he stepped straight into a puddle of muddy slush. He brushed the freezing mush off his shiny Hugo Boss shoes with his fingers, then peered around hopefully for a seat.

281

It looked unlikely, the train was rammed – standing room only with the usual cluster of people by the doors. He squinted down the carriage and could just about see a free rectangle of blue upholstery at the end. He made a beeline for it, stepping through an obstacle course of outstretched legs and stray bags.

Two men with beards wearing robes were sat engrossed in conversation. A woman in a nurse's uniform was opposite by the window, talking loudly into her mobile with a strong Belfast accent. A moody-looking schoolgirl was sitting next to her with a pair of ear pods in. On the other side of the aisle was the vacant seat he'd spotted. He walked across and planted himself down. There was a family of three sitting next to him – a young man and woman together with their mother. She smiled politely at him and her son made a fuss of moving his bag to free up some leg space. He could feel the cold water soaking into his socks now. Some mornings were just more aggravation than they were worth.

'You've got to have them out, Jamie. If that's what the dentist is telling you . . .' Jo Corcoran stopped, looked at the snow-blanketed gardens whizzing past, exhaled in frustration as he argued back, then resumed. 'They're just a pair of wisdom teeth, don't be such a big baby. And there's no need to pay through the nose, you can get them done for free on the NHS.' There was some more resistance from the voice on the other end. Jo looked sideways at the schoolgirl next to her and rolled her eyes, but the girl looked away, pretending she hadn't noticed. 'We'll talk about it tonight. What time do you think you'll be home?' She listened as he explained. 'No need to give me chapter and verse, just give me a time . . . okay, seven? Perfect. See you then. Love you.'

Jo tucked her phone inside her bag and looked around as if suddenly aware she'd been speaking too loudly. There were two men with long beards talking to each other who didn't seem bothered. The schoolgirl was now sitting eyes closed, lost in music. Across the aisle a grumpy-looking man in a sharp suit and designer raincoat was squeezing himself into a spare seat. She caught his eye for a moment – he was giving her a filthy look. She returned it and looked away. So she'd made a loud phone call – big deal. His precious ears would survive another ten minutes before the train finally heaved into Victoria.

'What's wrong with my clothes?' said Mikey. He and Hayden were standing by the doors of the packed carriage, talking across a man with bulky headphones whose face was buried in a copy of the *Metro*.

'What's right with them? You're letting Dad dress you. It's not cool. It's a long way from cool,' said Hayden. 'But don't worry, I'm going to sort you out today.'

'Can't we sit down?'

His tone was full-on whiny, his face screwed up as if they were standing in a field of manure. It was a reminder to Hayden that for all his little brother's quick wits and smart mouth, he was still just a kid.

'Train's full, what do you want me to do?' Mikey rolled his eyes and turned his head sulkily towards the doors. 'Come on then, let's walk. There might be some seats up the front.'

The boy turned and grinned again. They went to the end of the carriage and through the doors into the next one, which wasn't any better. They moved on again to the front carriage, but it was standing room only there as well. Hayden shrugged.

'It's not far now. I'll buy you a Maccy D's when we get into London.'

'Now you're talking.'

Hayden was pleased to see the brief flash of petulance had passed. The boy pulled out his phone and started playing a game. Hayden glanced around, looked at the faces of the commuters and briefly wondered about the lives they were all living. He tried to imagine himself in a nine-to-five job and couldn't, a world he never wanted to know.

A schoolgirl at the far end of the carriage rose and walked over to the doors, freeing up a seat. Hayden decided to teach his brother a lesson.

'Wait here, I'll be back in a minute,' he said casually.

Mikey nodded, still engrossed in his phone. Hayden grinned as he sat down. The nurse next to him squeezed herself closer to the window to give him a few extra millimetres of space. Mikey was glaring down the aisle at him as he finally cottoned on. Hayden raised a hand and gave him a little wave. Ten minutes on his feet wouldn't kill him.

Hannah Knolls looked out of the train window and watched the rain pockmark the snowy rooftops and gardens. Weather like this always reminded her of her father. He'd been a man who enjoyed a drink. And when he was drunk he became someone else. He'd never been physical with his kids though; it was always Mum he turned on. Even as a child Hannah could see how much he seemed to actively enjoy hurting her – the small invented reasons he'd use as a pretext. And then it had ended suddenly and mercifully on a cold and snowy night just before Christmas. He'd fallen down a flight of stairs, the whisky bottle he'd been holding shattering under his weight. They'd found him the next morning with a shard of glass embedded in his abdomen. He'd bled out slowly, alone and in agony. Yes, there was a definite reason Hannah liked this time of year.

It'd been their mother who'd raised them after that. She'd emerged from under the shadow of her husband and slowly blossomed. You could hear it in her laugh, Hannah always thought. The relaxed expression of pleasure when she enjoyed something now was a world away from that timid, mousy noise she used to try and pacify him with. But she was beginning to look her age, and there was a sense they needed to wrap her up in cotton wool a little. She'd been looking forward to today though, even if her taste in musicals was rather conservative.

'So it's not *The Wizard of Oz* then?' she said, as Tony gave an exaggerated eye-roll.

'No, Mum, as I've already told you. It's sort of set *before* the film.'

'And the witch isn't bad any more?'

'No – that's the whole point.'

'It sounds silly.'

'It'll make sense when you see it, I promise,' said Hannah, smiling at her bemusement.

'Isn't *Fiddler on the Roof* on somewhere? I like *Fiddler on the Roof.*'

Tony and Hannah exchanged glances, shaking their heads with a mock 'what can you do'. Hannah reached down into her bag, grabbed a bottle of water and took a deep sip. A businessman in expensive clothes was bagging the empty seat next to Tony, who was now hastily moving his backpack out of the way to accommodate him. The guy seemed to be in a foul mood, randomly shooting her brother a filthy look as he sat down. The Irish nurse on the other side of the aisle who'd been talking loudly into her phone also caught a glare.

It seemed to be infectious; the sullen-looking schoolgirl sat opposite the two men in robes gave *them* a dirty look, grabbed her bag and went to stand by the doors. Charming, thought Hannah. A small slice of everyday racism if she wasn't mistaken, but at least the men seemed too engrossed in conversation to notice. She drained her water and looked around for a spot to dump the bottle, but couldn't see anywhere. A muscular young black man was taking the newly vacated seat and smirking at a friend further down the carriage. Hannah rose, walked down to the doors and dropped the bottle into a bin. She turned, and the world changed.

What happened next seemed to take place in slow motion. There was a loud screech of iron on iron; the train was braking hard and she felt her breakfast buffeting around her stomach. This wasn't normal though. The train was howling as its driver tried to bring it under control. The standing passengers were toppling into each other like bowling pins. Tree branches were smashing loudly against the side of the carriage – *thud, thud, thud* and then a thump – an impact of some sort. Hannah let out an involuntary scream. Now the carriage was twisting too, shaking with the sort of turbulence you'd expect on a plane. Bags were falling from the overhead shelves, and she saw a man in a seat thrown forwards, smashing his jaw into an armrest, a sudden spray of blood exploding upwards. The train was almost bouncing now at a diagonal. People were screaming, aware that something extraordinary was happening, something utterly terrifying. Hannah's heart was pounding with fear. A pane of glass shattered, a tree branch protruding through it, and still the train seemed to be careering on. Until finally it stopped.

'What the fuck just happened' was her first thought. Mum and Tony were her second. The way back to them at the end of the aisle was blocked by the mass of bodies who'd either fallen or been thrown from their seats. She levered herself to her feet and could hear angry shouting now, more screaming. But as far she could see nobody was too seriously injured, even the man who'd hurt his chin.

'Mum . . .' she said out loud, almost instinctively.

She looked up and, through the gaps, saw her mother at the far end. There was no way through to her, and she found herself pushed to the ground again as someone tried to get to the emergency lever.

Joyce Knolls was standing, terrified and confused. The businessman who'd been sitting next to her forced his way past, shoving her out of the way with his hand. She stumbled and fell across the aisle, smashing her head into the metal frame of one of the seats. Hannah screamed and tried to rise to her feet again, but there were too many people blocking her. Now she could see the uniform of the nurse who'd been sitting in the far corner. The woman made no effort to help her mother up, stepping instead across her prone body, joining the melee heading for the doors.

'*No!*' yelled Hannah, helplessly. She could hear shouting somewhere – a row of some sort. All she could see now were her mum's legs on the ground, twisted at an angle. She pulled herself up again, pressed her back against the glass partition as people converged on the doors. With a surge of strength, she forced her way past and made it through into the aisle. The big young guy at the back pushed one of the men in robes out of the way, his face wild-eyed and feral. His huge, heavy-booted foot came down on Joyce Knolls' head; a second plunged into her chest as he trampled across her torso. They looked like the kind of boots a soldier would wear, crashing down with pneumatic strength on the frail bone and flesh beneath. For a split second Hannah found herself directly in front of him, but he didn't seem to even see her. His eyes were fixed only on the doors.

It had all taken place in seconds. But she would remember those faces: the businessman who pushed her mother off her feet; the nurse who stepped across and didn't help; the young man who stamped on her head and chest like so much dirt on the ground. The people who broke her.

38

He'd picked his victim carefully; Hayden knew the man was weak. He'd seen him dealing over the years and had never liked him. After the gang who ran the Hope Estate were smashed apart by the police raids he'd transferred his allegiances to another group, like a footballer changing clubs. Except this wasn't sport as far as Hayden was concerned.

'Come on, H, we're all just trying to make a living. What's wrong with that?' he was saying, with just enough fear in his eyes.

'Where's Gary Ritchie right now?'

Ritchie was the nominal leader of the Thornton Boys. He was the only person Hayden could think might be behind all of this. With Andy seemingly off-grid, he was sick of feeling powerless.

'I don't know – it's not like he checks in with me.'

'You know how to find him though; you work for him.'

Hayden slapped his face. It was a deliberate move, designed to shock and humiliate rather than hurt. It got the response he was hoping for.

'He doesn't tell me where he goes, why would he?'

They were interrupted by Hayden's phone. Not the normal ringtone but the distinctive one he used for Jade. He snatched an arm out, held the dealer tightly by the shoulder and took the call.

'Hayden . . .'

Relief coursed through him. She sounded distressed, like she'd been crying. It didn't matter – to hear her voice again meant everything.

'Where are you?' he asked.

'I've been so scared.'

'What happened – are you okay?'

'I am now. It was Andy. He said he wanted to help you, but then he . . .'

She broke off, upset. It took a moment for her words to penetrate.

'What do you mean, it was Andy?'

'He had a gun, said you were weak for not fighting back against these other guys – that you needed to be taught a lesson.'

It felt like a punch to the solar plexus. He considered Andy family; they went back years, had been through so much together. Their loyalty to one another was total. Yet this still felt credible. He knew how frustrated Andy had been with him recently. But could he have really shot Isiah? The dealer was twitching in his grip now, proper fear in his eyes. He could see what was developing on Hayden's face.

'Please,' said Jade, 'you need to get here. Before he finds me again.'

Wherever 'here' was – she still hadn't told him. But she was right. Retribution could wait, Jade was the most important thing. He needed to hear the full story and see that she was safe. And then . . . whatever was going to happen, would happen.

'I'm coming. Go back to my flat, you'll be safe there. I'll meet you there.'

Finn dispatched a team to the Knolls' house in Bromley where a search was now underway. A sample of Hannah's DNA had been retrieved from a hairbrush and they were now looking to see if they could find a match on the items recovered from Andy Forbes's flat. At Cedar House there'd been a short debrief as Finn explained his theory about the derailment. Finding Hannah was now their top priority. The CCTV from the McDonald's in Forest Hill had confirmed Andy's alibi for the previous night. But with plenty of new questions now forming around Hannah, Finn was keen to question him a second time.

'Why am I still here? You know where I was last night?' asked Andy, sitting across from Finn and Paulsen again in the interview room.

'Because there's two other murders you don't have an alibi for, because we found clothing that matches the killer's description in your flat, and because there's a sodding great machete with your fingerprints on it,' said Finn.

'I told you, I don't know how they got there.'

'Does Jade have access to your flat?' said Paulsen.

Andy looked surprised.

'What's she got to do with it?'

'Just answer me.'

He seemed uncertain, the implication of it starting to dawn on him.

'Is there something you want to tell us, Andy?' said Finn.

His solicitor whispered in his ear. He digested the advice, nodded. The look on his face was telling though. The very fact he was considering it was pretty much an answer in itself.

'She came to me earlier this week. Told me a few things about Hayden – that he'd been behaving weirdly. He's been a bit odd with me too. All I said to her was that trying to get him out of all this shit might not be the worst thing. I was trying to *help* him – not hurt him.'

'Very thoughtful. Or did you just want him out of the way?' said Finn. Andy glowered back at him.

'It was Jade's idea to try and bring Hayden and Isiah together. It seemed like a good thing. Why would I have a problem with that? He's been wanting out – and yeah, I saw the chance to make some more money. But what are you saying? *She* planted all that stuff on me?'

'It's just a theory at this point. All we know for certain is she's been lying about her real name. It's not Jade, it's Hannah Knolls.'

Andy looked a little like a cricketer who'd just been bowled, belatedly realising his stumps were now strewn on the ground behind him.

'So has she been in your flat?' repeated Finn.

'Yeah.'

Finn exchanged a look with Paulsen.

'You can't believe *she* shot Hayden's dad? Why?' said Andy.

Finn actually felt some sympathy for him now. They'd all accepted Karl and Jo's assumption about the killer's gender without challenging it. They should have done. Interesting how innate your own sexism could be, he thought. Even when his own long experience should have taught him otherwise.

'We don't know, that's what we're trying to establish,' said Paulsen. 'Do you know where she might have got a gun from?'

Andy looked across at his solicitor for guidance again, but this time she shook her head firmly. Finn had expected that.

'No comment.'

It wasn't hard to read his thoughts now; the growing fury at how easily he'd been duped.

'Did you see her last night, at any time?' said Finn.

'No comment.'

'Not even to tell you that Hayden was meeting with his father?'

He shifted uncomfortably in his seat.

291

'No comment.'

'Was the gun yours, Andy?'

'No comment.'

Finn looked over at Paulsen again, and they exchanged a wry smile.

As he sprinted down the walkway to his flat, Hayden was relieved to see everything was quiet. There was still a heavy police presence in the area, but just for once they were working to his advantage, keeping Jade safe while he'd travelled back. The sight of the cordoned-off crime scene, his father's blood still staining the concourse, hadn't upset him as much as he thought it would. Instead, it fuelled his growing anger. He was still trying to get his head round the idea that Andy was to blame for all this.

Once he got home he went straight through to the toilet. He carefully lifted up the lid of the cistern and pulled out a transparent, waterproof bag. He shook the excess water off and unknotted the tie at the top. Inside was a bundle of sour-smelling damp rags. He slowly peeled them apart until he could see the black barrel of a gun peeking out. Smoothly, he removed the weapon and slipped it down the back of his trousers so it sat snugly against the small of his back. He reached inside the bag again and picked out another, smaller bundle. He emptied its contents into his palm and stared at the heap of bullets. Andy had given him the weapon right at the beginning. He'd never imagined using it – but then he'd never imagined a day like this one.

'So you're telling me Hannah Knolls killed Leah Suleman and Jamie Baker – and shot Isiah Simms?' said John Skegman.

'That's my working theory at this point, yes.'

'Let me get this straight then: Karl, Jo and Hayden trampled over Hannah's mother and she blames them for her stroke and by association her death?'

The words came out as if he was stress-testing the concept rather than buying it.

'The only way those three could have got to the doors is by getting past – or *over* – Joyce Knolls. If I'm right about where they all were sitting in that carriage,' said Finn.

'So, why did she offer these choices each time? Why kill their loved ones, not them?'

'I've been thinking about that,' said Paulsen. 'We know she was by the train doors and couldn't get to her mother. She was helpless, but clearly saw what happened and who was responsible. I think that's what she wanted *them* to feel. Knowing something awful was happening to someone they cared about, but unable to stop it.'

'Didn't any of these people notice she was female?' said Skegman. 'Suleman, the nurse?'

'I doubt it even crossed their minds,' said Paulsen. 'All they'd have been thinking about was the choice, not what gender the person under the mask was. In Karl's case she threatened to rape his daughter – it was pure misdirection.'

Finn nodded in agreement.

'She was trying to control the narrative from the start, nudging him – nudging us – into making the assumption.'

'What about Hayden? They're in a relationship. You can't tell me he didn't notice,' said Skegman.

Finn shrugged.

'We don't have him. We don't have her. Until we do – or some hard evidence connecting her – it's all just a theory.'

Skegman was deep in thought.

'So why is Andy going all no-comment on us if he hasn't got anything to hide?' he said.

Finn smiled.

'Because I'm certain the gun used to shoot Isiah was his. I think she stole it from him, shot Isiah, then put it with the coat and mask for us to find covered in his DNA.'

Skegman nodded as he followed the logic.

'And she knew we'd be coming for him because of the fingerprints on the knife. She left us a breadcrumb trail.'

'Exactly. We have to find Hannah Knolls first and get her into an interview room. There's boots on the ground looking for her. We've contacted the phone companies and we've circulated her description. In the meantime, I want to talk to Jo Corcoran again. I've got questions for her, and I want to look her in the eye when I ask them.'

Hayden was sitting at his table, looking, as he so often did in these quiet moments, at the large colourful canvas of Donald Duck above his sofa. It helped him think. Could Andy really have betrayed him? They'd shared so much together, survived so much because of each other. Why would Andy want to hurt him? Had he really gone full-on gangster? It was almost impossible to get his head round it.

There was an urgent knock at the door and he sprang to his feet. Through the spyhole, he could see Jade waiting outside. Tear-streaked, her make-up a mess, she looked exhausted. He could see an ugly wheal on her forehead, crusted in dried blood. He opened the door and she ran to embrace him. He held her then ushered her in.

'I thought I'd lost you,' he whispered.

'It was terrifying. He's gone mad.'

'Andy? You're talking about Andy?'

She nodded.

'You need to tell me what happened.'

'I will, I promise. But Hayden – I know where he is. He's meeting someone right now. Same place he took me to.'

'Where?'

She tried to remember, shook her head.

'I don't know the address, but I can take you there.'

He looked at her thoughtfully.

'Alright. But then we'll talk, yeah?'

'Of course. But you've got to deal with him. He wants you gone. I think he wants you dead. Come on – we haven't got much time. He'll know I've told you.'

She strode to the front door and he felt his phone vibrate in his pocket. He pulled it out, saw it was the police again and ignored it, before following Jade out of the door.

39

'I bloody loved the Olympics. One big party. Before we all got dragged into leave or remain – and everything that came after,' mused Finn.

He and Paulsen were in a backstreet of Stratford, where the imposing structure of the London Stadium, formerly the Olympic Stadium, stood in the middle distance.

'Nancy made me go to the table tennis with her. Not my thing,' said Paulsen, only stopping briefly to admire the view. 'But then sport's not really my thing.'

'You have no soul.'

'Iyengar yoga's more my cup of tea. You should try it.'

She grinned at the look of unfolding horror on his face, then checked her phone to see if they were in the right place. She stopped and pointed at a Victorian house on the other side of the road. They crossed and descended a wrought-iron staircase. They were standing in front of a basement flat with a dirty white peeling frontage, its net curtains drawn. Finn rang the bell and a smartly dressed woman in her late forties opened the door.

'How are we, Nishat – going stir-crazy yet?'

DC Nishat Adams was one of the two family liaison officers looking after Jo and her mother. They weren't required to stay there full-time, but after what had happened with Karl, Finn hadn't been prepared to take any chances. It wasn't quite 24/7 coverage, but there weren't many hours of the day the

Corcorans found themselves alone. Jo's phone had also been taken, though no further messages had been received on it. Finn guessed Hannah was ahead of them on that front too, aware that after Karl's death stronger measures would be taken to safeguard Jo.

They entered and Nishat swiftly closed the door behind them. Paulsen winced at the wall of stuffy heat they'd stepped into.

'Welcome to my world. It's Maeve, she insists on having the heating on full,' said Adams.

They followed her into a sparse, functional living room. Maeve Corcoran was sitting in a battered leather easy chair, a side table next to her with a chipped teapot on it and some mugs. Jo was on a sofa close by, reading a magazine. She looked up and greeted Finn and Paulsen with a flat expression as they entered.

'Hello Jo, how are you doing?' said Paulsen.

'How do you think she's doing?' snapped her mother with an accent even broader than her daughter's.

'Mum . . .' said Jo, and the older woman shook her head disapprovingly. The tension and misery was almost tangible, stifling in the heat. Another reminder, thought Finn, of what the killer was trying to achieve.

'I'm sorry about my mum,' said Jo. They'd moved to the kitchen next door while Nishat stayed with Maeve in the living room. 'Do you want a coffee or something? There's instant in the cupboards, I think there's still some milk left.'

Finn and Paulsen shook their heads and they all sat down around a wooden table that looked like it had seen better days.

'How are you getting on?' said Paulsen, trying again.

'Oh, just champion, y'know.' She looked up at them. 'Don't worry, I'm not contemplating stringing myself up if that's what you're worried about. When you know that's what they

297

want, it gives you a little bit of power back. I wouldn't give the bastard the satisfaction.'

'Good. I'm sorry you've had to stay here for so long,' said Finn.

Jo looked up hopefully.

'Nishat said you'd arrested someone?'

'We've made an arrest, but we haven't charged them yet. It's partly why we've come – we've some more questions, if that's okay.'

'Sure. Whatever you need.'

'Is there any chance the person who killed Jamie might have been female?' asked Paulsen, diving straight in.

Jo exhaled, surprised.

'Well, I wasn't expecting that.' She thought about it for a moment. 'It's hard to say – their face was covered. I suppose they could have been. I was terrified, concentrating on the situation more than anything. He was kind of whispering – I thought it was because he didn't want Jamie to hear us talking. The TV was coming through the wall as well . . .' She shrugged helplessly. 'It sounded like a young lad to me, but I'm not a hundred per cent certain. Is there someone you've got in mind?'

'We think this might be connected to the train derailment you were on,' said Finn.

Both officers watched Jo's reaction carefully, but she just seemed bemused by the suggestion.

'Really? How did you arrive at that?'

Finn reached into his pocket and pulled out a brown envelope. Inside was a picture of Hannah Knolls, taken from her Facebook profile and blown up.

'Do you recognise this woman?'

Jo took the piece of paper and studied it closely. She shook her head.

'No, can't say that I do.'

'She was one of the other passengers on the train with you,' said Paulsen.

'I don't remember her. But it's a bit like the night Jamie died – when you're that scared, the fear distorts things.'

'I know you've already spoken to us about that morning. But it's specifically the time between the derailment and when you actually got off the train we're interested in,' said Finn, again watching her closely as he said the words. She looked out of the kitchen window and thought about it.

'Everyone was still for a moment, like nobody knew how to react or what to do. Then someone pointed at these two men – Muslim fellas, I think – said it was an attack. There was pandemonium. As I said before, it was absolutely terrifying. I didn't know what was happening.'

'What did you do next?' said Paulsen, keeping her voice neutral.

'I ran for the doors like everyone else. Stupid, really. Of course it wasn't an attack. But in the heat of the moment, you look at these guys . . .' she faltered again, embarrassed. Finn pulled out another image from the brown envelope.

'Do you recognise this woman?' he said, sliding a picture of Joyce Knolls across to her. She held it up and nodded instantly.

'Yes, she was sat by the window on the other side of the aisle – the lady who had the stroke afterwards, wasn't she?'

'You saw that?' said Paulsen.

'Not really, not properly.'

'You're a nurse though. Didn't you feel like you could help her?' said Finn.

'Well, of course. But the paramedics were already there by that point. I know better than anyone you don't want someone getting in the way in those situations.' She picked up the picture of Hannah, looked at it again. 'I do remember this one now. She was outside with the other lady. Her daughter?'

Finn nodded.

'When you were trying to get off the train – in that moment of panic you described – do you remember seeing either of these two?' said Finn.

'No. Should I?'

Jade was leading Hayden through a series of backstreets on the perimeter of the estate. They'd been walking for a good ten minutes now, in silence. Part of the reason for the route was the police presence in the area. Given what he was carrying, Hayden knew he couldn't afford to be stopped and searched. Every now and then they'd see a pair of officers walking in tandem and duck out of sight.

'Where are we going?' he whispered as they stood in a doorway, watching two more police pass on the opposite side of the road.

'I'm trying to remember. It's hard. This way . . .' She pointed, and they moved on again.

'You still haven't told me what happened last night with Andy. How you got that cut?'

'What do you *think* happened? What do you think he did?'

'What are you telling me?'

She stopped, gave him a look as if he were being deliberately stupid. He put both hands on her shoulders, looked her deep in the eye.

'Do I have to spell it out for you?' she said.

She turned and walked on.

'Do you believe Jo?' said Paulsen as she and Finn drove back to Cedar House.

300

'I don't disbelieve her.'

'What's that supposed to mean?'

'She's a nurse, she's hardwired to help people. If she'd seen Joyce Knolls on the floor of that train, I don't believe she *wouldn't* have helped. Do you?'

'But your whole theory about Hannah relies on the fact she didn't. And I'm thinking about that care home, what Sami discovered – that she turned a blind eye to what was going on there . . .'

Finn considered it.

'Put it this way: I can buy in the heat of the moment, terrified for her life, that she didn't see Joyce and can't remember what happened. Fear does that to you.'

'So you're giving her the benefit of the doubt?'

'I'm trying to imagine every scenario. And how things would have looked to Hannah Knolls.'

His phone rang and he activated the hands-free.

'What is it, Jacks?'

'There's been a sighting of Hannah near the estate. Sounds like she's with Hayden.'

He swore, turned on the unmarked car's flashing blue lights and put his foot down.

'In there? You're sure?' said Hayden. They were standing opposite a building site. Where once there'd been an old pub, a nascent new housing development was in mid-construction. The only clue to its past was the dark wooden trap doors out the front where the beer barrels used to be delivered.

'Yes. There's no one there. We were on the top floor. I heard him call someone last night, arrange a deal for today.'

Hayden looked sceptical.

'Why would he do it here?' She shrugged and he squinted up at the structure. 'I can't see anyone.'

'He's up there, I'm telling you. Come on,' she said and ran across the road. She moved a corrugated iron fence at the front to create a small gap, lifted some tarpaulin out of the way and they slipped in. It was deserted, the only noise some traffic in the distance, the air claggy with dust. Hayden stopped.

'There isn't anybody here, Jade. Is there?'

The multistorey building stood open in front of them like the cross section of a doll's house. The ground floor was subdivided into boxy rooms, the old brickwork in the process of being given a makeover of smooth new plaster.

'Why are you lying to me?' he said.

'I'm not. How could you even say that?'

He shook his head. He already knew the answer to his question, part of it anyway. A suspicion which was growing by the minute. His eyes were stinging. He could take anything from anyone, come back stronger. But not this. He could feel his hand beginning to tremble again and ignored it.

'Hayden – I don't know what you're talking about.'

'You're the only person who knew I was meeting my dad last night. I didn't recognise you, because it never crossed my mind it could even *be* you. But it was, wasn't it? You really think I don't know your voice?'

Her whole face seemed to change in front of him. Heavily lidded eyes, looking at him with a contempt he'd never seen before. He grabbed for the gun tucked in the back of his trousers, and watched in confusion as it clattered to the ground. He stared at it, unsure how it had got there, then looked down and saw the knife handle jutting from his chest and the blood leaking from the wound. He could feel the pain spreading like heat.

'Come on,' she said gently. She led him a few steps to the nearest wall almost tenderly, and he slid down it until he was sitting upright on the ground. He made an effort to grab at the knife, raising his arm uselessly towards it. She took his hand and restrained him like a mother with a toddler, then sat down next to him as the wind whistled around them.

'I want you to know why.'

40

Finn and Paulsen drove straight to the site where a witness claimed to have seen Hannah and Hayden together; a small Polish delicatessen on a street corner just minutes from the Hope Estate. Paulsen was now inside talking to the owner, while Finn was out the front, speaking to a police constable.

'How long ago was this?'

'Maybe half an hour, give or take. We've been asking all the shopkeepers if they've seen anyone who matches Hannah Knolls' description. This one said she'd seen two people walk past and the female was a possible fit. We've redeployed a few more numbers just in case.'

Finn sighed. It could be any young man and woman. He never trusted the public when it came to descriptions. Karl and Jo, after all, had both been convinced their attacker was a young man. Paulsen emerged from the store's entrance and marched over.

'The description's a decent match for Hannah. She says the woman had some sort of cut to her face, while the man had an older scar.'

Finn perked up.

'Any idea which direction they went in?' he said to the PC.

'That way apparently . . .'

He pointed towards a junction which split off into two separate residential roads. Even from where they were standing, the lack of street cameras was obvious.

'And we've got people looking down both those streets?'

The PC nodded.

'So what now?' said Paulsen as they jumped back into the car.

'We have to find them. Hannah wants to kill Hayden, I'm sure of it. Now she's shot Isiah in front of him I can't see what's holding her back – she'll want to finish this.'

The police radio in the car crackled into life.

'Break-in reported at the Whitegate housing development on Cantwell Lane. Any unit deal?'

'That's only a few minutes from here,' said Finn. 'Tell them we're responding and call for armed back-up just in case. Make sure no one goes in until we get there.'

He started the car and skidded away.

'The thing about killing someone is it isn't all that,' said Jade. Hayden's head was lolling now. Blood was soaking through his shirt, dripping down his trousers and pooling around them, but she barely seemed to notice.

'The first time I did it was years ago. But that was easy – I pushed a drunken old man down a flight of stairs.'

Hayden's eyes rolled towards her and she nodded with a smile, as if to confirm the claim.

'I learnt three things from that. One – that you really *can* get away with murder. Two – that when you're female, people will always underestimate you. And three . . . that if you want it, you *can* have real justice. You just have to take it.'

Hayden was barely listening. It didn't really matter to him why this was happening now. He needed immediate help or he was going to die. He could neither speak nor move to any great degree, and could feel the blood bubbling in his throat. But it was Mikey he was thinking of. If these really were his last moments, and with Isiah in the state he was, what would

305

happen to him if they both died? He could feel himself losing consciousness, and was fighting it with every ounce of strength he had left.

'I saw on that train who you were, Hayden. You didn't remember me, but I remembered you. I heard you give your name to the transport police when they took your statement. And you weren't hard to find.'

She shifted round so she could look him directly in the eye. 'When that train came off the rails, all you were thinking about was how to save your own sorry arse.' She lifted a bloodied hand off the ground, shook it for him. '*This* – these tremors – that's guilt. That's the poison coming to the surface.'

'I don't . . . understand,' he managed to croak.

'Of course you don't.' She pulled out her phone, held up a picture. 'Does this face ring a bell?' She moved it closer so he could see properly. 'That's my mum – and you killed her.' She leant in almost tenderly, put her hand on to the knife handle and pushed it further in.

Finn pulled up on the opposite side of the road to the building site. He could see the wind puffing out the plastic sheeting in the windows on the top floor. It looked deserted and moribund – the perfect place to lure someone. The armed police who'd been patrolling the area hadn't taken long to scramble, and were holding back as per his instructions. It could just be a couple of kids who'd chosen the wrong day to break into a building site. But if it was Hannah and Hayden in there, one or both could be carrying a weapon. They might just as easily be unarmed, and it was also a distinct possibility he'd got all this completely wrong. As usual he was running all the permutations at once – he didn't want two young lives snuffed out unnecessarily.

'Come on, you're with me,' he said to Paulsen. He radioed the commander in charge of the armed team and they waited as a single officer ran over to join them. Together, they walked across the road.

Protective fences and tarpaulin prevented them from seeing inside the site, but there was a makeshift wooden door that served as an entrance. Finn produced some skeleton keys and after some fiddling managed to gain access. Immediately they saw Hayden and Hannah sitting against a far wall together. The ground was drenched in blood and it was quickly obvious that Hayden was hurt. Paulsen called for an ambulance and Finn told the armed officer to hold back. She nodded and held her position, keeping her fingers wrapped around the trigger of her Heckler & Koch G36 assault rifle. The two detectives walked over, and as they got closer saw the knife handle extending from Hayden's chest. Hannah looked at them, like someone whose Sunday afternoon picnic was being rudely interrupted. Paulsen moved to try and help Hayden.

'I wouldn't do that,' said Hannah.

As if picking up a paperback, she reached down next to her and raised a gun. She put it straight to Hayden's temple, the barrel jerking his head upright.

'Tell her to go.' She nodded at the armed officer. 'Or I'll finish this.'

Finn signalled at the woman, who turned and walked, and they waited until she disappeared from view. The team outside would at least now know what they were dealing with. Finn looked down at Hayden who was still just about conscious. He wouldn't be for long though – he was bleeding out in front of them and desperately needed medical attention.

'So, what now, Hannah? That's all of them, isn't it? Karl, Jo and Hayden . . . three people on a train.'

Hannah looked surprised.

'I didn't think you'd work that out. Didn't think anyone would.'

'I'm not sure that I have. Not entirely, anyway. I know you were all on the same carriage, but I don't know the exact details of what happened.'

As he spoke Finn was watching her closely and could see the fury behind her eyes. They'd spent so much time trying to understand this killer – now it was written across her face. The rage that had killed two people.

'Suleman pushed my mum to the ground, the nurse trampled over her. And this one,' she motioned at Hayden, 'stamped on her head and chest . . . they killed her between them.'

'Why didn't you speak out? You didn't even tell your own brother what happened.'

'Because I know what everyone would have said: "one of those things", "heat of the moment". But that's bullshit – they were only thinking of themselves and if some woman got in the way, then so what.'

She got to her feet. Hayden was now unconscious and slumped sideways as she rose, the blood leaking like a tap from his midriff.

'But why get so close to him – I don't understand?' said Paulsen, unable to contain herself.

'Because he was the worst. The first two put her down. Kept her down. But him?' She kicked his shoulder. 'He did the damage, I'm sure of it. And don't tell me he doesn't know. What do you think that PTSD's all about?'

Finn nodded, more to himself, the pieces falling into place now.

'You wanted to punish Karl and Jo, but you wanted to do more than that to Hayden?'

She smiled grimly.

'It was easy hooking him in. I got close enough to understand his world – so I could *break* his world.' She held her foot above Hayden's head. 'So I could put my foot on *his* head.'

Just as it looked like she was going stamp on his skull, Hayden's eyes blearily flicked open again. He tried to speak, but could only manage a gurgled croak.

'Sorry, hun – didn't quite catch that?' said Hannah, leaning over. She lowered her foot on to his head, like a hunter posing with a slain animal.

'You don't understand . . .' said Finn quietly.

'No, *you* don't understand. Easy enough to show you though.'

She swung the gun at Finn's face.

'I'll make you an offer – walk away and you can live.'

He held up his hands, palms facing out.

'Please, I really do need to explain something to you.'

He took a step forwards. Paulsen, who'd been watching with mounting concern, decided she'd seen enough.

'*Finn . . .*'

Hannah kept the gun on him.

'You walk, or these two die. You stay, and you die. Your choice.'

And here it was, thought Finn. He was finally standing in the same place Karl and Jo had. But he wasn't feeling the same paralysing fear they must have experienced, and he knew why. The threat didn't worry him and so he was in control. If he was removed from this earth in the next few moments, the waters would close over his head quickly enough. A new DI would lead the major investigations team and a small flat near Wandsworth Common would find itself a new owner. And that was just about it. The world would carry on turning and this horrible, aching pain would finally come to an end.

'*Decide!*' shouted Hannah.

Paulsen looked at Finn, unsure what to do. She and Hannah were both waiting on him, but he remained still, his face like stone.

'Fine,' said Hannah, and steadied herself, still with one foot grinding Hayden's skull into the dirt.

Finn took a step forwards. There was nothing aggressive or sudden about the movement. It was slow and measured. He stopped millimetres from the barrel of the gun, pushed his forehead into it and looked Hannah in the eye. Paulsen was watching on in horror. This wasn't a ploy to resolve the situation. It was a man ready to end it right there, and even Hannah seemed taken aback.

'When I said you don't understand, I meant it,' he said. 'Because I think there's something you don't know about that day.'

Hannah stepped backwards, finally releasing Hayden's head. It lolled to one side, his eyes still just about open.

'Don't try and play games. I was there. You weren't,' said Hannah.

'And I've gone through every witness statement, spoken to the rail accident investigator, watched the trackside CCTV.'

He let the words hang.

'You're lying,' she said.

'Michael Simms. He was on that train too. Standing behind you by the doors when it came off the tracks.'

'Mikey wasn't there . . .' she said uncertainly.

'*He was.* You don't remember him because you didn't know him then – if you even saw him. Didn't you ever talk about it with Hayden?'

'Of course not. I didn't want him to remember me.'

Paulsen had already worked it out.

'Don't you get it? You were both doing the *same* thing. He wasn't trying to save himself. He wasn't running for the doors – he was trying to find his brother.'

For the first time Hannah looked unsure and Paulsen seized her moment. She leapt forwards and grabbed her arm, attempting to wrestle the gun from her grip. Finn moved in to help, but Hannah's finger was already closing around the trigger. The blast whip-cracked around the building site. Hannah staggered back and Paulsen pulled the weapon from her, quickly pinning her to the ground. A stream of armed officers was now pouring in through the single door. When she turned to look for Finn he was lying behind her, motionless on the ground.

4I

Finn was pissed off. He'd been sitting in a small curtained-off area of the Mayday for what seemed like hours and his heavily strapped shoulder was throbbing. Out of sight, but certainly not out of earshot, a very loud man with a honking laugh was jabbering on to his equally voluble wife. Finn didn't know which of them was ill, or what the problem was, but he hoped it was painful.

'At least he's got someone,' said Karin.

The bullet had sailed through the top of his right arm. It hadn't actually been that painful – more like a hard punch, the metal slicing through muscle, leaving a clean exit wound behind it. He'd been bandaged up, given antibiotics and painkillers, and told to wait. That'd been a while ago and impatience was now overtaking the physical discomfort. He wanted to know what condition both Isiah and Hayden Simms were in, and needed to get back to Cedar House to interview Hannah Knolls. Instead he was stuck here, listening to two very stupid people talking.

'You could have died. And who'd mourn you then?'

He ignored his late wife and, with difficulty, used his spare hand to pluck his phone from his jacket, which was draped over a nearby chair. There was a large sign on the wall in front with the words 'Please keep mobile phones turned off at all times'. He stared balefully at it and turned his phone on. He waited for an avalanche of messages to arrive, but they didn't and he sighed.

★　★　★

It'd felt like a pyrrhic victory to Paulsen. As she was processed at Cedar House, Hannah had been surprisingly cooperative, answering the custody sergeant's questions without backchat. Whether that was because the reality of her situation was now dawning on her, or because she felt she'd accomplished what she'd set out to do, it was hard to tell. To Paulsen's surprise she felt some sympathy for Hannah, the loss of a parent all too prominent in her thoughts right now. But then she remembered the time she'd spent with Karl and Claire, the eyes of their daughter staring down from the framed pictures on the living room wall. That haunted last image of Karl on the front page of the *Standard*.

Now Paulsen was back at the Mayday, checking in on Michael Simms. Dave McElligott, it seemed, had formed an unlikely bond with the boy. God knows what state the kid's mind was in – but there'd been some much-needed good news regarding his father. Isiah was now out of danger and under sedation. Hayden's situation was less clear. The paramedics worked furiously on him at the building site, and at one point Paulsen thought it was all too late. But they'd managed to keep him alive and now he was undergoing surgery, as Michael – again – was forced to wait. Perhaps it was because Dave was a child at heart too, but he seemed to be doing a decent job of distracting him, which was something. As with Hannah, there were unanswered questions. Did Hayden know what he'd done that morning on the train? Had he even seen Joyce Knolls? He surely must have *felt* her underfoot. Or had his mind blotted out everything except his brother's safety? Like Jo, only he really knew, and it might stay that way now.

Having checked McElligott was okay, Paulsen went to find Finn. Arriving at the ward she'd been directed to, a nurse pointed at a curtained-off bed midway down. She strode over, pulled the curtain to one side and found what appeared to be a sullen schoolboy sitting on his own.

'I was beginning to think you didn't care,' he said.

'I don't, I was looking for Dave.'

He rolled his eyes.

'You look like shit,' she said, because he did.

'Thanks.'

'How's the shoulder?'

'Sore. What's been happening?'

She brought him up to speed about Isiah and Hayden and he nodded sadly. While Hayden's life remained in the balance it was hard to feel any sense of accomplishment over Hannah's arrest.

'Do you think Hayden knew what he did to Hannah's mother?' said Paulsen.

It was something Finn had been giving a lot of thought to while he'd been waiting. The episode in the interview room was a powerful memory, and the sense that there was an essential decency to the man wouldn't quite shift.

'I think Hannah might have been right about his PTSD,' he said slowly. 'Something brought it on. Maybe the guilt was always there, buried beneath the surface.'

He grabbed his jacket off the chair, thought about wrapping it around himself and gave up on the idea.

'Shouldn't you wait for the doctors to give you the all-clear?' said Paulsen.

'Probably.'

He moved to leave, but Paulsen stayed where she was.

'Do you want to tell me what the fuck you were doing back there, by the way?' she said.

Finn turned to her wearily. There was another burst of honking laughter from the other side of the ward.

'Calling her bluff.'

She looked at him levelly.

'Didn't look like that. Looked like you were deadly serious.'

'Worked out though, didn't it?'

He pulled the curtain aside with his good hand and didn't wait for a response.

The interview with Hannah provided answers to some of the outstanding questions; how she'd tracked down three strangers on a train, for one. Karl and Hayden she'd overheard giving their statements to the BTP. Jo's name she'd seen trackside, pinned to her tunic. A little Googling was all it took to find out who they were, where they lived and, more importantly, who they cared about.

Every time Finn thought he understood grief, it seemed to find a new face to show him. As he listened to Hannah, it struck him just how well she'd planned all this. Two generations of the Simms family fell for her act, not to mention the hapless Andy Forbes. It was clear she intended to plead not guilty in court too, to enable her to give her side of the story to a jury and the watching media. It would be an interesting occasion. As powerful as Hannah's righteous fury was, it would be counterbalanced by the victims' impact statements – Claire Suleman and Jo Corcoran would have their chance to speak too, their pain and loss every bit as vivid as hers.

Finn was in no doubt that he'd be called upon to talk through the derailment and explain where all the significant players on the carriage were that morning. He wondered how Jo would receive that – confronted by the truth of her own actions in clear, forensic terms. More guilt piled on for a woman who'd walked away while her partner died. He thought too about Tony Knolls, forced now to confront two new truths.

The awful reality of what happened to his mother that morning, and the horrifying revenge his sister had taken. Another family reduced to one and all this because of a points failure on some frozen rail tracks.

Afterwards Finn and Paulsen reconvened in Skegman's office and while the DCI showed a passing concern for Finn's health, he was clearly more interested in Hannah Knolls' confession. Her arrest would go a long way to calming the growing tensions on the Hope Estate.

'The other bonus, of course, is this disrupts whatever county lines operation Andy Forbes was building, for a fraction of the cost of a major operation.'

Finn winced, rubbing his shoulder carefully before perching on the end of Skegman's desk. His face was as white as a ghost.

'As long as we've saved a few bob, that's the main thing,' he said.

'Go home, Alex. You shouldn't be here,' said Skegman.

'Might just take you up on that,' said Finn.

There was a knock at the door and Ojo joined them without waiting to be invited.

'Thought you'd want to know: Isiah Simms is awake. We weren't going to tell him about Hayden yet, the doctors didn't want to cause him any distress . . .' She paused for a moment.

'But?' said Skegman.

'The boy – Michael – told him anyway, despite being asked not to. Isiah's pretty upset. Someone really should go and talk to him.'

Finn heaved himself to his feet.

'Not you, Alex,' said Skegman.

'I want to. Should do.'

He headed for the door.

'*Finn!*' shouted Skegman, but the door was already shutting behind him. Paulsen exchanged a glance with Skegman, both with the same look of concern.

'This can't go on,' she said quietly.

'Where's my son going to sleep tonight?' said Isiah. Finn and Paulsen were both by his bedside, having been granted the briefest of conversations by a very resistant medical staff. The consultant was with them to make sure they didn't overstep the mark. Like Finn, Isiah had been relatively fortunate, the surgeons managing to limit the damage done by the bullet. Unlike Finn, there'd been a delay getting him to hospital and he'd lost a lot of blood at the scene. He was weak after surgery, and it would be a while before he'd be back on his feet.

'There's emergency foster care in place,' said Finn. 'Just until you're back home,' he added quickly. 'It's what they're there for – situations like this.'

'How is he?'

'Happier – now that he knows you're on the mend.'

'And Hayden?'

The consultant stepped forwards, a big jowly man who looked more like a yachtsman in an ill-fitting suit.

'Your son's just come out of theatre. He was seriously hurt and there was a lot of damage, but he's alive and his condition's stable. The next twenty-four hours will be key, but I'm a lot more hopeful now than when he was first brought in,' he said.

'Who did this?' said Isiah.

The consultant glared a warning at the two detectives, the message unmistakable – *don't upset him.*

'We've caught the person responsible,' said Finn. 'We're still investigating the exact circumstances though,' he lied.

'Why did you meet with Hayden last night, if you don't mind me asking?' said Paulsen quickly. 'I thought you two were pretty irreconcilable.'

There was a long pause. Isiah was breathing heavily, the exertion already visibly taking its toll.

'Because a very persuasive young woman got through to me. I thought it was time to end all this stupidity. And look what happened – I think God was sending me a message.'

Finn and Paulsen exchanged a look. The consultant was now standing with his arms crossed, eyeballing them both.

'So what now?' said Finn.

'Mikey. It's all about him. He's already starting skipping school. We have to do better . . . Hayden and I.'

'It's what happens when you let things fester, I suppose,' said Paulsen. 'Other stuff gets neglected. And there are consequences.'

The words were directed at Isiah but she wasn't looking at him as she said them.

'I'm not letting anything "fester" or get "neglected",' said Finn as they headed for the exit. He was visibly irritated. 'We've got the killer in custody, together with a signed confession. I don't think this is the moment for petty sniping.'

Paulsen stopped, forcing Finn to stop too.

'Enough. You've been dodging this for too long.'

Finn rolled his eyes.

'Can't this wait? Enough people have been taking shots at me today, don't you think?'

'You want me to keep it brief – fine. You're still in a state of deep grief, and more than that, I think you're suffering from depression. It needs saying to your face—'

'Someone's beaten you to it . . .' said Finn, interrupting.

'So start listening and get some help.'

She turned and walked, and this time it was Finn who was left on his own.

42

Mattie looked out of the window at the Norfolk countryside and yawned as she listened to Nancy murdering Paloma Faith in the shower. She'd been summoned back to East Anglia by her mother, who'd wanted a family summit. Decisions on the future needed to be made. Jonas was there and the atmosphere was surprisingly light given the circumstances. Perhaps it was because they'd all Googled, seen the future and arrived at a form of basic acceptance.

'So what are we doing today?' said Nancy, re-entering the bedroom, a towel wrapped around her.

'Mum wants us all to go for a walk on Brancaster beach this morning. She's got a massive lunch prepared for afterwards, then she wants to have a big sit-down.'

Nancy nodded and started choosing a top from the selection she'd laid out on the bed.

'All sounds nice.' She was about to start dressing but stopped, noticing the frown developing on her partner's face.

'You okay?'

'I'm not sure,' said Mattie, almost with surprise.

'What is it?'

'I don't know.' She half smiled as the tears began to come. First a trickle, then a flood.

'Jesus, Mat.' Nancy came over, wiping damp hair out of her eyes. 'What's the matter?'

'I don't know,' she said, still in the strange hinterland between embarrassed confusion and sudden unexpected pain. 'All of it, I suppose. The last few weeks. Karl Suleman, the cemetery, Dad . . .'

'Oh Mat . . .'

Nancy put her arms around her and held her. They were interrupted by a knock at the door.

'Are you two nearly ready?' shouted Jonas from outside.

'Yes!' bellowed Mattie, almost deafening Nancy in the process. They both found a smile from somewhere. Mattie sniffed, wiping some snot from under her nose with the back of her hand.

'Sorry, I don't know where that came from.'

'Don't be stupid. Everything's just caught up with you, that's all.'

Mattie produced one of her unexpected smiles. She always seemed to pull one out when Nancy least expected it, like sunshine after rain.

'We're alright though, aren't we?' said Mattie. She was aware that when she felt under pressure it was Nancy who tended to suffer the most.

'We're always alright, but what could have happened in that graveyard scares me stupid.'

'Me too.'

'And yet you keep getting yourself into these situations.'

'I know.'

They looked at each other. The conversation almost negated itself. One day that temper *would* cost her, and both of them knew it – knew too how futile previous promises to change her ways had proven.

'John Skegman only cares about saving money,' said Jackie Ojo, washing the assessment down with a swig of Malbec. She

320

and Finn were in the same bar in Clapham where he'd met Cally Hunter on the night of Leah Suleman's murder. He was starting to warm to the place. He and Jackie were enjoying one of their infrequent blowouts. They didn't do it often, but when they did there was an unspoken agreement to check their ranks in at the door. It allowed Ojo to speak her mind, which she certainly took full advantage of. Finn knew her well enough to know what was said in the bar stayed in the bar. The alcohol was also helping to numb the pain of his still-aching shoulder.

'You're hard on him. I've known him a long time – his heart's in the right place. Don't let his demeanour give you a false impression of what he's about.'

'He has the demeanour of a plotting ferret. And you're a Skegman apologist.'

Finn tried not to laugh, failed, took a sip of his scotch.

'He has to deal with a lot of politics. With the budget we have, you need someone sharp . . .'

'Sly . . .'

'. . . *sharp*, to manage them.'

Ojo gave a non-committal shrug.

'I'll take your word for it. Anyway, how are you? And I'm not talking about your shoulder.'

'I'm fine.'

She looked at him patiently, as if to give him a second chance to answer the question properly. Finn folded.

'According to Paulsen I'm cracking up. A little dramatic, I think.'

'No, it isn't. She's right,' said Ojo simply.

'You too?' said Finn.

'Do you really need all of us to tell you there's a problem?'

The words came out lightly, but her face told a different story. She'd been building to this. He didn't need telling, of course, he understood it only too well. A lot had happened in a short space of time. Before Karl and Leah Suleman had taken their ill-fated walk in the park, he'd just about managed to convince himself that his bereavement was a side issue. A sad distraction he was coping with. But now that a few days had passed since Hannah Knolls' arrest, he understood why he'd deteriorated so sharply. The whole investigation seemed to rotate around grief. Karl had been destroyed by it, Hannah consumed by it. Claire and Jo were just starting to learn to live with it. Ripples and reflections of emotions he was all too familiar with. It was no wonder the delicate eco-system of his own loss had been so sharply disturbed.

'It's under control,' he lied.

It didn't even shock him any more how easy it was to deceive the people he trusted and liked. But he felt possessive about his own grief; that it was his to deal with and no one else's.

'With respect, it's not.'

'I think you're all exaggerating this a bit. It's not affecting my work, is it? As this week amply shows.'

'You think? Paulsen told me what happened – that you stuck your head into the barrel of a gun. Are you telling me that's normal behaviour?'

Finn shifted uncomfortably on his seat.

'It was a play – in the heat of the moment. I was calling her bluff.'

'That's not a bluff, that's Russian roulette. Don't try and kid a kidder . . . and don't take me for an idiot.'

And just for a moment he remembered how he'd felt, his forehead pressing into the metal. How he'd almost willed Hannah to pull the trigger. He recalled what Murray had said to him in that AA meeting room, his prophecy: 'Eventually it'll reach a crisis point.'

'Okay,' he said quietly. 'I probably need to talk to a professional. Just for a steer.'

Her expression softened. She clearly trusted him to do the right thing, but it was a misplaced trust. He would address this – but he'd do it his own way and in his own time. He smiled as reassuringly as he could manage and she gave a small nod of acknowledgement back.

The rest of the evening was less strained. Ojo, realising she'd got her point across, spent the night refilling his glass. By the time they left, Finn was pleasantly tipsy rather than hammered. It had been a good choice to go out with Jackie and it seemed to have lifted rather than lowered his spirits.

He felt relaxed as he walked home and knew the call he now wanted to make. His intention had been to wait until he got back to the flat; prepare for the conversation, think through precisely what he wanted to say. Sober up a little, frankly. But as he walked on, against his every instinct, he made the call anyway.

'Hello you,' said Cally Hunter with some surprise. 'I thought I'd been binned off?'

Her tone immediately got up his nose.

'Of course not. Absolutely not. Do you talk to everyone like this, by the way?'

'Alex, are you drunk?'

'No. Well . . . *ish* . . .'

'Interesting. So what is it I can do for you?'

There was a long pause as he tried to gather his myriad thoughts together.

'I . . . it's kind of hard to explain, I suppose.'

'Has something happened?'

'I got shot, if you must know.'

'Jesus!'

'It's alright. Only in a small way.'

'*What the fuck?*'

He smiled.

'Just my shoulder – I'm fine. Sorry, I didn't mean to alarm you.'

There was a pause as he wrestled with his feelings. He was only doing this because Karin wanted it. Cally was a touchstone to the past, someone who could help him keep her alive.

'*That wasn't the idea . . .*' said Karin testily.

'What's going on, Alex?' said Cally.

'I'm sorry about before,' he said quickly.

Why was he ringing this woman – what did he want from her? Someone to help him *get through*. That was it. Just enough to take the edge off. To keep Skegman, Ojo, Paulsen and the rest off his back while he sorted himself out. He sounded like a drug addict begging for one more fix before he got clean, he thought.

'What I'm trying to say – rather badly – is I could use a friend. Someone who knows me, who knew Karin as well.'

'I think you need a damned sight more than that. But yes, of course I'll be there for you if you're asking – I think that was her intention. What do you want to do?'

'Just meet up and talk from time to time. How does that sound?'

'If that's what you need, of course.'

'Thanks, Cally, I appreciate it.'

'Are you *sure* you're alright?'

'I'm not going to do anything stupid, don't worry.'

'Good – take care of yourself. You can call me any time you want. And Alex . . . drink plenty of water when you get in.'

The line went dead. He waited for Karin to say something, some pithy judgement, a reassuring quip. But none came. His shoulder was throbbing again and he suddenly felt very tired.

'Come on ...' he said quietly. 'Say something.' He looked around the deserted street as if expecting to see someone. It was beginning to rain now and he shivered.

'Karin ... ?'

And still there was no reply, just the tap-tap of the rain. He waited for another moment, then strode off into the night.

43

The road looked the same as the taxi drove Jo and Maeve home, but it wasn't. Not any more, how could it be? The familiar old front door was now more foreboding than welcoming, the hallway chilly and haunted. The police had done a good job of tidying up though, and the place smelt of detergent.

'It's cold,' said Maeve.

'That's because the heating hasn't been on for a while, Ma. It'll soon warm up.'

The old woman looked unconvinced.

'I'm going upstairs – see what they've done to my room.'

'They won't have done anything, it'll be just as you left it.'

Maeve grumbled under her breath, pottered towards the staircase and began levering herself up.

Jo remained still, listening to her mother's footsteps. She heard the bedroom door open and waited for a complaint, but it didn't come. She exhaled and looked down the narrow hallway. This was where it happened. If she closed her eyes it would be easy to imagine Jamie in the adjacent room, feet up, watching TV, laughing that big throaty laugh of his. She knew now who'd killed him. Nishat had told her about Hannah Knolls. Who she was. Where she'd met Jo, and why she'd paid them a visit.

Upstairs Maeve had a small coughing fit. Jo imagined she'd adapt to being back in the house again quite quickly. She stayed up there most of the time anyway. If she wasn't in bed, she was sitting in her chair reading or listening to the radio. It was alright for her – the ghosts were downstairs. But it could all be so different. There wasn't a day when she didn't think that – what life would be like if she'd made another choice instead. Jamie would be here now, and the ghosts would be upstairs. The feeling she might have made the wrong choice was like a shadow that wouldn't quite leave.

She took a deep breath – better to get this over with than delay it any longer – and walked up to the living room door. Its handle, usually greasy with fingerprints, was shiny and clean as she turned it. The room itself had been scrubbed and tidied. They'd warned her about the carpet though. Despite their best efforts, it was still blotched with blood, a huge wine-coloured concentration on the spot where Jamie died. In her mind's eye, she could see his body there, superimposing itself. The blood, fresh and soaking, the spatter and spray all over the walls and furniture. The only sound the tick-tock of the mantelpiece clock, then as now.

She stood still, not entirely sure what to do. What was supposed to happen now? Did everything just go back to how it was before? Did she return to work as normal, come home, dish up shepherd's pie for two, rather than three, and pretend everything was okay?

Jamie's family were now conspicuously quiet after their initial burst of contact. Maybe they were dealing with their own grief, or simply giving her some space. Or maybe they now *knew* exactly what happened. Would they ever forgive her? Could she ever forgive herself? She was used to living with guilt, she thought. Back at the care home she'd ignored one or two things and found it remarkably easy to live with those choices. She'd been doing the same ever since that snowy morning on the train. She remembered what happened alright, hadn't lied about the fear. You don't forget terror like that when you think you're going to die; when your only thought is to save yourself. People could judge her, but they hadn't been there.

She'd seen Joyce Knolls fall, watched the man in front push her to the ground. His urgency had become hers – the only thing that mattered was getting to the doors. He'd almost given her permission, like when they tell you on a plane to put your own oxygen mask on first before helping anyone else. She'd trampled over that woman with her full force, seen her face contorting in pain below and hadn't cared. Later when she'd collapsed by the tracks, Jo could have helped. But the shame held her back. And the thing about carrying shame is how quickly you get used to it, and how quickly it dilutes. She looked up at the clock on the mantelpiece and saw a teardrop of dried blood on its face. Clocks and carpets could be cleaned or replaced. Over time, most things could be.

'I can't find my blanket,' shouted her mother through the floorboards.

'It's alright, Ma, I'm coming,' she shouted back. She took one last look around the room, and walked out.

The End

Acknowledgements

It goes without saying that 'stuff happened' during the writing of this book. There's not much mention of social distancing, facemasks or lockdown within these pages but you may frankly find that a bit of relief! Hopefully some of the themes the novel touches on are universal, and the story you've just read doesn't feel too much like a period drama from long ago.

As ever there are some people I owe some words of thanks to ...' Akua Gyamfi and Derrick Bennett for some important conversations and steers at the start. Police advisor Stuart Gibbon for keeping me on the straight and narrow with current Met Police procedures. Copy editor Joe Hall for some critical tweaks at the end and Lewis Csizmazia the designer of the quite magnificent covers to both this book and also 'The Burning Men.' I love both pieces of art to bits.

Special thanks are also due to my editor Eve Hall. It takes real skill to make sense of my ridiculously overcomplicated first drafts and find ways to declutter them. She most definitely has the happy knack – don't put your feet up Eve, Book 3's on its way ...

Huge thanks too, to my agent Hayley Steed without whom I simply would not be typing these words and for propping me up through the periodic moments of self-doubt. There were a few this time round!

And one last thank you to my friend Nishat for critical advice on wisdom tooth removal. Trust me, it mattered.

Finn, Paulsen, Jackie O and the team will return ...